PRINCE RUPERT'S
TEARDROP

Dear Pat and Dave
Hope you enjoy the book!
Lots of love
Lisa Glass
xxx.

Lisa Glass

TWO RAVENS
P R E S S

Published by Two Ravens Press Ltd.
Green Willow Croft
Rhiroy
Lochbroom
Ullapool
Ross-shire IV23 2SF

www.tworavenspress.com

ISBN: 978-1-906120-15-3

British Library Cataloguing in Publication Data. A CIP record for this book can be obtained from the British Library.

Designed and typeset in Sabon by Two Ravens Press.
Cover design by David Knowles and Sharon Blackie.

Printed on Forest Stewardship Council-accredited paper by Biddles Ltd., King's Lynn, Norfolk.

About the Author

Lisa Glass studied English at Swansea University, until she eloped to Cyprus with her RAF boyfriend. Several months later they married and she finished her degree. She went back to Swansea for her MA in Creative Writing, which she passed with distinction. She has worked as a cleaner, a bookseller and a promotional model. She lives on the north Cornish coast where she takes inspiration from the dramatic scenery and drunken tourists. She has two cats, and a collie puppy.

Acknowledgements

With thanks to Jonathan Cann for endless patience and true love.

My parents Alicia and Geoff, for wisdom, and humour, and for giving me their library tickets that I might borrow thrice the books.

Richard Glass, for glassmaking advice.

John M Douglas and his spectacular book *The Armenians* – a terrifying, remarkable read.

Ann Heilmann, for her provocative and moving class: 'Gender and Monstrosity.'

Claire Mainwaring, lovely girl and first reader.

Rosy Barnes, for sound thinking in moments of panic.

Ger Nichol, David Smith, Margaret and Steven Cann for greatly appreciated enthusiasm about this book.

Nigel Jenkins and Stevie Davies – terrific writers and teachers.

Digger and Domino. Dear friends, first listeners, and the greatest collie/spaniel mutts the world has seen.

Sharon Blackie, for believing in this book.

For my grandmother, Makrouhi Kardjian, whose experiences inspired me to research a piece of forgotten history.

One

M ary could never have been expected to guess what was to come, because there was no precursor, no warning, nothing indicative of a change. A sibyl would have been needed to foresee such exceptional events. A sibyl, as Mary is ruefully aware, is a woman prophet, an oracle to the ancient Greeks, and the name for this woman is so close to her own name – Sibly – that it seems both ironic and outrageous that she possesses no prophetic powers at all, and so did not foresee a shred of the coming events.

For more than half a century things were the same; she and her mother lived prosaically and then, out of nowhere, her mother vanished. Not in the manner of a magician's assistant: not glibly, with a flourish, only to materialise in the basement two seconds later. On the contrary: on May 28th, a typically wet and windy summer's day, her mother vanished in a profound sense, and Mary could do nothing except wait for her to reappear.

There had been nothing to suggest that May 28th would be different from any other day in all the years that had preceded it – but it was. Because her mother, aged ninety-four, disappeared from an unremarkable precinct of Plymouth, city of pirates and plunderers and nautical heroes, and there was nobody to remark upon her absence but Mary.

It was, in fact, the day of May 27th that unfolded differently: Mary woke up happy.

Today is the happiest that Mary has been for a long time. Surprising, really, since it's her birthday: fifty-eight years down, no party, four cards, two presents – but she's wangled a month of sick leave from work, and that's something to be celebrated. Her colleagues say there was an incident, an episode on the shop floor. Swearing! Screaming like a banshee!

They say it was certainly a first – they've never seen a grown woman go on the rampage through the shop like that before, and they have certainly never seen anyone treat an item of knitwear with such disrespect – not in all their years in Fashion.

They think it's best that she takes some time, has some rest.

1

In the emergency Personnel meeting, which they called while she convalesced in the sickroom next door (she pressed her empty glass to the wall), she heard them sincerely hoping that they were wrong – after all, she's worked in Bodwicks for forty-two years – and yet they simply could not deny the available facts: all signs indicated, quite clearly, that Mary Sibly of Knitwear had cracked up.

Mary can't help but care what they think, ignoramuses though they are, and she harbours vast reservoirs of bitterness. For one thing, she is adamant that her colleagues and employers have conspired against her, for she has never achieved a salary commensurate with her performance.

It is as if some higher power has kept The Automaton from Knitwear, The Cardigan Queen, fixed at the bottom rung of the ladder. She knows without a shadow of a doubt that Management has underestimated her – for forty-two years, no less.

Well, no more. Her hour is nigh; if obloquy and whispers of schizophrenia are the price she has to pay for being heard, it is a price worth paying.

Perhaps their term 'cracked up' is not too far from the mark, after all.

Of course, she hasn't cracked up in the way they mean: she's not insane, but she is different, destroyed and remade – sloughing off the old stuff to herald in the new, like an adder who's slithered out of her old skin and feels the sun on her new scales for the first time.

Well, no matter what they think, no matter what stories they tell, she intends to enjoy every moment of her commeatus. She has cut herself loose from work with all its worry and she is at last unconstrained and disencumbered.

Mary lies in her bed with a whole day of autonomy stretching before her, and she remembers just how proud her mother was when she was accepted into the fold of fashion. Her mother has always been admired for her sartorial elegance, and she no doubt cherished a hope that working with department store *haute couture* would elevate her daughter's appearance to her own exacting standards.

She was disappointed, Mary presumes, given the subsequent decades of solicitude she clearly felt – and verbalised – with regard to Mary's attire. Still, she reminds herself, it is impossible to please all of the people all of the time. So she will settle instead for pleasing herself, and she does: she spends one whole day wallowing in the luxurious sludge of freedom; one day of reprieve, one day of hope.

Mary is faintly repulsed by her mother at the best of times, for a number of reasons that begin and end with the fact that her mother eats Crackerbreads, which she spreads with margarine and Marmite using her bare fingers. Who wouldn't be repulsed? – and for the umpteenth time Mary racks her brain ineffectually, seeking the reason her mother can't manoeuvre a knife.

And is it her fault that it makes her skin crawl to see her mother scrabble on hands and knees up the stairs? Like an insect, using her sticky fingers to feel her way?

Mary has suggested a stair-lift, some basic funicular device to get her up the steps that she finds so insurmountable – but she'll not have it, she'll not be coddled. She'll not be treated as an old person – except when it suits her, notes Mary, which is generally when there's something to be gained, some argument to be won, some moral high ground to be commandeered. Then Mary hears about the aches and pains, the constant torture of arthritic hips and a curved spine; then Mary hears about the purblind eyes that are little more than symbols for sight.

It's regrettable that she feels such disrelish for her mother, but she can't help it. Familiarity has bred contempt on both their parts – as she has often admitted to herself whilst watching her mother in the garden, squinting in the crepuscular light. Hunched over the flower-bed attending to her dear roses: blooms that are beautiful and fragrant beyond belief; blooms that must wince under her infirm and quivering touch.

Her mother is famous for these roses; people look at them in awe and sniff with closed eyes, and yet, thinks Mary unrelentingly, at the advanced age of ninety-four, isn't it time to throw in the trowel? Isn't it time to give up on those flowers? Isn't it time to let them wilt and die? Those old companions who have bloomed year after year, for as long as she can remember; wasn't it really time to let them go years before now?

So instead of spending quality time with her mother, she suits herself and goes out. She has no desire to be mured up in a frowsty old house with a nonagenarian: foreign old Meghranoush, so proud to be Armenian but pretending to be Polish when it suits her, sitting in the front room at this very moment, stitching a hole in the jeans of Him from Two Doors Up.

She's covering the knee in tiny black stitches, a swarm of biting ants on the attack, working their way up to the groin. Mary suspects they're Mr Merafield's 'knocking about' jeans, judging by their fetid inelegance: marbled bleached denim with oily stains from his street-side pottering.

Mary views him as being of a chronically ergophobic disposition: he has a deep and unshakeable fear of any type of work. She feels acutely that he is the sort of graceless baboon who would have flourished if born into an aristocratic family – but, sadly for him, he was not.

Whilst Mr Merafield is an ergophobe, Mary is a coulrophobe: she has a deep and unshakeable fear of clowns. Hence, Mary and Mr Merafield have never hit it off. He has made a point of telling her mother that he doesn't want any more big denim patches because they look 'bloody stupid,' so her mother is stitching instead. Mr Merafield – in Mary's august opinion – is not worth the bother; he is a troglodyte, a philistine, a barbarian and a rascal of the highest order; prodigiously obese, right down to his pasty ankles, a titan of pure lard. But he's one of her mother's best customers and so Mary is forced to be obliging because customers, no matter how unrefined and vulgar, have always been of greater importance to her mother than she.

'More of that louche man's offerings?' Mary asks, good-naturedly.

'He good man, good customer, he give good tip.'

'I'm sure, and did he give you that thing as well? I expect he found it at a jumble sale.' Mary points to a new ornament sitting on the coffee table.

'Is not from Mr Merafield,' says her mother, abstrusely.

'Well, where did you get it?'

'Someone else give to me.'

'Who?'

'Mind your business.' Her mother stares at her with pursed lips, as if underscoring the fact that she will not be led into divulging any of her precious secrets.

'A glass robin is a Christmas ornament, not a summer one. It'll bring you bad luck, mark my words.'

'Silly Mary,' is her mother's intelligent reply.

Mary can tell by the recalcitrant cast of her mother's face that she'll make no progress with her today, so she rids her mind of kitsch glass tat and casts her eyes back to the stitch-infested jeans. There'll be trouble; Mr Merafield's boozing cronies won't be impressed with the ant hill, although at least he has no workmates to ridicule him.

When Mary finds her mother missing, and before her thoughts turn to the mysterious ornament, they fixate upon Mr Merafield – for if there is such a thing as the murderer countenance, Mr Merafield has it: sly piggy eyes peeping out of a flabby face. Yet Mr Merafield will not be to blame; it will be someone entirely different who will take her mother, and this individual will turn out to be someone respectable, someone liked.

As she prepares to leave for her hike, Mary reminds herself that her mother will probably be glad of some time to herself, glad to have some space. When she's alone, when the house is empty, her mother talks to herself. Mary knows because she comes in with her key and before her mother sees her there, she hears her foreign lilt filling the air. Sometimes, the one or two sentences she hears are filled with vitriol and spite and Mary has come to think that her mother finds it comforting to verbalise these terrible memories – of genocide, of ethnic cleansing, of racial homogenisation, of human rights abuse, of mass execution – if only to the air.

She speaks to herself and perhaps to imaginary listeners, and she speaks in Pidgin English, as she hasn't spoken Armenian since the day she left Jerusalem. There is no Armenian Society in Plymouth – there are barely any foreigners. When she first came here she was a novelty in the town, a pet, and people still stop Mary in the street to ask:

'Are you the daughter of the Foreign Sewing Lady?'

'Yes, my mother's Meghranoush Sibly.'

'Megan, I thought it was?'

'Immigration made her change her name: they couldn't say Meghranoush so they vetoed it. It could've been worse: she could have been made a Maggie.'

'Is that right? Well now, how is she?'

'Still sewing.'

'Is she? At her age? Well, I never!'

'Tough as old boots, my mother.'

These little old ladies seem delighted and comforted that she's still alive – which is ironic since Mary's mother hates all English people – and they still sing the praises of her dressmaking to Mary, after all this time.

'Your mother's sewing is the best I ever saw, and cheap! The most beautiful suits, she made. All stitched together by hand, too; none of your machine stuff then. Always had her head held high, your mum. Friendly as you like, but always a lady.'

'I can imagine.'

'A real lady. Everything always matching. Hat, gloves, handbag – always in a hat, she was. Always in a hat.'

Mary casts her mind back and tries to grab a still of her mother as she was then ... and yes, they are right: even when visiting the fish market or a neighbour, Mary remembers her mother pausing in front of the hall mirror to pin her hat in place.

'She got them free off the milliner, in exchange for silk waistcoats.'

'Did she? That explains it, then.'

'I suppose she was an advert for her dressmaking business.'

'Oh no, she was more than that. Used to give us hope, did your mum.'

'Hope?'

'Oh, yes. If we had a do coming up, and no money, she'd deck us out like ladies for a few pound. She'd even let us have it on tick, and pay her bit by bit. She had this way of cutting cloth: could make the plainest woman look marvellous.'

As she stands there, trying to muster enthusiasm for their nostalgia, she finds that she is shocked – for she'd forgotten how they adored her, forgotten how the shabby street women whispered about Megan Sibly: foreign but beautiful, a dead ringer for Greta Garbo, and how they called her *The Film Star* (probably wondering all the while how such a stylish woman could produce such a lumpish and dreary daughter).

The authorities would vaunt Meghranoush as the perfect example of integration into Devonshire life: starting her own business, adhering to the principles of capitalism and self-interest, displaying traits of innate entrepreneurial talent.

However, the drawback of her successful integration is that she's forgotten her language. She's ashamed, deeply ashamed to admit it, but the words have almost all gone; they've slipped through her fingers like the Syrian Desert sands. A few grains remain, some isolated phrases here and there, but she's forgotten how to string them together.

It's funny, the words she remembers. Mary had her write them down for her one day and she was amazed at the ancient flowing script, so much more beautiful to look at than English, and yet wasn't it utterly odd how some words stayed when thousands of others fled?

Her mother knew for instance that համբուրել meant kiss and that ճչալ was scream and that կարել was sew.

She remembered that բալիկ was baby, that սեր was love and that թուրքական was Turk. Words like մարդասպան: murderer and դարանակալություն: ambush, stayed with her through everything and she said she could never forget that օծել was Christ, եկեղեցի was church and աստված was God.

But what was ամերիկա? She wrote this word down and they looked at it a long time but she couldn't remember what it said. A country; she felt sure it was a country, but which one? America or Egypt, she decided at last, her face set in a frown, and likewise she was adamant that օձ was snake.

'I never forget Farouk, beautiful Farouk. My friend. She bitten two day before wedding. It hot, she sleep on terrace where cool, when Devil's օձ get her.'

'Terrible.'

'Snake there on terrace: Farouk father kill it, he bash it, but poor Farouk gone. He suck bite, but it too late; he shake her until blood come from mouth, but she already gone. They bury her in wedding dress.'

'Such a shame.' Mary would listen to these snippets of her mother's life in the same way she listened to people talking of the Romans: there were battles, there were victories, but when it came down to it, it was all just ancient history.

Her mother's siblings – the five out of twelve who lived through the genocide and fled to Los Angeles, San Francisco and New York – are the only remaining connection she has to her people; octogenarians and nonagenarians all of them, but they still keep in touch, they send her cards with pressed purple flowers in them and these flower cards, which have the power to so greatly elevate her mother's spirits, arrive through the letterbox at Christmas and Easter and sometimes they have Armenian words in them.

Some, like զատիկ and քրիստոսի ծնունդը look familiar, she says, but she's old and her brain can't pick out the meanings. The purple flowers which flutter out of these cards are special: they're pretty, but their value is far greater than just aesthetics.

Mary witnesses her mother's face light up when she holds these desiccated blooms in her hand, for they are sanctified, they are descended from plants which grew in the Holy Land, in Jerusalem. Her mother wishes she'd taken one of these sacred plants with her, a little bit of colour and fragrance in the dreary country she's ended up in, but she didn't think of it at the time. Why would she? – she was going to a land of plenty, with blue skies and green fields. Who knew it was all so grey? Grey faces in grey clothes under grey skies. Still, while she may have forgotten Armenian words, at least she has her accent and Mary knows her mother takes some comfort from this; her accent's never left her, there's no sound of Plymothian in her speech, no sound of Janner, and when she talks to herself, her heavy Armenian lilt must bring her comfort.

Every so often, her mother begins to tell her things. She drops dark hints about ruthless soldiers, about burning churches, and then she stops and won't be drawn. Mary is sure that deep down her mother wants to tell people the full story, but she's abashed because she senses that no-one wants to hear it. They want to hear the interesting things, the entertaining things, but they would find it distasteful to hear the pain.

'So much hate, so bitter,' they would say. 'Let it go. Let it go!'

It's sad for her, though; Mary acknowledges that much. Her customers don't even believe her when they ask what race she is, and when she says her race was massacred ninety years ago they think she's fibbing. How can it have happened without them knowing about it?

If only they knew what she knew – saw the blood, smelled the flesh burn, heard the children's screams – they would not, perhaps, expect her to let it go so very lightly.

Still, furloughs from the retail industry are not meant to be wasted on thinking and so Mary calls *tally ho* to her mother and departs the stifling confines of the house. And this day, the 27th of

May, is superb: she spends seven blissful hours tramping through the unpeopled woods of the River Plym, ascending to the shelter of spinneys topping hills, crossing granite viaducts and striding along ancient railway paths, and this day of deer sightings, of echoic jay calls, of ponderous reflections cast in still green waters is a day filled with extempore moments of bliss.

When she lays her head down to sleep she feels contentment and happiness in rations not usually allotted her: May 27th is the nearest she will ever come to a perfect day.

With the crushing sense of hindsight, she feels that to go through such a change in twenty-four hours is unbelievable; to go from sunny optimism to the terra incognita of confusion and loss is unbearable. The absence of her small mother's small presence has left a void so huge that Mary can hardly bear to think about it. Such thoughts seem to score her brain with a thousand paper cuts leaving it a stinging, throbbing mass.

Although they were never exactly friends, they were companions. Her mother was not just part of the furniture; her mother was the entire house, her mother was the essence of Mary's life – neither particularly good, nor bad; just a constant in the tragicomedy of her existence.

And so the stripping away of her mother is like the stripping away of skin: it is a constant flagellation, an unremitting whip that delights in finding tenderness. In losing her mother, Mary will lose her protection, her armour, her surface, and the anatomical jelly beneath will have to be enough; she will have to make it enough to find her mother and bring her back where she belongs.

Two

His dwelling is dark and decorated with trinkets collected from exotic countries: small paintings hang on the wall, impressions of religious scenes, Christ and the children, the *mater dolorosa*, Saul on the road to Damascus. A mass of cheap *passepartout* dots the walls: Kodak impressions of children, for in the absence of his own flesh and blood children, he furnishes these walls with the staring children of strangers – snaps taken in parks, on beaches, outside school gates – and there are no pictures of women save a small picture of a very old woman whose translucent skin and purplish hands seem to mark her as on the brink of death. And this is a new picture, one he has taken with a Polaroid this very day. He finds it calming to examine this picture: the bright old eyes, the soft wrinkled cheek, the wattle of flesh hanging loosely at the neck, the smallness of hunched shoulders.

He has her just where he wants her, in the beautifully carved antique armoire in the cellar, tied and gagged, and she's quiet: she's not struggling, not caterwauling, not even trying to mouth muffled screams; not fighting, just breathing. She's cooperating, she's very confused and she's putting up no defence because she wants to make no waves, she wants not to anger him. True to those exemplars of passive aggression – the Armenians – she is desperately keeping the peace.

He is not neglecting her: he feeds her and waters her like a plant, and although soon enough he will cut her throat, burn her bag of bones in his furnace and use her essence to flavour a vase, for now he asks nothing of her other than compliance. For now, he's just biding his time, and struggling with his overwhelming attraction to her anility. It is sad for her, he thinks, that the qualities of the aged female are so alluring to him, so overpowering that his brain will burst if he denies himself; and in the struggle that will come it is sad for her that she will die, for die she will, as he is certain of the ineluctable superiority of his desire to kill over her desire to live.

Sitting at the kitchen table in the empty house, he holds aloft her brown and green polka-dot headscarf, twirling it in a pirouette, like the Brummagem tornado reported in the newspaper. He balls it in his fist to inspect it: it has a bilious hue in the low light. It is pure silk, and the lubricious fabric slips through his fingers and turns his stomach. Generally, he'd rather clutch a ball of fibreglass loft insulation than any of his victim's accoutrements, but needs must. He raises the scarf to his nose and takes a whiff of her scent. It is perhaps the least fragrant garment in the world, but it'll make a decent ligature.

He wasn't always like this. He didn't always have this hunger, he thinks; he used to be different. He was not haunted by thoughts of soft decrepit flesh; he used to cope with the emotional disfigurements of his mother, he used not to be angry ... he used to be a lot of things that he lost. Yet it is not his fault; he has been trespassed against, and he forgives in his own style, and for him forgiveness begins with recompense, and so he takes as others have taken from him. He would not be this way were it not for certain events. He has been ill-used, and this ill-treatment has fed the wellspring of his anger and desire. He closes his eyes and he allows himself to see that gauche young boy as he was then, so very long ago, yet so near in his mind's eye, still.

He is so heart-rendingly young, so awkwardly callow, so guileless, so small and he is so very unsophisticated that he eats his fish and chips and mushy peas with his bare fingers and wipes oily smears onto his trouser legs without a thought. He has a long neck, his skin is pale and his bright eyes are large and oval and strangely penetrating. He knows that people find them unnerving, as they often avoid his gaze, and this saddens him. He is an ardent fan of Tolkien but he's not Elven in the slightest: he's too puny, even for an elf. If anything, he must admit that he is more akin to an emaciated hobbit: scrawny, destitute, Gollum eating raw fishes with bony hands. His face is not haggard yet; the bloom still lingers, but his mouth is small and unfashionable, thin-lipped and tight. On his bad days he thinks he resembles the subjects of the creepy eighteenth-century portraits bedecking Saltram House: a 'Vlad the Impaler' look, an anachronistic face that nothing in the world can change. There's nothing to admire on his body, either: he's short and narrow-shouldered and thin – but not the sort of thin that's attractive; not the sort which his mum aspires to be. No, he's too thin; his bones are too big for his body, his hip bones jut and his ribs push angrily out of his chest.

11

However, despite his natural drawbacks, he is teetering on the edge of acceptance with a like-minded cabal of boys and, accompanied by these enthralling new friends, he ventures out into the wilds. They've conspired to deceive their parents about their true whereabouts, and unbeknown to their guardians they have slunk onto the moors. Just a handful of boys, just a radio, just several bottles of beer and vast quantities of purloined peach schnapps. It's a beautiful summer day. Too beautiful. So beautiful that he can taste the beauty in his mouth, and he swallows it so that it doesn't escape him, so that a small piece of beauty resides within him.

The six-week holidays are stretching ahead – holidays that he normally dreads because of his mother, but on this day he's blocking out her face and beckoning only the beautiful. A delicious breeze soothes his hot skin and the cerulean sky is punctuated by fluffy nimbus clouds which bring moments of relief from the eye-needling glare of the sun. They pick out their camp location carefully; they want to be a few miles from the village for easy access to bus stops and corner shops, but they don't want to be too close, because they'll be playing their music pretty loud and they don't want the coppers coming to call.

With their tents on their backs, they wander around the fields until one of the other boys decides it's too hot to go any further, so they set up camp at the edge of the woods, in a field even more verdant than him. The landscape here is more Shire than Lothlórien, but pretty and fresh, away from the grey of the city. They're here alone, overlooked by no adults: they're young and they're free. Their esoteric interests include drinking alcohol, playing poker – strip poker – and conversing for hours on end. They know that these experiences will form memories that will quicken their hearts in old age, because they know that being young is the freest they'll ever be, and that it's all downhill from here. He quivers, actually *quivers*, at the prospect of such freedom. The feeling begins with butterflies in the abdomen: butterflies that flutter through his chest and fingertips, down through his groin and on towards the soles of his feet.

They light a spluttering fire and he's drinking something he's never drunk before and never drunk since: overripe sweetness that seems like nectar to his previously abstemious palate. The peachiness comes back to him, even now; it surges in his mouth and manages still to turn his stomach. He wrongly thinks he's only had one glass, but someone must be refilling it while he's dancing, because before long he's drunketty-drunk-drunk. He dances around the fire with the other boys, and if he was less innocent, he'd shed his clothes and dance like a pagan under the silver sky that arcs above him – a summons to the empyrean.

The sky is luminous with stars. He dances and his blood throbs – and even in his moment of abandon, he's aware that he's watched. But he doesn't care, for in his glory he's immune to those who choose to stare. It must be the music; it keeps him dancing when he should be thinking: the music dopes his mind. Then the exuberance leaves him, quick as a flash, and the energy drifts out of him as the music slows. He lies back and closes his eyes; tries to get a lock on the spinning, but he can't stop it unless he open his eyes, so he focuses on the silver band of the Milky Way, which is so much brighter out here.

He awakens to find a soft face kissing him, fierce passionate kisses. He's not sure who it is, or if any of this is real, or if he can move. He tries to roll away but whoever is upon him is heavy and he's not sure, but he thinks he might be kissing that person back. He might be, but he's paralytic, heavy-legged, deadened. His head is thumping and he doesn't have control of his betraying lips. His mind whirls and for a moment he's up with the stars again, but then the darkness beckons and he accedes.

He can only imagine what he must have looked like to that person who kissed him: so young, so pathetically emasculate, his white face illuminated by the stars. Lifeless, he must have looked: supine. Inviting, he suspects. He's thought of this at great length – just what was it about him that invited attention? Was it that he was so alone, so vulnerable, so innocent-looking? He was innocent, he recollects, once; back then, he was innocent. This thought repeats in his head and the irony won't stop revealing itself, because he was innocent at the time he felt most disgusting; he was more innocent then than he ever would be again.

He was so thin, shorn of puppy fat, shorn of any fat. His body had retreated from its childhood curvaceousness and he was almost skeletal. His arms were incipient, budding; only his larynx was fulsome. Perhaps that was the attraction – naïveté, pure and simple? He wonders how long that man sat there watching him, taking hungry eyefuls of concave stomach and bony face. He might've touched him – very gently, of course, running his fingers over sleeping skin. He can't know for sure if this occurred: he was certainly drunk enough to have slept through such a delicate molestation, but he likes to think he'd have woken had that been the case. Then again, he likes to think he'd have had the sense to stay away from alcohol when he was four years underage.

When he awakens the world is a blur, and when he reaches for his glasses they are not to be found. He looks into the gloom and finds that he's alone – or so it seems at first. The others have retreated to tents – in pairs, probably, for kissing and perhaps mutual masturbation, but nothing more. As far as he knows, none of them have crossed that line yet: it seems more trouble than it's worth, and at least this way, they don't have to lie to their mothers when they maintain that they're virgins. He's thirsty and freezing, he can barely move his hands for the cold, and the goose-bumps are out all over his body; he's rolled away from the fire and he faces the darkness. His first thought: why have they left him here alone, these so-called friends? Couldn't they have woken him, couldn't one of the gits have given him a shake, or even a boot? It never occurs to him that they've not left him alone, that they've left him with someone. It doesn't occur because he doesn't remember yet; he doesn't remember the young man with the alien accent who came to their campfire, attracted by the flames, presumably, with a bottle of whisky and a rag-tag bag of traveller's tales. The man who carried a guitar, who adored Lennon and Janis Joplin and who claimed to have travelled in exotic places such as India and Thailand. Just what he was doing out on the moors on his own on a summer's night was a question that had not occurred to any of them.

His next thought is his hair, which is matted and soaked in something – alcohol of some sort, acrid, fumy – and his face is also sticky: a foreign substance glues his cheek taut. It smells. He thinks he must've spilled something over himself, or rolled in something nasty. Using the back of his hand he wipes the goo from his face as best he can and begins to move. The fire has burnt low, but for a moment he thinks he sees something move across from him, just out of the reach of the glow. He peers over the cinders but is lost without his spectacles.

'Shit. Bugger. Shit,' he says out loud, hoping perhaps that the movement was an animal, an animal that will be scared by his profanities – although he's pretty sure that for a second he saw a person lurking beyond the flames, because his heart is frozen. Don't be pathetic, he warns himself; it's stupid to get the creeps for no reason. At fourteen he should be past being afraid of the dark, past being afraid of aloneness. He feels his face and realises that he cannot turn in for bed in such a state. His tent would be polluted by the fumes emanating from his face, for one thing. And so, bending awkwardly at the waist and groaning as his intoxicated legs falter, he begins to stumble across the field towards the water pump, the jagged line of tents growing steadily smaller behind him in the distance. Slipping across substances that foul his plimsolls, he's uncomfortably aware that every step leads him deeper into silence and he suddenly feels very little, as if in some dark way he's bitten off more than he can chew. For a moment he considers turning back, forgetting his filthiness, and heading back for the tents. But no, he's unsightly; he's covered in what feels like excrement, and what if some of the boys are still awake? He doesn't want them to see him like this. He'll clean himself up, wash his face before bed, as his mum always advocates.

He takes a wrong step and he trips over something heavy. He hears a crack and falls hard, his grasping fingers disappearing into the muddy soil. He realises too late that his glasses were in his trouser pocket. He pulls them out and sees that one of the arms has snapped clean off. He's in trouble now; that was his only pair of glasses and his mum's skint, so unless he wants to walk around for the rest of the trip in blurry-vision, he'll have to wear them lopsidedly, one arm on, one arm off. He puts them on tentatively and decides that he'll just have to make do.

When he is through with his panicking, he looks downwards and sees a red trickle creeping down his thigh; he has landed on the spiky branch of a severed tree and it has cut a rent in his trousers. Pulling himself up and mopping his stinging leg with his palm, he catches the gleam of the silver pump in the starlight, not more than fifty yards away. 'Nearly there,' he says aloud and it seems, in his state of frightened paranoia, that a twig cracks.

His footsteps drag achingly slow now; he seems to be inching towards the pump – when suddenly the back of his neck prickles. Lifting his face upward, he looks into a yellow-eyed face. A Little

Owl watches him; its stripy head swivelled unnaturally. For a moment this bizarre creature peers into him, probing him, assessing in a way that scares him. It looks down and seems to rebuke him, for a young man with a frightened face shouldn't be out here, this night, alone. It shoots him what can only be construed as a deeply disapproving look and then it pierces his ears. The hoot is violent and makes him flinch; it cuts through the air like a scream. In a second it's gone, sweeping low over the field into the darkness, and he shivers before letting loose a string of expletives aimed solely at creepy nocturnal predators.

Thankfully, he reaches the shining tap, bends double and runs the stream over his head. The coldness eats into his flesh and chills him, it cuts into his neck and travels down his spine painfully. It's all he can do to stay still; his reflex is to bolt, to get out of here – but he forces his body still, for doesn't he have a head and a face full of filth that needs to be cleansed? And then they come, the hands that seize quietly from behind and grip him.

There's a legend on Dartmoor of two hairy hands that attack those foolish enough to be out alone on the moor. These severed hands throttle murderously, they jump through car windows, they clutch at motorcycle handlebars, and they steer the hapless vehicles into ditches before finding the throats of the occupants. He's heard various theories about these hands: that they once belonged to a thief who was punished with amputation, or to a labourer whose hands were severed by a threshing machine and were never found. There are many witnesses – reputable ones, too, who claim to have seen the devilish pair running along the roadside or in dells and bogs, using fingers for legs, and so he's embarrassed to admit that when he feels the hands on him, for a split second he does wonder. But the fabled hairy hands only attack on the stretch of road between Postbridge and Two Bridges, and he's in a field somewhere near Yelverton. Even more sinister, these hands clearly have a body attached, because there's strength and weight behind them; if they were severed he could throw them to the floor and kick them or stamp on them until every one of the little finger-legs was bloody and broken.

Then, at last, something comes back to him. He knows, if only vaguely, who these hands belong to; he can smell that twang of whisky – the same smell, he realises too late, that's emanating from his hair. He fights them mutely, not wanting to break the silence, not wanting to dignify the violation with speech. He doesn't turn to see the face. His primary concern is to escape. If he can just wriggle free, he'll take off, running fast in his well-worn plimsolls. He'll get the hell out of here. He's not particularly speedy, but he'll make an exception on this occasion and he'll run like the wind. And he'll never give up: his forte is distance running and he's stubborn as hell. He'll keep going all the way across the moor, ten miles to his door and he won't stop once.

Miraculously, one of the hands weakens for a moment and releases him. He cups the remaining hand, gouging his nails deep into the white flesh.

A branch, maybe. It's swung powerfully and catches him full across the chest. He slumps, panting, waiting for the next move, which he knows will come. He can see the face now, coming to him out of the darkness. It's not an evil face, it's not mad; it doesn't seem to hate him, even. It looks lachrymose, as if the whole world has conspired against it and this is what it's been reduced to. It is a round face with lost blue eyes: eyes that look and don't see; eyes that see him as only as a thing and not a person. The face doesn't speak, but he begins to yell as it moves closer. Now that he knows that he's beaten, at last he finds his voice. 'What do you think you're doing you leave me alone who do you think you are fuck off fuck off.'

Temporarily blinded by rage, he strikes out, ferocious, cat-like, scratching, arms flailing, searching for the eyes, like you're supposed to with sharks: gouge their eyes out and avoid being eaten. But he can't find the eyes; he finds instead the mouth, which doesn't bite him but seems instead to curl around his finger in a warm lick. Then he loses the face again and loses his voice, as strong arms wrap around his throat and slowly, almost leisurely, drag him across the field and into the woods, away from the camp.

He doesn't fully understand why his body is suddenly limp, and why his will evaporates when he so desperately needs it. This betrayal of his body, this cowardice in the face of aggression is the most confusing thing to him at this moment. But in hindsight, perhaps it's the fear that deadens him so completely, a reflex to avoid further injury – in the same way that his drunken mother escapes injury when falling down flights of stairs. Her body so limp that she doesn't reach out to steady herself and therefore doesn't break her arms and wrists and spine, but lands instead in a crumpled and rubbery heap. His body is doing the same; it is regrouping, protecting itself, holding its limbs close.

By the time his attacker has him where he wants him, he can barely breathe and his heart is loud in his head. As if he has asthma, he's gasping hoarsely and the bones in his neck feel shattered. He keeps swallowing. There's blood in his mouth, put there by the punches to his face.

They're in a clearing, the pale blue eyes loom over him and he's crouching on the floor now, retching. A knife appears, quite banally, almost as an afterthought. A back-up plan, in case his victim suddenly acquires a spine, some fight.

'You know what's going to happen here. It'll be quick. Don't think about fighting. You won't win.'

No questions, just facts, but he can't respond to that sad face, that monotone speech even if he wanted to.

'I won't hurt you, unless you make me. Be nice to me, and I'll be nice to you.' These words are dull and lifeless; they are the words of a robot.

An alien hand, smooth and moisturised, reaches downwards to unzip his trousers, the ones his aunt made him for his birthday. They're blue, fitted at the waist with strong elastic and cut from the softest, lightest denim. As they come off he can see the newly acquired mud and grass stains, stains which will never wash out, stains which will mar it forever, and he feels sorry for them. Then comes his black vest. The eyes don't look straight at him; they look instead at this dark garment and the hands feel out the shape, lingeringly, curiously, then they are back on him, burning a hole into his breast tissue. Hands reach out again to touch him and these fingers are hot.

'Don't,' he says, hoarsely.

'Take off the pants,' he is instructed, softly.

He shakes his head determinedly. He will not take off his pants for anybody; he would rather have red hot pokers inserted into his eyeballs.

'Stand up.'

He shakes his head again. He's not even sure if he can stand up, and what does this madman want him standing up for, anyway?

The answer comes to him forcibly in a flash of repugnant insight.

'Do it.'

'Don't, please.'

'Make me angry and I'll hurt you, properly.'

He gets up.

'Now take off your pants.'

'Why are you doing this to me?'

'You shouldn't have kissed me if you didn't want it.'

'I didn't mean to.'

'Course not.'

'Please, don't,' he persists, finding solace in this powerless plea.

'Off.'

He no longer feels cold; there's numbness, but he doesn't feel cold. Like when he has gone bathing in the sea off Cornwall and it is freezing, so cold that it burns his ankles and knees and groin, and then suddenly he feels nothing. That's when he's supposed to get out: when he stops feeling the cold he's in trouble. He knows he's in trouble now. If he screams, even if he screams loud enough to wake the others, it'll take them at least ten minutes in their drunken states to run here, and then they'll have to find him, and by then he might've been stabbed to death. He must survive; he must not be killed as a result of his shameful pride and self-consciousness.

His pants are ridiculously loose, 'tents,' his mum calls them and now he's utterly ashamed of these white tents, disgusted that those awful eyes have seen his pants and that they are the pants of a child. Those eyes already have enough power without the superiority of adulthood, without relegating him to the ranks of the juvenile.

'Bend over,' come the two words that he has been dreading, and these words are no longer robotic, they are husky, they are thick with emotion.

This is it, he thinks; this is what happens to him, and after all the horror that he has been through with his mother, this is what is meant for him, the divine plan adding insult to injury: he will be raped doggedly by a whisky-drinking stranger. Raped and probably murdered. But at this point, rape seems trivial compared to the prospect of being murdered. He has to think he'll survive; he has to believe that when his attacker is done, he'll leave him alone, for he is sincere in this. He must be; if not he could have killed him first and penetrated him when he was dead: he'd still have been warm.

19

It is clear to him now that if he doesn't fight, he won't be hurt and like his mum says, if it doesn't kill you, it makes you stronger. He's heard this phrase so often from his mum that it pops into his head now and he doesn't see the grotesqueness of the application in such a context. He is told two unremarkable names, a Christian name and a middle name – out of politeness? As a nod to propriety? A token of guilt? A show of chivalry? – and then he is informed that it will be quick.

His captor doesn't even bother to undress; there is the sound of unzipping but no clothes fall to the ground. He is behind him; he feels hot breath on his naked lower back so he knows he's crouching somewhere behind his buttocks. There's some probing, some manoeuvring, the hoiking of phlegm onto fingers, and then dampness, and the pain that hits him like a machete, like a knife, like an axe and his seams are torn, so torn that everything must unravel because he has split all the way up the middle and then crossways and he's so fragmented that he's surprised his head hasn't rolled off. He is disenfranchised, he is no longer even a person, he is just mush, he is a tacked-together garment of flesh and bone that can be unmade.

It cannot go on forever, it cannot go forever, and then, in a heartbeat, a deafening, rib-shaking heartbeat, his attacker is done and he's gone. The moon is bright tonight, but now it disappears behind a cloud and he can't be sure that the eyes are not turning back; they could be on their way even now. He should go for help, make his way back to the tents, but he can't, he can't wake them, he doesn't want them to know, and anyway he hates them, they're all bastards for leaving him on his own, for leaving him with a psychopath. He'll never speak to any of them again, he vows, and he doesn't; he keeps to his word and they call him frigid, a freak, miserable-as-sin.

There's no going back to the tents, so he goes for cover; he walks deep into the wood, selects a tree and climbs it. He wraps his arms around the bough and he cries for a while, and then he stops. He feels calmer up here, so he stays in the tree, watching. He sees a fox and a badger and ten thousand rabbits, but no men. His legs fall asleep and he attracts a number of deep splinters. He stays until he can stay no more and he leaves in the hour before dawn. He walks alone, and he's calm. He's no longer afraid and the rage has yet to hit. The world is changed, but he's alive and even if he's alone, in this case aloneness is better than accompaniment. Still, the world looks different; there are things he's never seen before. There are faces of plants; trees reach down to touch him, and the beads of morning dew watch him like the eyes of river fish. He stops at a twist in the river. The water deep and dark green: an invitation. Stepping out of his stained plimsolls, he submerges himself into the magic of the river, feeling the chill creep through his body. He lets it swallow him. The current whirls him around and he feels his body sucked down until his feet bleed on broken slates. Thin tendrils of his hair eddy around him and he sees the blurred film of the water's surface high above.

Then the river has its fill and spits him out. Gaping at the surface, he ululates and vomits onto the water. He watches it float and swirl on the oily surface, catching in the seaweed tresses of his hair; he treads water hysterically as tiny fish mouth the water's skin and eat his puke; he crawls out of the river and sits on the slime of the bank, shivering from the cold clinging of wet clothes; he leaks his way up to the village. He has sought cleansing from the river, but the river is not enough, and as he stands under the battered shelter of the bus stop, amongst the shattered panes of glass, he struggles under the weight of damnation, for he feels with absolute clarity that he is damned. The glass is shattered and there is no mending it. And then he considers, for a moment, the merits of broken shards of glass, and then he disregards them.

No-one is about; the curtains of cosy village houses are pulled shut and his eyes fix on the mouth of the lane, terrified lest they've wakened and followed him, seeking answers. He stares at the mouth and kills the cold hours with dread but no-one comes.

At the centre of him he knows he is broken, broken and remade in the image of his attacker, leeched of all his natural colours. He is scrubbed clean and started afresh, a canvas in the service of an oil painter peeling off old layers, scraping away past errors and starting again from scratch. This newly-thinned canvas, no matter what he builds upon it, will always be stained from this fresh deep scrawl and its imprint will remain, a Turin Shroud of lees and marks.

The changes creep upon him slowly, the rage that turns into insolence and eventually remorselessness. He will come to be fascinated with war, with arcane theories of death-infliction, and he will come to be bored of his sickening, powerless reflection and so he will make dramatic fashion statements, he will experiment with weight loss, with hair colorants, with plucked and then with grown-out eyebrows, with changing glasses and, in time, with coloured contact lenses. Some people will think he is psychologically damaged for wanting to change himself so drastically, but he will enjoy the fact that people do not recognise him – it will give him the upper hand and he will find it comforting to employ disguises, comforting to fool people so absolutely. As the years progress, he will come to despise mastication; he will abhor his postprandial distended stomach, which he will see as a tumour-like protrusion. Food will become a burden, like an advanced pregnancy, and so to his mum's scathing ridicule he will opt to be light and mobile and empty. He himself will accept his appetite impairment unquestioningly, but he will seek other ways to nourish himself, and this search for fulfilment will fuel his twin passions: the arts of creation and destruction and, contrary to matriarchal expectation, he will find himself to be a prodigy.

Three

May 28th: when Mary opens her eyes at 5am, she feels an unusual glimmer of hope – the memories of the preceding day are still warm in her mind – but when she pulls back the curtain there is rain and the cherry blossom falls, bested by drizzle, fluttering to the ground in animate sheaths.

And the avifauna are diving. But their peace will be short-lived: the rain-slicked marmalade tom watches them, prowling nearer, skulking, flanks down, chin in the grass, green eyes on the fragile twitching of a blackbird who finishes the tail-end of a worm.

The rain strengthens and it continues unabatedly for an hour, and the sky is cloven: burgundy clouds to the east, blue skies to the west.

But she is not deterred from venturing out, and when she returns from her daily dawn amble, she is soaked to the skin. She removes her walking boots and socks and leaves them perpendicular to the rush doormat to dry out, and it is then that she sees that the heavy oak-panelled door leading from the hall to the kitchen, which is always shut on account of draughts, is open.

Her mother never rises early, and so Mary is immediately on her guard, considering the twin possibilities of burglars and rapists. With a surge of uncharacteristic bravery, she pads across the floor in bare feet, hot flesh leaving opaque prints on the black tiles. She looks through the gap between door and frame. To her utter astonishment she sees her mother, awake, and bending over something. She is dressed only in her night robes and the patchy white and orange hair flowing to her waist is unfettered by pins. The elbows work fiercely as she crushes – no, grinds – something that is set in a heavy bowl on the counter-top.

Mary's arthritic knees, worn from walking, creak loudly as her body tenses, but her mother, silenced by deafness, hears nothing. She watches, enthralled, as her mother turns and reveals the suspicious white powder that she's grinding with a pestle and mortar. Her mother finishes her preparations, pinches the powder between thumb and forefinger, drops the dust into the rose teacup, struggles with the heavy pot and fills the cup with tea. She washes and dries her grinding implements, and then stoops to return them to their home beneath the sink.

Can it be, Mary thinks incredulously, that her mother is trying to hurt her, deliberately poison her? Is this a form of medication that some busy-body has advised her mother to surreptitiously administer? But it seems so out of character, so devious, and who would have encouraged her to act with such vulpine cunning?

Mary turns away from the opening and back into the hall. She stands in front of the hall mirror, thinking, but she is not unaware of her own eyes, the oddity of which are compounded by the enlarging effect of thick tortoiseshell glasses.

At a loss as to how best to proceed, it seems to Mary that the only thing to do is feign ignorance, which will give her sufficient time to discover what her mother is up to. And so she slams the front door loudly enough to register even in her mother's aged wing-nuts, and pushes open the kitchen door to find the old lady sitting down to a bowl of oats and cup of tea. An identical bowl of oats sits waiting on Mary's 'Secret Garden' placemat, the rose teacup set on the matching coaster.

'Mary, Godsake, why you always make such noises? Bang, bang, bang at such time of morning.'

Meghranoush's Armenian accent has many shades, the most common being the tone of irritation she reserves specifically for Mary; even so, today her mother seems especially irate.

'Where you been, anyway? Don't tell me: walking?'

'I've been getting some exercise, yes.' Mary eyes the pink teacup and a faint suggestion of white powder is perceptible.

'Always walking. So early! It still night! You not normal, you should be sleeping, get beauty sleep, you need, Jesus know you need that kind sleep.' Her mother has built up steam and Mary braces herself for its inevitable release.

'Walking, always around stinking pond, stinking water make you ill!'

Her mother has not put in her teeth and her empty mouth leers, pink, gummy and rubbery. She hates her dentures with a passion, the shiny ivory traps bits of food in the hinterland between teeth and gums and the itching drives her mad. She saves her teeth for neighbours and customers but as soon as the front door shuts, the teeth are back in their glass of water, grinning from the sideboard.

'It's good for me, Mother. I need air,' Mary says, trying to sound breezy.

'Not stinking air. I tell you what you need, what you need is man. Now you not go to work, you should try to get man.' The old woman purses parched lips and shakes her head with exaggerated disapproval.

'What I need is peace and quiet away from you,' Mary says, low enough for her mother only to catch a murmur.

'Look at you, you old. No Husband, no Baby. You never make Baby now. Too late. You nearly fifty-eight. You old.'

'Oak trees don't grow acorns until they're fifty,' Mary ripostes, looking into her mother's eyes, forcing a smile.

'What you say? Tree?' The elder woman turns her neck, straining to hear.

'Oaks don't grow acorns until they're fifty. Shall I repeat it for you again, Mother?'

'You not tree, Mary,' Meghranoush answers.

'I know that, but if I was, I'd be an oak.'

'Shut up. Eat food,' Meghranoush says, with a repellently full mouth. Mary watches empty gums mash cereal, and flakes of milky oats stick to pale lips.

'Your command is, as ever, my wish,' she says, picking up her spoon.

After the first mouthful, however, she finds that the vessel of poison, the china teacup, brushes against her elbow, flies to the floor and smashes into a thousand satisfying fragments.

'Dear me, look what I've done.'

'Stupid, clumsy girl. God, I hurt. You hurt me, stupid, clumsy Mary.' A shard of china has torn through the papery skin enveloping her shin and a slow trickle of blood runs from the gash.

'Silly me, silly little Mary. Want a pestle and mortar?' Mary asks quietly. The old woman looks at her.

'What you say, Mary?'

'Want a plaster, Mother?'

'Leave me alone, stupid, clumsy girl. I get myself.'

Her mother stoops to a cupboard, her shin still bleeding, and scrabbles for the First-Aid box. A synthetic smile stretches Mary's face; she picks up her spoon and one small and ladylike mouthful at a time, she finishes her oats.

'Why you always hurting me?' her mother mews plaintively.

'It was an accident.'

'How you say such lie, to your own mother?' Meghranoush hobbles to her feet, friable joints cracking from the effort. She moves towards Mary, to face her. She totters on atrophied legs, swaying, but standing nonetheless.

'How could you poison me?' Mary asks uncertainly. 'Don't deny it, I saw you.'

Her mother looks up to the heavens and sighs.

'Silly, silly Mary. Poison? Pah! Who want poison you?'

'You, evidently.'

'Shush, not so loud, we okay. No need be angry.'

The fact of her mother's mendacity in response to direct questioning angers Mary more than she would have expected.

'Sit down, Mother.'

'I stand.'

'I'm warning you.' Mary waves her spoon in her mother's face. 'Sit down.'

'No.'

Mary stands and towers. She scorns the weak imploring face and she feels no hesitation for what she will do, because she is strengthened by justification and the knowledge that her disputatious mother must be put in her place.

The old woman raises her hand and reaches up to touch Mary's cheek, which is her first mistake, because her daughter chooses to misconstrue the gesture as an attack. Mary regards the papery hand and whilst on another day she might turn the other cheek, today she is hot with temper and the old trick fails in efficacy: Mary brushes away the mottled paw.

'Leave me and my cheeks alone. You don't deserve a daughter. You deserve to be alone,' Mary spits and she hopes her mother's hearing aid is cranked up to full throttle.

There is fear in the old eyes but Mary registers only a provoking head shake, and she watches, almost as a bystander, as her own hands reach out. With the slightest push Mary nudges her mother back down on her chair, and turns to gather momentum. Spinning on the spot, she whirls with dervish alacrity until she is dizzy, and she doesn't want to scream, she wants to laugh because she feels that her slewing is unravelling the spool of her mother's existence.

Lifting her arm, the back of her hand finds her mother's cold cheek and there is the crack of a slap. Mary is sick that her arms aren't stronger, and as she sees a small bright nose-slick, she is sick that she can't hurt her more than she has, and she triumphs to see her mother's face crumple, and she sneers at those crocodile tears.

'He tell me to. You hear? He tell me put tablet in teas.'

'Who? That unctuous lickspittle of a general practitioner?'

'I no know what you say,' Meghranoush says in a tiny voice.

'Who told you to poison me?'

'I confuse, I say silly thing.'

'Tell me!'

But she is wordless. Mary detects the stubbornness in her mother's countenance and she knows she'll not get answers, not now, but she expects something in the way of retaliation – at the very least a personal attack, a litany of criticisms, remonstrance – but there is deep silence, so deep it seems she's forgotten what's passed, sitting so still, so craggy, so silent. A limestone bust strafed by acid rain.

This torpor is the newest strain of her mother's senility and perhaps, thinks Mary, these moments are the positive effects of antiquity, because her mother is liable to forget everything. Mary could lash her with maledictions, smite her with blasphemy, and within an hour she would show no sign of remembering any of it.

And so, by a twist of fate, it happened that the day on which her mother disappeared was also the day that Mary took her hand to her mother for the first time in her life – a coincidence that led Mary to believe for the first brutal week that her mother had run away to escape brutality, that her mother was afraid of her.

And these thoughts were very painful. That decades of frustration could lead her to hit her own mother, her own 94-year-old mother, was appalling.

Trapped in a quagmire of doubt, it seemed possible in those first days that her mother had checked herself into a nursing home, or was living rough as a bag-lady, to spite her. It was only when her searches came to nothing that the panic began to gore.

If Mary were less religious she might deem her mother's disappearance to be an act of revenge on the part of the Great Almighty, a wake-up call. 'You took her for granted, you little bitch, so let's see how you manage without her.'

Taking for granted is a strangely human phenomenon, Mary will decide later. Marauding lions never take for granted an antelope corpse, not even for a second, as they delve their bloody noses into comforting wetness and consume entrails by the bucket-load. They glance over their shoulders with a weather eye to impostors, who they expect to steal their kill at every moment. This, Mary postulates, is why lions are the king of the jungle and why there are so few human kings.

After endless minutes of stony-faced silence, Meghranoush mops her bloody nose, and with recriminating glances at the portrait of Mary's father, she stuffs her nostrils with Kleenex and pretends that nothing untoward has happened. Instead of fighting her corner, she sets about her work of sewing a wedding dress, the first one she's done in years. It's for a rich lady who wears a fur coat which smells of dust and moths and wet dogs. The lady's eldest daughter is to be married and insists on a handmade dress, and everyone knows that Mary's mother is the best dressmaker around, despite being decrepit. She's also the cheapest, but she's foreign and glad to get a few pounds for her work where others would charge a few hundred. In the Homeland she'd have got little for any of her services.

Meghranoush's old hands shake and she can't thread the needle.

Mary surmises that the current threading problem lies in the eyes, which were once brown but now are turning blue.

'Let me do it.' Mary swipes the needle and threads it, waves of anger ebbing away and leaving only an imprint of curlicues.

'You've got cataracts,' Mary suggests sulkily. 'Not waterfalls – opaqueness of the eyes.'

Her mother rejects this with the information that: 'I not old enough to get old-lady disease.'

She can't see the stitches, though; only last week her mother accidentally sewed a puffball sleeve to her apron, but Mary said nothing, she didn't want to embarrass her, and her mother noticed it eventually.

'I can sew blindfold,' she says taciturnly.

'So then,' Mary rationalises, 'it won't be too difficult for you when your cataracts make you completely blind.'

'I sew in dark all my life,' Meghranoush replies.

Mary is touched by the briefest pang of guilt – the blood has begun to seep through her mother's makeshift nostril tampon – and she considers offering to help with the sewing. She could maybe hold the fabric straight while her mother ran it through the machine, but she's well aware of her own failures in the tailoring department: she's a shoddy seamstress, abysmal; the fabric would end up in a snarled, apocalyptic mess. As for hand-sewing, a tacking stitch is the best she can manage.

Her mother professes not to know how Mary can be her child with stitches like that. 'You like your father,' Meghranoush says with barely-disguised disgust, following this revelation with: 'Your father good-for-nothing, always smoking drunk.'

Mary cannot keep track of her mother's meandering moods, and it is not just her mother who is inconsistent: her own moods are quicksilver, up and down every other minute.

She believes at this moment that she is better off alone; she believes that her mother is an annoyance; that no-one in their right mind would want to loll around with a sententious nonagenarian, day-in, day-out. She is haunted by the notion that her home is a theocratic state ruled by her mother's religious authority, and within this acidic atmosphere she finds that her thoughts are unacceptably interrupted. The Armenian's penetrating voice is a continuing noise that fills the air with words tending towards the spiteful. It is a voice whose missteps in English rasp unbearably upon her ear and it is time for it to diminish.

With every day that passes, Mary's antediluvian grows older, weaker, more shrivelled: she's a fossil of her former self.

Mary thanks the Lord that at least her mother can still drag herself up the stairs and to the toilet – she dreads her becoming one of those urogenous old women who sit in chairs all day, producing piss by the barrel, leaving their poor daughters to scrub defiled furnishings. Heaven forfend that she'll be called upon to succour her. She doesn't think she could do it; she would faint in horror.

It's only a matter of time before the inevitability of death, but she's ninety-plus already, far beyond her life expectancy. How much longer will it be? – and when will her own halcyon years be upon her?

And Mary prays that her mother will not outlive her, for so many children die, she tells herself, and yet here is this Armenian greedily clinging on, gasping good clean air, snuffling like a hog at the life trough.

Good God, thinks Mary. Go gentle into that good night. Fizzle at the close of day; don't bother to rage against the dying of the light.

She forgets the old adage that you should be careful what you wish for, but then she doesn't know what is to come, and so she is unaware of the poisonous nature of her own thoughts. Instead, she blames her mother, whose obstinacy and moralising have surely forced her into such uncharitable ideas.

As unbearable as this encounter was, Mary will later find comfort in the fact that her mother at least tried to reach out to her with that gentle touching of cheek. That some semblance of love was in her mother's heart on the day she was taken. That it was a soft, feeling heart, that it was not already dead, is a blessing.

If only, she wishes with clarion hindsight, she had known that another person – a man – had even more uncharitable ideas about her mother, that he had been having terrible thoughts about her for a long time and that he was about to obey his own violent and perverse instincts, then Mary would have rushed her mother out of the house, deposited her in some safe, untraceable place.

Instead of abject grovelling, though – instead of begging her mother's forgiveness for splitting both shin and nose – Mary attempts to make amends by going to the kitchen and slicing a sun-blushed pomegranate in two. She places it on the arm of her mother's chair but Meghranoush is too absorbed to notice at first and when she does, she nods, unsmilingly.

All of her tacking stitches are in place and she's set to sewing a new line in her tiny formal stitch. She's not using the sewing machine; perhaps her legs are hurting her. She sits huddled in the morning sunshine, prisms of light flashing off her needle. Every hundred stitches or so, she needles a pink jellied eye from the pomegranate. Half a pomegranate or an orange persimmon can keep her going all day and she loves them, she says it's fast food: it requires no cooking, she doesn't need her teeth in, and the sweetness reminds her of the Homeland.

Mary has often heard her mother say that the only real benefit of sewing is that it busies the hands and leaves the mind free to remember. Armenian to the core, her mother is, and as an Armenian she knows how important it is to recall.

'Forgetting wicked,' she tells Mary, breaking the silence.

'So you said yesterday, and the day before that, if memory serves.'

'Forgetting thing make thing history, make thing less real. If people forget, past never happen. Too many people forget already.'

'Yes, you told me already.'

'Armenians remember.' And she does remember, because there is so much to remember: Igdir, Van, Constantinople, Syria, Palestine, Jerusalem, Bethlehem. Heat and rocky deserts, stinking camels and stinging scorpions in little shoes. With every stitch, it is as if her mother remembers a difference face, a difference place. She sees them as vividly now as she did when she was five years old.

Her memories are not vague or blurred, they have razor-sharp outlines. They come to her like the first film she ever saw, they come to her like *The Wizard of Oz* in Technicolor: the hot summers, the icy winters, the fruit trees; panning for gold at the edges of fast flowing rivers, the village women weaving the brightest of silks and the softest of woollen tunics; the smell of the air as she walked high up in the mountains with her family, under the shadow of Little Ararat.

There was nothing to be afraid of; she wandered where her feet took her and only looked back to see the sky.

'I never forget churches,' Meghranoush promises, hand on heart. 'They say there five thousand churches in Motherland. Five thousand!'

'I know. You told me.'

'Wondrous church and monument dedicate to Jesus. Figures that alive, carve by great sculptors from ancient rock, beautiful yellow stone of Homeland.'

Mary doesn't answer because her mother is not really talking to her; she is running through a list of safeguards that steel her against loss. So Mary only half-listens to her mother's talk of the homeland, and she only listens at all because her mother's nose is still bleeding and so is her shin, and because she cannot pretend that they are not.

In all this talk of the homeland, though, it occurs to Mary that once upon a time her mother didn't use such expressions as the Homeland, or the Motherland, or Armenia: she only began to use those names when she left. Back then she was Meghranoush, not

31

Megan, and just like everyone else, little Meghranoush Zorabedian called the Homeland *Hayastan*.

She watches her mother trying to suppress her yawn because it's only morning, and the lower palate of her own mouth fills with the juice of unripe apples as she thinks about what her mother's endured. What her mother's hidden from her, because she didn't trust her, because Mary is not one of her people, because – and she has made this clear – Mary is not Armenian.

Suddenly, it occurs to Mary that her mother should not be sewing in her nightgown at this time of day: she should be washed and dressed and brushing her hat in anticipation of her daily hobble to the Post Office. Her mother insists upon this daily pilgrimage, where she exchanges pleasantries with Glenda the post-mistress who, after sixty years, still cannot make out Mrs. Sibly's halting attempts at English.

'Why aren't you going to the Post Office?' Mary asks tentatively.

'I go later.'

'But you go at ten.'

'I go later.'

'But you always go at ten.'

'Man coming to collect suit trouser at eleven. Better nose stop bleed before he come.'

Her mother is strong; stronger than she herself is.

Mary watches as the old lady shifts in her seat and wobbles her way to the black Singer sewing machine. Her mother turns her back and whirring fills the air as she pumps the foot peddle.

Mary stands for a moment, watching. The old house suddenly feels suffocating, prehensile, as if it is clawing at her like the tentacles of a giant squid, suckering her all over. She must leave. She scratches the tender skin of her wrist agitatedly, and bends to peck her mother on the cheek in wordless apology, smoothing out a crumpled but clean tissue which her mother takes sniffily. Not sure what to say, Mary turns to leave.

'Where you go, Mary?' her mother asks, without looking up.

'Out.'

'Out to where?'

'I don't know.'

'When you back?'

'I'm not sure.'

'Back for tea?'

'Yes, back for tea.'

'See you teatime,' her mother rumbles continently.

'I'll bring us some buns,' Mary says, attempting an olive branch.

'I get fat. I on diet, I no want no buns.'

Mary hazards an unreturned backward glance at her mother. Meghranoush's hair is free around her sloping shoulders, the tresses marred with patches of orange hair dye. Harmony Hair Dye, she uses, in Copper. Mary sees it in the bathroom; hears the neighbours' children whisper that Mrs Sibly is rusting.

A small distended belly pushes out of Meghranoush's fragile four foot-eight frame and rests on her lap: a cruel mockery of pregnancy. Old Meghranoush is a state, no longer the Film Star; she's shrunk and bent from decades of sewing abuse. A Superannuated Sewer is what she's become – it's always tickled Mary that the word 'sewer' is used both for consummate needlewomen like her mother and the underground conduits that carry sewage – a point that her mother, with her limited grasp of English, would never be able to appreciate.

And so Mary takes a lingering look at her mother and turns her back again and leaves the room – but then she does something that she will later come to cherish, an act of procrastination that will result in her knowing her mother infinitely better than before.

She does not leave the house straight away, feeling, in her state of irritable guilt, that she must wash and dry the remainder of the breakfast dishes. Mary hovers in the house and suddenly she hears a disembodied sound: the small voice of her mother emanating from the sitting room. But her mother is not talking to her; she's not talking to anybody.

Mary discerns the shrill note of distress in her voice, and although she feels instinctively that she mustn't intrude upon her mother's hard-won privacy, she's desperate to know whatever it is that her mother can tell to the air. She throws down the tea-towel and listens.

Four

I getting be old. Mary, she not know what it mean to be old woman. She still young, she not know what it is to have pain in your bones. She not understand what it like to wake up and feel tired, more tired than when you lay down at night.

She say I strong; she never know I weak. She need me be strong to look after her, she need me always be her mum, but I old and I not live forever. I try live forever but I can't.

We all have our time, then it time to die. I know it, and I know my time comes soon. She a good girl, maybe I should tell her she is good girl more. She could make a good wife, it still not too late. Or even be modern, maybe not even be wife, maybe just have love for a man would be enough. But how I tell her? How you tell someone fall in love if they not know what love is? If they never felt pain, never felt happiness in they heart?

Mary my biggest mistake. When she in womb I so sick, I sick every day. I had such nightmare. Maybe I poison her, like rat. She not die, but when she come out, she look at me so sad. I go doctor and tell him. Doctor think I stupid, but I not. I know she not right then, she never smiling, never crying, always quiet. Not sleep, but not scream, she lay quiet in baby-bed, just looking, big baby, big eyes looking at ceiling, looking for heaven.

Then when she is little girl she is always talking to her friends, but friends that not there. So many imaginary friend, people say normal for little girl, say not to worry about such thing, but she talking to people not there, she dancing music not in air.

I should have done something. My poor Mary.

If only I know then what I know now. But that life, that life, there no go back when you want, only go forward. I maybe should not come to this country, this England that everyone is so proud to live in. This Plymouth, they say so historic, you sit on Hoe with all statue of famous people and big red and white lighthouse. They say Francis Drake live here, Darwin leave from here and go Galapagos, and Founding Father leave from Mayflower Step to go America.

Well, is this thing to be proud of? They so quick tell you these thing but when you ask question you find truth not nice. Founding

34

Father go to America, bring disease to peoples who live there, then come more English people who kill buffalo so nothing to eat for anyone else, they take gold and get rich and they kill Indians. Indians, they call them. They not even in India. They so stupid they think they in India, when really in America. Now look America. It better if they leave people who live there alone.

Then Francis Drake, he make money from Africa slave, he take slave for America, take free people and sell them for slave. He start slave trade, millions poor African stole from they land and this begin in Plymouth. Nothing be proud of! If Armenian man do this we be ashamed to speak his name, we not make statue.

Slaves make Drake rich man, Elizabeth Queen knight him and he is her favourite; then he is pirate, picaroon, he sail around, steal thing from places and other ship. Spanish coming to invade, they say, and he finish bowling game before trying to save his people. He not nice man to me.

Then they got statue for Darwin who go to foreign islands and make new idea for how people come to live and he come back and ideas go around from mouth to mouth and then nobody believe in God. What these Plymouth people proud for? All these famous people, what they done good? Killing people who minding own business, selling them, stealing gold and taking for themself, making idea which killing people faith, which killing God?

They say we foreigner uncivilised.

Mary never be way she is if I stay in Jerusalem, if I go back to Motherland I would been happier too. But there no going back home: once you out, you out. People say there no Armenians in old places, even now, they still not allow go back.

These English, they tell me how grateful I am for living in they great country. They say what relief it be to come to 'civilised' place with food on table and television in front room.

They ask me if I ever seen television in Homeland. I tell them no, they not invented until after I come here.

They think my family don't have one back home. I tell them none my family in Homeland anymore, we all must leave, but that they have many television where they live in America, and bigger television than you have, as my brother families all rich and own jewellery business.

They look me, shock, they not believe I got rich relative, me, foreigner, got family richer than they. They think if it true, then I be rich too, that my family send money; they know nothing.

My family always send money and present, and I give money to charity and give present away to neighbour. It not Armenian way to take charity, we take what we earn. I have enough; I no need trinket, silly luxury, to make me happy. We not like English, we not 'buy, buy, buy, more, more, more.' We glad what we got. If we get more, okay; if we work for, but if not get more, we no mind.

I never know greed until I come to this country: people steal handbag, come in house when you sleep, take your thing and sell to buy drug. In Homeland, and in Jerusalem, nobody lock door, nobody need. Everyone know neighbour; if someone got more money, more thing than we, we happy, we not want to steal. No point be jealous; more thing you have, more thing you dust; more thing you watch here in England and worry be stolen.

I tell Mary I want live like tramp, give up all thing and just go, be free. I look at old men sitting in blankets on Hoe and Barbican and I think, 'you are free.'

I try to tell Mary this and she laugh. She say I not last two minute, she say I small, she call me 'short-ass' and she smiling. Today not like old day, she says, real world different. More danger. Tramp sleep one night and boy, sixteen maybe, come out nightclub and set fire to him, Mary say. Pour petrol and throw match. Tramp almost die, but survive with bad burn, and old lady tramp sleeping in bus station is stab to death by spotty boy who on drugs. This life, she say, not silly dream. I tell Mary: 'Tramp is free. He free, he sits under star and he worry for nothing.'

My daughter. How you have children who so different from you? She not like me, she not stone enough to survive what I do. She call me silly and little, she think she blow and I fall. Papa used say, 'Meghranoush, you strong, more strong than all boy; you sent from angels to protect us.'

He not think small is same as weak; he not think young is same as silly. Papa and Mami know. But then, they Armenian. These English, they only know tea and ballgame, and silly joke. My husband used to ask me, 'What is difference between blonde lady and Panama canal?' I say, 'One is canal and one is lady?' He say I have no sense of humour but that answer is that Panama canal is a 'busy ditch' and he laugh and I am in dark.

And he spend all the hour doing silly little newspaper puzzle, they 'crossword,' they call. It funny that 'cross' mean 'angry' and angry word is all they say when they do crossword.

I try to tell George, but he not smile. Instead, he asks what is anagram for 'Vile Dog.' I ask him, 'What is anagram?' and he ignore. I look in dictionary and anagram is mixed-up word that not make sense, so that you have to find back again.

English people got time to waste.

Only anagram I find for 'Vile Dog' is 'God Live,' and also 'Evil Dog,' but I not like 'Evil Dog,' so not write down. There no other anagram, I tell George, but he say I wrong and that 'God Live' is not right, but close to the one he mean. I look for long time, but I not find answer.

George tell me he love me every day; I never believe him.

I no know why. Maybe because he no love God. When I go to church, he say, 'why you go church? Why not pray God here?' he not understand why I love God more than I love him. But he say 'I love you' every day. He not liar man normally, but on this thing, I think he lie.

I think he like me, I good sewing, good cook, make him happy night time, but he not love me.

Once he bring me this country, he seem forget me, sequin fall off. I only interesting when I new, or when he can't have me. He like me when I exotic, in exotic country. When I exotic in England, I just pain in backside. He always say how long it take me to learn English – I stupid for not speaking stupid language. English no sense language, so I no care. Anyway, I know more English than he know Armenian.

When I first here, I want George learn one Armenian thing, just so I can talk little bit with him, which remind me home. He say, 'I not speak mumbo-jumbo.' Mumbo-jumbo, he call. I angry and tell him I have to learn stupid English. He blow his nose and say that if I in his country, I must speak 'lingo' that he speak, then he talk about Romans being in Rome. Not one Armenian word he learn; more I try make him, more angry he get, as if I make some crime against him. If he love me, he learn one word.

My neighbour say I lucky, they hear him call 'Love you' as he leave for dirty pub. They say they husband never say such thing in street; never say it ever. But saying not meaning always. Quiet husband might feel, I wish George feel. But there. God have plan.

I wonder when I die, what happen up there. George there? Or just Mami be there, with Papa, and how old they be? I try talk this thing with Mary, but she say I never die. I try talk to Mary and she say I should not think these thing. She say I should live one day as it comes. Always off in world of own, Mary; empty in eyes. Off with fairy, George use to say. Never look like fairyland. Look like she somewhere sad to me.

What happen my daughter? Why I not have boys that live? I never know. It my punishment maybe. I punish for what I do in war, I should not run away and leave Mami with bad men. I should stand and fight and die, if that what meant for me, even though I only little.

Boy dying is punishment for what I can never make better.

I save myself and leave Mami, I deserve to be punish. I lucky to make any children, with what I done. But it bad men, bad men that hate Armenians, they do these thing. If they not do bad thing, I be in Homeland. I would grow up with Papa and Mami and brothers; not run always. I wish bad men death, pain.

If only I can go home! Sit in hot sun and feel warm in bones, all quiet, no rush. I can listen to voices of old men who sit all day under trees, they sit and talk and laugh all day through. They play domino until dark. Other men bet on fighting spider and they drinking white pomegranate juice. Summer so hot, we children play all afternoon in beautiful river. So happy, before what come.

We walk into mountain, Mami, Papa, brothers; we collect nut and berry, Papa use stick to frighten snake. We make fire in cave in mountain and eat hot nut. All warm inside and big cloud make rains outside. Big mountain and beautiful music of Papa's duduk is floating in air. He play into our hearts and bring Armenian people into air.

There is no instrument that is beautiful like duduk. They make by hand from apricot woods. Beautiful sounds, and we have high zurna to float happy sound on winds, and shvi, which like flute, and then thump, thump of dhol, which is Armenian drum. You not hear any these sound in England, not once I hear duduk since I come here, but no matter, I still remember in heart.

My brother tell me one Armenian musician very rich and famous, he composer Aram Khatchadourian and Aram say to world that duduk is only instrument that ever make him cry. All should hear duduk, and then they understand: is no music like Armenian music – is music made by God.

I dream of they in night, they come to me in dream, they hurt Mami, they kill baby, he shoot pregnant lady, he cut baby from belly.

When I wake I still hear they laughing: laugh they do, as they kill. I try tell Mary, in genocide I say, they laugh as they kill. Armenians never laugh, even if we kill animal, rabbit maybe, we respectful when we take even rabbit life. That's what Turks call us, little rabbits, because Turk word for rabbit, they say, is nearly same word as they word for Armenian.

Even in Jerusalem Turks laugh at us, they call us little rabbits. Little rabbits, making baby in Armenian quarter which they call 'warren,' they say we too meek to fight, timid, always run away.

Little rabbits. I wish I show them, but one day they all die and God will see them and punish them for what they done. This make me happy. This thoughts give peace.

Oh God, I wish I not talk to Mary, she never comfort, she never kind. You know what she say? She say, 'Yes. They laugh as they kill, so do the English. Only one little letter separate Slaughter from Laughter in this language.'

I cry, I cry for long time. Slaughter, laughter, these thing must be wide apart, must stay one on one side, one on other side. I wish there someone I can talk to. Mary laugh and leave, and I glad when she gone.

So much gone wrong for me. Five babies grow in me and one living still, from five. All the boy gone now, Nishan, Tigris, Luke and Leo: all gone, Nishan come out of belly dead, Tigris and Luke come out belly too soon and not last – and Leo, my beautiful, strong Leo is dead in baby bed: blue faces all four. Mary: she almost dead, not living; she is still walking, always walking, but face is going blue.

Poor Mary, silly Mary. Should be good things for Mary, husband, baby, friend, but she getting old, it too late maybe. Out of all, she only one to stay home. I not believe she is my daughter. Hair all dry and grey like old lady, she won't dye, she say no Harmony Hair Dyes. She just keeps it big and grey like old bush. And glasses, they so thick! How she see through them? Make her eyes big like fish. Not nice nut brown eyes like Meghranoush eyes – staring, pale eye and they not match: one blue eye have patch of green in it. Patchy eye – I should known when I see this baby that she go bad.

She got no style, she wear plastic mackintosh, blue one and purple one and silver one, no hat, just grey hair and yellow bag around waist, she call bumbag. Bumbag! Daughter of Meghranoush is wearing bumbag, not holding nice leather handbag.

How she get husband when she look like that? And she have no figure. She so thin, thin like beggar woman, but she no eat food. I catch her eating sponge! Kitchen sponge! Why she eat sponge? Maybe she think keep her thin but she already thin. Too thin. She never still, always walk: walk around lake, walk on beach, walk in Kiddie Park.

She gone funny. She not right. She always looking at big red dictionary, always dictionary. She know enough English word already, better she learn Armenian or reading Bible! And she see thing, she see thing and talk voices not there. I try help, but she no listen, why she listen to me? I only her Mami, what I know?

Lucky she is, lucky, but Mary listen? No. 'I no need your words,' she say, but she do need. She scratching herself, she scratch face until it bleeding, she scratch backside and she screaming like animal, some nights. Always shouting at me, shouting like mad man and she eat me with her eyes. Where is my Mary gone? She miss me when I gone.

I can't help her when I gone, then I up in heaven and I no help to her up there. After I die, all river and well might run dry and there nothing I can do. So angry, even she shouting at wall. And I hear her at night and she swearing. She say bad thing, blasphemy thing against God. I tell her beware those who not fear God. Neighbours can hear she say these thing, they will talk; and who can stop the talk of the people? Mary, she know she is in all the neighbour mouth, but she no care. What I done to get this daughter? Why she do this to us? Why she angry, what she know of hurting? If she go through what I go through, she know when be happy and when be angry.

I never forget. In English year is Nineteen-Fifteen when it is starting. The year is Four-Thousand, Four-Hundred Seven in Armenian calendar, which different from English calendar. That year they come for us.

Mami told us, things they changing. But I so small, only five year old, how I know that in two days, eight hundred Armenian people dead and only beginning. If we knew what to do! We think God save us, we not fight.

We should have made fight. The day brings bread to one, woe to another – Mami said on the day we hear the horses coming. We none of us eat bread for many month. They want to kill all Armenians living in Turkey and West Armenia. Mary used to say, 'Mum, why you live in Turkey then, why are not Armenians living in Armenia?'

'We are,' I say. 'Yes, is Turkey now, but once it was Armenia. Armenians live where they have always live, even if border change, land not change. Our country on maps is one in ten of what it is one time. Our land one time stretch from Arapgir in West to Baku in East. We have beautiful Karabagh before Azeri come and make war, we had Tabritz in South and Ardahan in north before Turk take. They take all Armenian lands, but no matter, just because they think is theirs, they still ours.'

Poor Mary, she not know anything. How I make her see what happen in 1915? It too late now, poor Mary.

Everything upside down when I little. They already taken Papa many month before, they take clever Armenian men to make thing for war. Papa is good tailor so they come take him in night. Bang, bang, bang on door. They need him make uniform for Turk Army. He not want to, but they got gun, they say they kill us if he not go. They take axe and gun and bow from village, so we little lamb. When bad men come back to village in Nineteen-Fifteen, Papa gone and we women have not enough men protect us, and men we got, they kill. They want kill all Armenians. We women, how we fight such men?

Central Committee of Young Turks make laws, their Jemiyet, they call them; they say lands should be rid of Armenians, we infidels, we Christian. Greeks too they want out, they want dead. They say they want to free they 'Fatherland' from Armenians. They Fatherland is our Motherland.

They make gang murderers do dirty work, they 'Special Organisation,' they convicts and crazymen, they say is Jihad and we Christian infidel, we dogs must die. How women fight?

You no make axe from thousand needles. They flew their brains. Our church they burn, yellow rock tumble down, gone all black, smoke filling sky, it fly up and away to Ararat. Smoke in Noah mountain. We taste burnt church in mouth. Our priests they kill. They spit on holy men then smash sculls with axe.

Stuffed my priest mouth – I know him since I baby – they stuff his holy mouth with pages from Bible and he choking. They make us watch them cut his head with knife. In square where everyone can see. The blood come and spray far, spray donkey who tie up, it making donkey mad, he try to run but he tied. Priest still screaming as head coming off. God help us.

They kill politician, priest, lawyer, teacher, writer, painter, smart thinker, then they start to kill merchant. They chop they heads and keep for souvenir – some of they take pictures, they say if you look on computer you can see photo of these thing, row and row of dead heads sitting on kitchen shelf, where plate should be. And they take many head and push on stick, and wave in air like torch, they wave at us so we must see.

Five thousand taken from beds and murdered. They start deporting Armenians, force them to go to Syria, millions going, then we still too many so they beginning Extermination Camp. Oh God. Mary think she got pain? Mary got food, water, work, doctor. She got mother; what I got?

All gone long time. Children screaming, beaten to death. Mullahs shouting. Christian Infidel, they call us. Who helped us? Who even heard of my people?

It start with men, they ordered to go to government houses and they shot. Thank God my Papa not there. Brothers gone too: Mami made they go south to Arda Aunty and cousin Arkina in Van – such beautiful lands there, shining Lake Van, like Paradise; we once visit pretty Arkina there, who I love like sister. Mami know boy not safe where we live near Igdir. Mami right. They shoot all men and boys. We not know then that in Van is just as bad, they kill twenty-five thousand in three day.

I stay with Mami. I am only girl and Arda Aunty got no room for me. Anyway I no want to leave Mami. Turk no waste bullets on women and children, they send us on march through desert. Turk got food and drink, but nothing for Armenian peoples, only whip. Heat gets us, no drink kills us. Hot sun up here, hot sand down here. Any too tired to walk? Murder: they use knife, hammer, rope, never waste gun on girl.

Woman, pretty woman, still young, who come from Mersin, is

big with baby, she can't walk fast. They whip her but she still not move, she no breath left and she is stone because of the fear. Turk push her to ground, take dress up and cut belly with knife while she screaming.

He cut and cut and put hand in and he get baby. Use knife to cut cord and he throw little baby on floor. He stamp on it. Baby only born one minute and he die like nothing. Man turn to woman, who bleeding bad, and say 'Now you walk.' And we can do nothing

Me and Mami we walking together with thousand other Armenian girl and lady. We starving, we walk long way, many die, all bones, most behind us, dead on road, flies on they faces, we can't help, we look away, God help us.

But we strong and one Turk, he like Mami, he gives us water. Mami: she so pretty, everyone love her. Long hair all the way down to ground. Sometimes she put vinegar in hair to make it shine. I brush it and help her rinse vinegar out, then tie and plait and turn in big coil. We walking through village in south when they see us. Not many Armenian left. The men see us, Mami beautiful face bit their eye. They come; they do her nose and mouth in one. They beat her like dog.

She look them in eyes and say: 'I pity your city. Your king a child.'

They laugh then they lay on her and make her scream. One at time. My Mami, they squashing her. I try help but the men laugh and point knife, I only little, more little than now. I so small, I can't fight them. Mami say, 'Run Meghranoush,' and one day she will find me. So I run, I not know where I going, but I run. I see they hurting Mami. I want fight. But I run away, too many men to fight. Mami say run, so I run.

I never saw Mami again until I am in England ten year. Not know if she live or die until twenty-seven year have gone in Jerusalem and ten year have gone in England. Poor Mami, why they hurt you? Bastard. But we find her. All the year, I always hope, never stop hope. I not believe at first, letter from Mami!

George sending money so she can come England and she come, all smiling, but looking old lady, so little and eating only fig and olive. She talking Armenian to me and I remember Armenian when she there and I talking back.

But I forget again when she go. It in paper, on face of Evening

Herald. It say: Reunite! Foreign woman not seen Mami in thirty-seven year. But she can't stay long and have to go back. We not talk much about genocide when I see her. She cry when I try tell her how I run away from Mullah and go through desert and come Jerusalem. I try find out what happen to her after she hurt. What happen when I run? She goes quiet.

I ask again and she cry and say they make her prisoner long time, she live in big Turkish house with big land and big wall. She not know where she is but at least she with other Armenian lady, she say there many Armenian lady. I don't know what she do, she no say, maybe house cleaner.

But she made speak Islam, she even read Koran. No money, not allowed out, but then one year, she escape and she come on foot to Palestine and then she track me and she write me letter. God, how I cry when she go back to Palestine, I want her stay in Plymouth with me, but poverty is bitter pit, you can't spit it out, you can't swallow it. I cry so long, but Mary happy, Mary want her to go back, Mary jealous. This English, they think guest is like fish; both start to smell after few day.

I want Mami stay with me always, stay with me forever so I can look after her. Poor Mami, she dead now, they say she have big heart like me that give her pain, she no breathe and she die.

When I little I am on own, on own running, on own like now. I only little but I fast, I run from village and keep running until I far away, feels like body burst. I look back and see burning behind, where is village. Black smokes go up to heaven. God: he know what they done to us. I run long, so I stop to rest, I hiding in haystack and waiting to feel stronger. Across valley in field I see haystack burning, hear little voices, they screaming. They hid like me.

Next to me in haystack is pregnant lady, she hold my hand and smile and tell me things be okay. I hear men coming for my field, they got fire sticks, and again I run. She too fat to run, she sweating, tired, so she stay. They find her, I watch from barn, they throw her down, one spread her legs and shoot bullets up. I hear the screams now, loud in my ears.

I see burning and in firelight Mullah is coming, I see him in his big clothes walking fast to barn, I not wait for him, so cruel, I run. Mullahs have knife. They take nipple, slicing them like blade through fig, they threading nipple on strings. I see they necklaces,

44

see them sit and sew, they sing foreign songs, songs from Koran, they singing as they sewing.

Even babies they take, stuck they things in them, rape and put on ropes, they hung baby from trees like winter meat. Just baby.

They hate all Armenian. They find new ways to kill us each day; they cut off baby hands and feet, leave babies in fields, not dead: dying, they eaten alive, they left for dogs to finish. Why baby? What harm they do? What crime they done? Being Armenian baby, that is it. My neighbour baby, little Nazar, the men they take him. Take him gently, we think he might be save, might give to Turkish family who want baby.

His little body, dead meat, dragged back into town next day, being eaten by wild dog. They know the clothes Papa made him, little shirt with brown bear sewn on. Nazar little mouth wide open, they can't get him away from dog to bury him and dog run away with him. He so little and dog so strong. He like rag doll I make. We no guns or money, can't defend ourselves, they taken them all from us long time ago, we got nothing.

Stranger move into our houses, take our thing, eat our chicken and our goat, take our money, our coat, nothing left to us. Any things they can't use they burning. Four week it take, four week and all Armenians pushed from village and town. Four week and everywhere empty or burning. My cousin Vahan, he live in Trabizond. I see him long time after in Jerusalem. He say it go crazy in Trabizond, they made Armenian boys eat shit, animal shit. They eat it, what they can do?

Old men, old women sent to church. Soldier do they business down on floor and make old people clean, down on knees. Why? Old people no hurt anybody. Push people from village in, lock door and window. Burn church, Armenians inside. Smells like burnt goat meat in air, everywhere you go is smell, can taste always in mouth.

At Deyirmini river. My God. Beautiful green river. They got women, took them there, rip down they dresses, cut off they bosom with sword and knife, red and hanging like bad sewing, then they throw women in river. I see they eyes, old eyes, young eyes, all eyes. Is blood everywhere, on rock, on sand, on leaf of tree. Screaming, bosoms hanging off. Bright eyes burning me, faces sinking.

Make me think of one time I see young goat eaten by pack of

wild dogs, it try cross river but they catch it and drag to shore. My God, river gone red. People tell me, don't hate, it all in past, forget it. I never forget. I see Armenians beat to death, all cracked, they not look like people. One man open mouth to scream and red come out, like fish belly, and then I see all teeth is gone. All broken and he can't breathe – nose flat like English bulldog.

Ones that still breathing, still crying, they take to stables, put on hook, they push hook in broken backs, they hang there like butcher pig. They die on hook. I vow then I never forgive. How I can forget? Money for him who hurt most Armenians, like meat, like pig. Mullah gave good reward to Turk who brought pee-pee of young boys, more they bring, the better. They pin notice on our church door which say 'This village will purge of Armenians. This land it ours.'

In desert, there still too many children alive, so they drag them by little feet and stab with knives. Blood paths on sand, then they throw in well, still half-alive. Hundreds they do like this, until well is full and then they force more refugee to come and press down body, so there more room.

There is disease in refugee camp, cholera, typhus killing people; it Hell and people go like Judas and they say there is no God, no son. Armenians are saying this! They say this is Hell; this is our reward for believing Jesus. In Rakka, Turk take Armenian children and pour sand down throat until they die. In Jarabluss Turk troops on horses pick out refugee girls they want, tie girl necks to horses' tails and ride horses, dragging poor girls behind, for joke, until girls die or backs break, so they not walk anymore.

Millions Armenian dead and nobody know. They say some report travel abroad but no help come, not from England, they busy fighting Germans. No help from America, it good friends with Turkey then, and we got nothing it wants, no gas, no oil. We got diamond and some gold, some gold, but not much, just dusts shining in river. America not wanting get involved in first war, so not come help us. American missionaries only, they living in Turkey and they try to help Armenian people but they only small and they have no money, how they take us all to safe places?

Anyway, they not allowed to see. American missionaries forbid to come in Armenian places, Turks not want them seeing. Some do see though, they come to towns. American minister saw, he riding on horse in outskirts of Aintab, he sees big field full with new bodies. Smells blood in air. He sick, he can't look. He tell his friend to look for survivor. Some hurt bad, but still alive, sitting on top of dead ones. Missionaries try help, they find baby, he still alive, he sucking breast of dead lady, they almost get him, but Turks come, they point gun and order them away.

I on my own, I see these thing, easy hide when just you. Everywhere I go, they been there, they kill us, dead peoples all places. I see such thing, I child before, but when I on own I forced to be adult.

Little village, near Everek, Armenian women and they children made go to meadow. Children chopped with swords and they mothers forced to bury them. Too many soldier: women can't fight. Soldier shoot those who not dig. Women cry and throw dirt on baby, try keep body away from dog. Suddenly little voice from pile, he shouting 'Mami, Mami, I still alive.' Soldier put gun to her head and he shout 'don't stop.' She shovel. What she can do?

Turk not all bad, I had Turk friend once, Mihr, he called, I play with him and he so kind, so beautiful, older than me, he would bring me food when my belly rumble, when my brothers tell me: 'my belly closer to me than yours, Sister' even when I starving. I love Mihr, he tell such beautiful stories, kind boy ... but one flower not make spring, and even Mihr change, his papa not let him help us, they make him turn away.

They not allowed to help us. Any Turk they catch helping Armenians is dead as us. Friendly Turks gone cold or mad, lost senses. Everyone know story of Armenian priest, still alive, he crawl out of dead bodies in big grave. One leg smashed, all bent, and blood in his eyes, but he walk in night to home of Turkish friend, they friends since children. Turk gave priest something eat, then Turk give him to Turk police, they come and take priest back to grave and they crush priest's skull.

World gone mad for us. When nobody there to help, what you can do? They dead in Igdir, in Siva, in Mush, in Marsin, in Adana, in Kharpert, in Derende, in Divrigi, in Trabizond, in Tomarza, even in beautiful Van. We dying everywhere, so many dead; my brother who live now in San Francisco, he send me numbers, numbers of dead Armenian peoples: many, many little circles.

I walk south, hundreds miles, I cross border, it hot in Syria, burning me, no water, I have to beg everything. Girl give me old donkey to carry me, he skinny, his rib stick out, she say if I no take him then her brother eat him. I take him and call him Tiri. He take me all way through desert. I share my food, my water with Tiri.

Armenian peoples everywhere I go, they living in tents in desert, like nomad, they run away from Armenia, from Turkey. They give me food and water, but I can't stay in desert, so hot and disease, so I go on with Tiri. Eventually get to Jerusalem, find other refugee like me in Armenian quarter. Nun take me and cut hair and use sticks hit us when we bad.

One day Papa he come rescue me. He been looking for me, I think he dead but he looking for us. Brothers come later, but not all, some die, God rest. Others not stay long; there no going back, so they go America. Papa start business in Jerusalem and I work too, he make man clothes and I make lady things: dress, skirt, blouse, coat. I work hard all my life, little hands always working; I not sit like English woman all day staring at box. Papa say, 'Meghranoush, if you want, you can make.'

Poor Papa, he dead now, bomb drop on his head long time ago, after I come here. He gone shopping in Jerusalem but it dark, it after curfew. He shouldn't be there. Jews are bombing the area. Everyone know you shouldn't be on the streets when it dark. He die before Mami come back from dead.

When Hitler is killing the Jews, he say, 'Who remembers the Armenians?' No-one in England heard of Armenia. 'Is that even country?' they say. 'What you speak, Spanish, Turkish – you got language? You wearing black? You Muslim? Jew? Arab?' Narrow mind got broad tongue. We Christian, we first Christian people, writing book and building church when English people they still living in cave, we believe Jesus, what they believe?

We pray, we read, we write, we know clever book and making statues. We got cathedral and fine building, take hundred years to build, but Turk take land; then they get thousand men to knock down. Sacred places, pretty statue, gone. No-one ever see them again. Why I survive? You want know why I survive? – fearful head survive. I run fast, faster than they can run, bad men not catch me.

Run away, always running, run from Turk and Kurd who want cut me, stab me.

I leave everyone, Mami, Papa, brother all behind.

Thank God for brothers get out, go America, thank God they don't come Plymouth. God hold close Arek, Hrant, Vahakn, Madteos, Dro, Nigol and Aram who never come out. God hope they bodies not wake up in earthquakes which hits Armenian lands.

Always Armenians dying, always people looking away from us, not wanting see us. These English they not see anything out of they own country. Always worry about themselves; well-fed never know what it like for the hungry, never feel cuts of the bleeding. They just looking at neighbours, and woman's hen looks like goose to neighbour. They never see simple thing, never see jealousy first hurts jealous.

Why English so simple?

Pigs, they never see the stars.

English tell me don't hold grudge. Forgive. How can I? They see their family cut, rape, burn? Where my lovely people gone? Dead, rotting. Refugee. Ninety years they say, forget! But for me, for me it yesterday.

And I am here in England where nobody know Armenia. English people tell me be quiet. What they know? They sit all day doing nothing, they going red in cold summer suns. They not have to walk in desert, with snake, and sand in noses. They eat what they like and they fat, every year I have to make they clothes bigger and bigger, and they never wearing hat, never looking clean. They smelling of cooking fat and smoking, and they got alcohol drink in their breaths when I taking they measurements.

I say nothing but I remember my people who know one drink is good, two is enough, three is sorrow. This English lock themselves in houses, put curtains in window to shut neighbour out.

Armenians trust, we love neighbour, we leave door open for breeze and never worry we be robbed. Here they put they names in everybody business, they talk, talk, always talking behind they backs and from mouth to mouth a splinter become a log. They too stupid to know that speech silver, silence golden. So much mess they make with they gossip; bad tongue sharper than razor and there no medicine for what tongue can cut. How I get to this place? Why I still here?

So poor here. I think there be money in rich country, but only people who rich are government, and they keep money. Rich country just mean more expensive for poor people to get food. Have no tree to give food. In Motherland and Holy Land in summer we reach up and take sweet grapes, figs, olives, peaches, pomegranate, pear, apple, orange, but here there is nothing, you must go to supermarket and pay big for one apple, and Armenians have Ishkhanatsoug which mean Prince Fish and is nicest fish in world; better than English stinking kipper and mackerel.

My Papa tell me, wherever there is bread, stay there. And he say it better to be wife for poor man than be maid for rich man. And he say it not shameful to live poor, it shameful to live dirty. He say a sweet tongue can bring a snake out of a hole, and he say that the later good things come, the sweeter it is.

I old and I think long on these things for many year and I have always listen, but now I keep remember what old gypsy lady tell me. She so clever; she must be dead long time now, she say so many things, she say: you go to England, you have many baby but only girl will live, and the last thing she tell me, as I walking out, is, 'Never be sad, because for mad people, every day is holiday.' I never know what this mean at the time. Mary, oh Mary. Why you are what you are?

Ah, my back it ache, my throat it cracked, but got to get on, man is coming soon, only twenty minutes for dressing now.

Pah, Turkish government, they never say sorry for what they did, never do they say it. Armenian lives cost nothing for them. How I forgive when they not think they do wrong? How I forgive all they done? I old, I not got much time, but I still here and while I still breathe, I remember. People they don't want hear, but Meghranoush Zorabedian will talk.

Five

Mary is nonplussed by what she has heard. Not the parts which relate to her: no, all of that is very old hat. But the terror, the escape, the drudgery of endless walking, the image of her young mother in the face of a murderous oncoming foe. Can it be true? The details of her mother's tale – be they true or false – stun her and sting her in ways she has never anticipated, and so as Meghranoush falls silent, Mary slips into the hall to breathe.

Can her mother be an out-and-out liar? She has an air of truthfulness, of innate honesty, but she could be a fabulist: maligner of Turkish people, falsifier of history.

The words poured forth in torrents as her mother extolled the virtues of the Armenian nation and berated the Turks, over and over, and she seemed so definite – and yet Mary is sure she has never come across an authoritative account of such claims in any history books. Yet why would her mother lie? She didn't know Mary was listening, and lying to oneself would be meaningless. It would be like cheating at Patience: an exercise in stupidity.

Yet Mary must consider Ockham's Razor: the simplest of two or more competing theories is preferable. Also called the Law of Parsimony. So in this case, what's the more likely possibility? – that a deluded old woman is fantasising untruths into existence, or that the whole world has hushed up a massacre perpetrated on a vast scale?

Mary honestly does not know what to think. Even if her mother isn't lying, they could be false memories that she's unwittingly fabricated over the course of many years – for it seems to Mary that memory is a wholly untrustworthy version of reality. There is no such thing as an accurate recollection of the past, as reminiscences are only ever subjective. They are coloured by emotions like guilt, bitterness, and hatred: they are mutable. Mary supposes that some of what her mother says is true, but much of it might be the product of years of bitter musing, the fruits of a maudlin mind. She also reminds herself to take into account the simple deterioration of an addled brain.

And what about the holes in the story? How was it that none

of these rampaging soldiers turned their sexual attentions towards little Meghranoush? Mary has often heard her mother grumbling to herself about the evil of pederast soldiers, abusing small Armenian boys as par for the course, yet she's never once mentioned the rape of girls. If – as she insists – some degree of ethnic cleansing did occur in 1915 Turkey, then the rape of girls must've occurred too, surely? Just as it did in Rwanda, in Kosovo, in Darfur and a hundred other places, for murder and concupiscence seem to go hand-in-hand in times of war, and Mary suspects there were just as many egregious episodes involving small girls as there were involving small boys, and perhaps her mother was one of them, for it is said that small girls are even more attractive to some gentlemen than sexually mature women.

Mary does not know at this point how relevant these thoughts of murder and rape are; she does not know that when she returns to the old house, her mother will be gone.

She does not know this because she only ever has the curse of hindsight to guide her. What she does know, however, is that she disappoints her mother. She knows that the old lady lets out a deep grateful sigh whenever she leaves, and she knows that the old wooden cabinet piled high with the bright limbs of various incomplete garments reminds Meghranoush of the soft sponginess of her own mother's lap.

Mary knows all of this because, oftentimes, when the anamnestic mood is upon her, Meghranoush says so. Yet these indulgences are few and far between and even after fifty years of lucubration on the subject of her mother, Mary feels that she is no nearer to knowing her. There are facts and tendencies and habits and patterns, but the person generating them is a mystery. Perhaps it is the cultural abyss, the distance brought about by foreignness that separates them.

At this moment Mary feels she is perhaps ready for her mother's demise; she has steeled herself to its inevitability.

Here, as she ponders in her hallway, she believes she would beckon the Grim Reaper and direct him with an index finger pointed at her moribund mother if she had but the chance, for she has lived for years with the expectation that her mother might keel over at any moment. But what she does not expect is that her mother will vanish. Kidnap is something reserved for the filthy rich and their obnoxious progeny, not for long-term pensioners.

Mary thrusts the tales of genocide into an unattended corner of her mind and, utterly unaware of what is to come, she decides to leave her mother to mawkish sentimentality, to leave her sewing hem after hem and collar after cuff in the shade. But Mary won't stay here in the shade: the sun is shining so she's going to the boating lake lickety-split. She slams the door and trips lightly down the garden path. Without meaning to, she pauses and turns to look back at the dark house, suffocating beneath tentacular ivy.

She half expects to see her mother in the kitchen window, pretending to clean, rubbing the white enamelled sink with a green sponge and a bottle of bleach, but secretly spying. Like Mata Hari. Mary has seen the 1931 version of Mata Hari, the one with Greta Garbo, and she found the German spy to look suspiciously like her mother did when she was young.

But no, the window is empty. Her mother must still be sewing, pumping away at the worn old foot-pedal – unless she's watching from the shadows, hiding where Mary can't see her.

Mary has lived all her life in the house on the hill, but it hasn't always been just her and her mother. They used to share it with Mary's father. The house was filled with smoke then, and didn't have any carpets, only thin rugs and splinters. It was cramped but there was always something going on, always something happening. But he left a long time ago, lifted out in a coffin and returned in a white oriental urn with blue trees upon it.

Mary does not ever consider that the house could be even emptier than it already is.

Still, the boating lake is the place to start her holidays, she feels. Hop over the mossy knee-high wall, and immerse herself in the sanctuary of the parkland. She has a notepad and a fountain pen to record this momentous trip; she'll watch the people and for once, *she'll* be the judge of *them*. She'll make a list (a list that she will refer to frequently over the next few weeks, determined that one of the persons listed is in fact her mother's abductor).

The boating lake is only a whisker away, but there are difficulties. For one thing, a road circumvallates the park like a moat and the traffic is constant, even in the rainy season when most of the tourists have crawled back under their rocks with their brightly-coloured Minis, Beetles and mephitic relics masquerading as camper vans.

She follows the pavement down to a series of mini-roundabouts devised solely to terrify tourists into travelling more slowly; she navigates her way between them, dodges a cyclist hurtling through, and waits for the blue and yellow tourist train to pass. It moseys along, chuffing and plinking.

She stands opposite the boating lake, and with a final dash she crosses the busy road dividing the lake from the pavement. The small gap that comprises the entrance is a hundred yards away, so she hooks her skirt into her knickers, skips over the wall and makes her way across the grassy verge and onto the brown winding pathways.

Wending her way through a passel of ducks and drakes, she tries to avoid eye contact. Natatorial birds have always fascinated her in principle with their rubbery webbed feet and sleek plumes, but she finds the reality of them disconcerting.

She counts the small ducky bodies dotting the reedy island in the centre of the lake. The rabble consists of Ruddy Shelducks, Mandarin Ducks, Shovelers, Teal, Eurasian Wigeons, Ferruginous Pochards, Pintails, Tufted Ducks and, of course, the odious Mallard. Then there are Moorhens, Coots, and Grebes. There are Brent Geese, Canadian Geese, Mute Swans and the vociferous Whooper Swans, trumpeting their call louder than all the other birds put together. Loudmouths.

It's no safe haven, either; Mary is not fooled about that. It's an avian dystopia where the strong oppress the weak, where the old starve, where the young are eaten, and where gang-rape is the approved method of procreation.

Well, perhaps she should befriend some of her local avifauna, for it is surely a case of 'better the devil you know.'

A group of mallards detach from their regiment and waddle in her direction, quacking offensively. The boating lake has become a veritable aviary, overflowing with the diminutive descendants of dinosaurs enacting their various comedies and tragedies. A jackdaw succumbs to a prolonged attack of laxity and Mary takes her cue to move on. She walks hastily to the commemorative rose garden and pauses to catch her breath. The benches here have small brass plaques screwed to their centres and she supposes that people must find these benches uncomfortable, since there's not a soul to be seen. It must be the plaques: they dig into the spine and speak of the dead. She lounges, and lets the metal voice of Gwen Turner graze her spine. She likes it. The cool brass oblongs are comforting; they remind her of the inexorable march of time that bring all to the same place. She's grateful that in this moment she's the sitter, not the sat-upon.

She chooses a bench under a splendid hazel tree – a nuciferous: a nut-bearing tree, as she duly notes on the first page of her notepad. Something draws her eye up into the foliage, and she sees that she's chosen well: this tree has special significance. Most people are blind when it comes to spotting skeogs; they can sense that a tree has a presence, but they can't fathom why.

Skeogs are fairy trees, and Mary has always been able to spot them. Anybody who tries to remove or harm this tree would place themselves in great peril. Which was precisely what happened in 1958 in Blunts Lane.

The good people of Blunts were outraged when road builders threatened to cut down a silver birch skeog to make way for a wider road. The contractors refused to destroy the tree, until one cocksure chap from the electricity board came along and unwisely agreed. He did the terrible deed: he cut the poor tree down, and the next day he fell off an electricity pole and was killed. Eventually, of course, the road was diverted and the man was lost for naught, but still the point was made.

From her vantage point under the skeog she has a good view of the main pathway outside the rose garden, and can muse and score without attracting too much attention. The first target wanders past: a curly-haired little girl, straining at her reins, her body drawn to the lake. Her grandparents – she assumes they're her grandparents, although IVF can't be ruled out – tug at the reins and haul her back.

What does she see in there? What's drawing her? Mary decides that the answer could be fish or ducks. On second thoughts, she crosses out Ducks and Fish and settles instead on Water. The water itself draws the girl; the liquid darkness invites her in. She gives her a score of eight for Commendable Audacity.

A breath of horse manure is tangible on the wind and the whickering, breathy whinnies of old mares fly across the water. The stables have been here for fifty years. She often watches from her bedroom window as young families take out palomino mares and dun colts to trot in circles around the boating lake, or to canter through the reedy estuary pathways on the other side of the sluice.

Upwind, she can hear those beasties stamping and clattering behind the high walls. She's never been in there; how could she hire a horse? No children to take with her, no companions, no husband? – They'd take one look at her and tell her to hop it.

Out of nowhere, two boys of eleven or twelve appear and bomb past on mountain bikes, one with an index finger inserted into his nostril, the other attempting a wheelie. They deliberately swerve for gulls who squawk splenetically. The boys stare at her. They score a zero, for Insolence to Elders and Malice to God's Seabirds.

There's a period of absolute quiet. The wind drops, and even the surrounding road becomes silent. She shifts uncomfortably and bites the nib of her fountain pen, tonguing metal and tasting ink. She twists and squats to check her reflection in the brass plate: blue seeps across her bottom lip and stains the corner of her mouth.

The froufrou of an old woman's dress is audible from the far side of the lake, the still water bouncing the sound across to her.

A solitary duck quacks. She squirms; the other ducks are dozing in the morning sun, clustered together on the lakesides.

Reaching into her pocket, she pulls out a pristine green kitchen sponge. She grasps it loosely in her hand for a moment, feeling its rough sponginess, and then she places it on the bench beside her. Carefully pulling out a pea-sized fragment from the centre, she rubs the morsel slowly between her thumb and forefinger. Clasping the fragment in her palm, she scratches the inflamed skin of her throat.

Finally there's a surge of walkers, and a bus rumbles by. With a deep inhalation, she flicks away the speck of sponge and watches an orange-eyed pigeon peck at it determinedly. She pockets the remainder.

The sickly scent of dog faeces is in the air. Not far from her bench, beneath a red bin illustrated with a graphic of a squatting (and, by the looks of it, constipated) canine, there is an unedifying pile of crispy excrement. A note is inserted into her book, and the absent dog scores a minus two for Obscenity.

A pack of shirtless students rides by on mountain bikes, rucksacks hooked on bare shoulders. Shirtless! In May! She observes them coolly until one of them flashes her what she supposes is intended to be a winning smile.

A blonde girl with the looks of a scullion passes by.

So, the winning smile was not aimed at her after all.

Lickerish louts. They score a two. It might've been more, but they're hampered by Vanity and Flirtatiousness.

A duck goes into a spasm of splashing for no apparent reason, half-flapping, half-flying over the surface of the dark water. It's male. He might be washing himself: some bizarre drake bathing ritual. Or he might be insane. There's no way of knowing, no way to tell. She is scoring him a zero – for obvious reasons – when someone unusual walks by: an urbane gentleman in a rather dapper outfit.

An enigma. He seems depressed, world-weary – *Mal-de- Siècle,* she writes neatly. Fiftyish, sporting a bright pink face and a salmon-coloured polo shirt tucked into tight shorts. His outfit is completed by white boat shoes – no socks – chosen to complement his carefully shaven legs. Thinking intently, almost consumed by his thoughts. Dejected – perhaps to the point of suicide. His feet barely clear the ground as he walks. He pauses for a moment at the water's edge, perusing the reedy wasteland of the lake. The weed is out of control. For a second her buttocks are on the edge of her seat, she's so positive that he'll throw himself in. He steps back.

She sighs; there might've been a chance of suicide if it weren't for the pondweed. The grossness of the noxious plant has put him off. She wonders just what sort of personal crisis the man is going through. He looks fit, healthy, spruce – if anything, a tad too spruce. He's fingering something in his hand: a glint of gold, a wedding band.

Suddenly, she understands. His problems are feminine. He's having problems with Her Upstairs, The Old Ball and Chain. He glances at her and she's startled to be looked at so directly, startled to be seen by this pompous man. He looks away and past her. His eyes rested on her for the merest moment before moving on. What did he see? How did she look through his eyes?

Ancient and *haggish* are the two adjectives that assault her mind. He scores a two for Depression – or, more accurately, for making her depressed.

The pink-shirted figure recedes and is replaced by a frail granny in a camel coat and silk headscarf; her tan-coloured support tights swathe thick varicose veins, and the low heels of her beige shoes sound an irregular tapping. This antediluvian is even frailer than Mary's own mother who is sequestered back there at the house, too contented with her fabric and threads to take a walk to the boating lake with her daughter.

Mary will come to realise that she is wrong here: that her mother is no longer sewing. That instead she is waiting, that she is placing several small cakes onto a glass plate, that soon her mother will no longer be in the house, that soon her mother will be in the vehicle of a man who has the very worst of intentions.

The granny is still in her view, tottering along the muddy pathways. In fifteen minutes she's barely gone a hundred yards. She's poorly: deep into decrepitude; dying, very probably. Walking slowly, one wobbly step after another, her face a rictus of pain, her elbow supported by a granddaughter who seems bored. Every step looks unpleasant – no, *excruciating*, Mary notes in her jotter.

What's the point? This old biddy can concentrate only on the patch of path in front of her, never looking up ahead of her or to the sides: only at the tiny spot around her small feet. She doesn't see anything. She could be walking in a landfill for all she knows. She's just walking and fighting the pain of walking.

But then maybe it's not about the surroundings. Maybe it's actually about proving something: that she's not old, that she hasn't got one foot in the grave just yet, since both her feet are free and walking! A nine for the granny, she decides, for Making An Effort (and not sitting sewing at home). On the grass verge, just a foot away, she spots a mutant duck. There's a plethora of bills and a grotesque webbed foot sprouts from the flank of the abomination. The bird wriggles and quacks at her.

A tiny beaky face appears. So it's not a freak after all, just a mother-duck warming her young, the weedy duckling cowering beneath its mother's soft belly. Three more diminutive ducklings wriggle out, to the chagrin of their mother, who's perhaps so used to nursing her eggs that she's reluctant to let them go, even after birth (*hatching*, she corrects her notes).

The scruffy fledglings waddle to her, leaving ochreous spatters in their wake and tweeting surprisingly loudly for such small creatures. Mum follows, nuzzles and shushes them away. Unsure whether she fully approves of such coddling maternal instincts, Mary gives Mum Duck a two for Clinginess.

The traffic surrounding the garden becomes louder. She feels a transient relief; she can't abide silence. With concentration and ambient noise she can sometimes blow internal noise away. Noise around her is fine; it drowns out the noise within, and inner calm is what she wishes for. She wishes the continual voices in her head – the chatter – would just stop. Even for a second. It's so exhausting to live with an ongoing cacophony. What she'd give to stare blankly at a wall and feel nothing, think nothing, hear nothing.

She pictures the ice-blue wind swirling around her mind, cleansing everything it touches, and for a moment there's silence. She looks up with fresh eyes and spots the tiny white cottage, long-abandoned, on the opposite side of the lake: an enchanted abode. One day, she'll creep down there in the depths of the night and discover its secrets. On second glance, she sees that the enchanted cottage is actually the newly-painted toilet block and she chastises herself for letting her imagination run amok, for letting it make a mockery of her.

A young man enters the rose garden and she stiffens. He's equipped with a large shoulder strap and customary camera. He has a wistful look about him, and without warning he stoops to smell a rose.

For some reason this innocuous gesture strikes her as odd, verging on the abnormal. She recollects that the only other rose sniffers she's witnessed are little girls and little old ladies. The young man moves on, perhaps aware of Mary's gaze. As he passes her, he says:

'Nice day, isn't it?'

There's no-one else nearby and so she assumes he must be talking to her.

'Yes, grand,' she replies and the two words come out husky and faint, as if her mouth is unused to words. This momentary dysphonia is disconcerting, but she has at least surprised herself: she's never said *grand* in conversation before, and she wonders where this new word sprang from. Certainly not from the dictionary; she'd never waste her eyes on such a puny offering. The man walks away and she awards her first ten. Earned, she decides, for Breaking the Mould of Masculinity.

It begins raining again, lightly at first, mizzling. It becomes steadily heavier until finally the heavens open and the lake and gardens empty. Mary remains, unabashed by a spot of rain, and unravels her blue pak-a-mac from her bum-bag. A young couple bound over the wall, coatless and sodden, rain streaming down their saturnine faces. They've come to the boating lake, it appears, to stand opposite each other and shout.

The rain in her ears muffles their voices and makes them seem farther off than they are. The girl looks angry, her face contorted unattractively. She seems to be asking him something, her hands flung up in the air dramatically – melodramatically, she notes mentally, as the rain precludes the use of her notebook, which she's secreted beneath her bottom.

The man sneers and turns away from the girl. He's closed, deaf to her taunts. He's slightly bent and might have a spinal deformity: a small hunchback. *Quasimodo*, she seems to hear the girl taunting, though she supposes she can't be an accurate judge from such a distance and with the pouring rain in her ears.

Suddenly they become aware that they're watched, and move closer together to regard her. They wander away and she sees the girl cast a backward glance in her direction, but she can't tell if it's hostile or simply curious.

A few steps farther on the man also turns to look at her, and then he reaches for the girl's hand and they slink off together. Mary doesn't bother to rate them; she's spent. She thrusts her hands into her pockets and rubs her sponge absentmindedly. She's enjoyed herself, but has worn herself out. She thinks she might've found a new hobby. It's so refreshing to be the judge and not the judged. She's percipient, she has acumen and she could take this new hobby to a variety of locations: beaches, fairgrounds, cliffs, promenades. All places with soothing ambient noise.

Of course, Mary sees that she has been observed, too. People have noticed her; they've a sixth sense when it comes to being watched, being written about. But who cares? From this moment onward Mary Sibly, aged fifty-eight, will do as she pleases. She does not know, though, that the person who has most carefully observed her is a man that she has not seen – a man who has not made her list, but who has been surveying her from the moment she entered the boating lake. He has been watching her intently from a position of camouflage, and when Mary decides that she's too tired at present to walk to the supermarket where she'd intended to purchase milk, but will instead sit under the fairy tree until the rain stops, it occurs to him that today could be the day.

Mary vows that the moment the rain stops, she'll make a move. The very second the rain stops, she'll be on her way. She'll walk all the way to the supermarket as punishment for resting there so long. She'll definitely not, under any circumstances, catch the bus. In the absence of passers-by, she wonders about her future. Where will she be in a year? Will she be back working at the shop? Or will they have given her the boot?

Hopefully they will have – and on medical grounds, which should at least result in a decent pension. She knows they think she's nuts, insane in the membrane; they've always thought so, in a way. They used to think her vapid, a pushover, a worthless bimbo who didn't have the sense, the guts, to tell them to get their own damn sandwiches at lunchtime.

They wouldn't allow that she liked walking to the shop, liked getting out into the open away from the chemical smell of fine knits, away from their gossip and catcalls. She relished the sandwich run; it was the only fresh air she breathed during her day on the stuffy shop floor, hawking her angora and lambswool to idiots. And she could stuff herself on cream cakes during the walk back to Bodwicks with none of them looking.

They wouldn't have it, though; they just thought she was a wimp, a dull passionless robot. Well, those days are over. They're gone, long gone. She'll do what she wants from now on, and no more cakes either. She'll eat like a sparrow and roam like a wolf; she'll shed a couple of stones. She'll start today, with the walk up the hill. She doesn't care if a bus is waiting there, she'll walk and she'll enjoy it. She'll become thinner and she'll become happier and people will treat her with respect.

Negativism? Negligible.

She smiles at the glistering droplets of rain on the bench, and though the rain has ceased and the sun is shining she thinks she'll sit here for a little longer, safe under the skeog.

When she finally drags herself off the bench, the slatted wood has forced grooves into her lower thighs and her hair steams with rain. Forgetting her notebook, which has warmed her bottom and still sits on the bench, she clambers back over the wall, dashes across the road and mounts the pavement with a little jump. She approaches the bus stop; she sits on the wall and waits.

While her back is turned, a small unremarkable man in a mackintosh that is almost as unfashionable as Mary's emerges from the shadows of the copse, walks to the skeog, pockets Mary's notebook, and begins to walk – via the backstreets, in a twisting, doubling-back route – towards her house.

Six

When Mary comes home there is no sign of her mother. She takes a cursory sweep of the sitting room. Her mother is not here. Neither is she in any of the bedrooms, nor the bathroom, nor the kitchen, nor the garden. She is not even in the cupboard under the stairs.

There is no note but there is no sign of a disturbance, so she has no reason to be worried – although she is. Her mother has just gone out, and so what if she hasn't left a note to explain where? She is an old woman and increasingly forgetful, so she has just forgotten to let Mary know where she's gone. Mary tells herself that she should be relieved by her mother's absence: she'll have the house to herself for a few precious hours, perhaps, if luck will allow. Mary reclines in her mother's armchair and notices something sticking into the stuffing, where her mother's needle is normally stowed. It is a bright feather: iridescent turquoise, with black and white bars.

Mary knows enough about birds to know that this is a jay feather, although how such a feather could have pierced her mother's armchair is not so easily understood. Perhaps, she thinks, her mother found it; or perhaps it was a gift from a customer.

Pacing to the door, Mary sees that her mother's green felt hat is still in its place on the hat stand. There is no knowing when her mother last left the house without her headgear, but surely such an occasion has never happened in Mary's lifetime. A further oddity in the empty house is the presence of small droplets of blood dotting the kitchen table – then she remembers her mother's cut nose and shin. Yet still it seems ominous that her mother hasn't taken the time to wipe the surfaces clean.

After a second check of the house, Mary ascends to her bedroom and perches on the blanket box in front of the window to await her mother's return.

Mary is still sitting on the blanket box when a bloody dawn splashes the sky. The night has been the longest of all nights, but it is over now, and Mary is certain that today will be the day that her mother returns. It has to be today, because the idea that this is not the day her mother returns is not feasible.

With eyes sore from watching, she checks the path leading to the house again, searching for the small figure; but the path is empty, save for pigeons.

In the absence of a sounding board, Mary talks to herself. The important thing, she reminds herself, is not to panic: panic leads to ridiculous behaviour and to the potential for incarceration. The police are sick to the eye teeth of her and she must not give them further cause for wrath. Their recalcitrance is not what is needed here; they are sceptical of every word she says. *Focus* is what is needed. Taking stock, and a cool, calm look at the facts: 1) Her mother was in the house yesterday morning, but is not now. 2) Her mother could be anywhere that is not the house.

If her mother has abandoned her, she'll pack up her things into black bin bags and she'll just live. She'll paint the house purple – her homely domicile transformed by perse paint – and she'll sit the way she wants to, knees apart, showing her knickers. She'll say what she wants and go where she wants. She'll go to the seaside and wear a bikini; she'll walk the promenade in Mary-Janes. She'll sit and watch the shags dive into the sea and she'll walk until she's fit to drop, and talk to everyone and make friends.

But what if her mother hasn't abandoned her? Her belly aches; a touch of dyspepsia has worsened into something more sinister, she fears. She is feeling fluey, the worms in her belly are wriggling, and her hip is aching: a dull, throbbing pain. Her throat is ragged and her head feels as if it has been immersed in a bubble of thick translucent fabric, blurring her vision and dulling her hearing.

The sickness is the hardest thing to bear at the moment, for this is not the self-inflicted variety: this sickness is not welcome. It doesn't bring freshly-eaten food happily back up: it brings the heavily-digested remains of fruit; it brings bile.

Hubble-bubble, toil and trouble. The sickness in her body is uncontrolled and running rampant; it needs to be reined in, pinned down and rationed. *Sick* when there's nothing left is depletive, not regenerative; it's the final straw, and her teeth are bad enough already – they don't need further battery. They started falling out years ago from the purging, and now she has hardly any left. Her mouth is cavernous and witch-like and she has heard the neighbours' children call her 'The Predator.' Some monster from a film, she gathers.

In times of stress Mary has found that, for the sake of her sanity, it is best to avoid thinking of the stressor: she focuses on the distant boating lake and watches the far-off swans. The swans have had babies: four cygnets bob on the lake. They're ghastly. People come to look at them, expecting them to be pretty, but are consistently disappointed when they see the dishevelled beaky faces looking up at them.

It is a fact that Mary's mother might be anywhere at all. Either she left of her own accord or she was taken – neither of which has any bearing on whether she is likely to come back. If she was taken by an unknown person, there is nothing to say that they will be of a mind to return her, and if she has left of her own accord then there is nothing to suggest that she will change the stubborn mind that led her away in the first place.

A dog approaches the cygnets: a mutt, some collie-cross-heaven-knows-what. It plunges into the water near them, and for a moment the mutt vacillates, contemplates attack or, at the very least, pursuit; but then the parent swans glide into view, craning their long necks, fluffing their feathers and spitting like camels.

The collie about-turns and skulks back to its owners, tail between its legs. 'A wise move,' Mary concedes to the dog from her overseeing position on the blanket box. 'Many a mangy mutt's been killed by a stroppy swan daddy – they force you under the water until your lungs fill with gunk and you're fish food. Not many males are so paternal; normally it's the mother who does the killing.'

Except in Mary's own case. It is not her mother who has done the killing, for if killing has been done at all it has been done to her mother. It might have been an angry Turk who, after having spent a lifetime tracking her mother, finally located the object of his desire and murdered her. But then, the majority of murders are committed by a friend or family member, as is the case with dolphins.

Mary saw a TV programme and so she knows all about dolphins. Harbour porpoises kept washing up in Scotland, and across the Atlantic baby dolphins would appear rotting on beaches, some with not a mark on them. Scientists thought it was underwater blasting or some horrible new disease, but when they opened the bodies up they saw they'd been devastated, clubbed to death – except there were no marks on the skin.

It was only when they found a few teeth-marks and matched

them to jaw samples in their database that they knew what had happened.

Bottle-nosed dolphins had been using porpoises as target practice, for they were exactly the same size as baby bottlenose dolphins, and baby bottlenose dolphins were what they liked to kill for fun. Flicking them out of the air at a hundred miles an hour; using their echolocation to target their babies' internal organs. A way of controlling the youth: infanticide, like lions. Stop them while they're young.

Never let them grow up and the young will never eat you.

Except Mary's mother is not young. Mary's mother is ninety-four, and who would want to stop a 94-year-old? – which leads Mary back to the 'family and friends' statistic. If family and friends form the majority of murderers, that pattern posits one person as the prime suspect: Mary herself. Which is why no-one must know that her mother has vanished.

Seven

Three days have passed. Mary dresses in a calf-length nubby green skirt and an old blue cardigan – another relic from the seventies, but one which is still soft, and light enough for a summer's day. Stretching over the back of her armchair, she finds the jag in the fabric and pulls free a handful of yellow stuffing. She crams the spongy wodge into her mouth and chews, swallows her mouthful, and leaves her sparse bedroom. Pausing for a moment, she listens at her mother's bedroom door and her ear meets silence.

Has the abductor killed her mother and submerged her at the bottom of the boating lake? Has he weighted her down with concrete pockets? Is she rotting a little more every day – is that what's causing the noxious odour around the place?

It's a possibility she hasn't countenanced before, but there it is and it's been right under her nose. She must know, and so she digs out the old snorkel and mask, and she follows her feet to the lake.

Beside the path hangs brightly-coloured litter dropped by careless tourists, like patchwork squares hung on bushes. Birds pulling at the remains of flattened rodents make off into the mist that has crept into the valley, and Mary hears the tiny train advancing along the road behind her.

She slews around and for a second she thinks she sees the far-off outline of a man loitering in the spinney. The wagons squeal past one by one with jerky movements, and the train curves away and when Mary turns back the man has gone.

She is here now: the boating lake, where the withered litter rolls and drops noiselessly into the black brackish water. The lure of that water. To swim, to feel wet, to feel cold – just to feel. Bare unadulterated water against her skin.

There can be no second-guessing, no hesitation, no analysing – she'll do it, and she'll do it this second. Clothes will be a burden, a slimy wrapping around the essence of her, and so she'll shed them.

She is wearing no shoes, so she unpeels her socks and lays them on a fruitless blackberry bush where they hang like a funny grey flower. The skirt is next: green and vibrant. Green is the colour that geniuses are drawn to, so they say. She acquired this skirt in a shop full of teenagers who stared at her and sniggered at her silver moon coat as she stood in line to pay.

Her lower half is nude now, for she gave up on daily underpants long ago. Underpants are not an expression: they symbolise that which must be hidden; they serve to wrap and enfold – they are fabric chains. When she took to wearing beautiful clothes, silky underpants did not follow, for even thongs – mere slips of silk and lace and sparkling crystals – are chains.

Women are so worried about their emissions, their natural discharges; they're obsessed with new ways of hiding them for reasons Mary can't fathom. 'Gusset,' originally signifying a piece of chain-mail, is a dirty word to Mary and a ludicrous concept. It is almost as ludicrous as the word 'vagina' which, she has discovered, originally meant 'sword sheath,' a receptacle for a man to plunge his weapon into: a concept that is distasteful to the point of being repugnant.

Naked from the waist down, she breathes in the acidic fumes that float on the air. The lake water is not wholesome, not virtuous like flowing rivers: it is stale and rank, which she feels is apt. Instead of repulsing her, it entices her. Her cardigan is off and her blouse is half-unbuttoned already, and the last two fasteners come undone with satisfying pops.

She prefers her breasts bra-less, unfettered by tight fabric the sole purpose of which is to convey a false sense of roundness. The v-shaped softness of her breasts' fall should not be hidden: the long teardrops are natural; they fall and point in an arrow to her belly and beyond. To think how once she worried that her adolescent breasts weren't perky enough, or round enough. If only she knew then what she knows now.

She stands on the verge, naked as the day she was born, the wind chilly on her skin. She extends her toes and tickles the edge of the water.

It's cold, but then what did she expect? The summers in Plymouth are arctic. People don't know it's so cold. They think it's like the French Riviera, or sunny, like Cornwall – but it's not, it's too close to Dartmoor and the sea-clouds hit the hills and spew their freezing contents onto the city on a daily basis. It always rains in Plymouth, even in the summer. Especially in the summer, though it is true that the hiemal rains are positively glacial.

She'll not be a wimp; she's hesitated already, when she promised herself that she wouldn't. How did she come to this? Having second thoughts, when there was never any option other than the one she must take? She'll just do it.

With the blackberry bush now fully adorned she's ready to submerge herself. She puts the mask to her face and clamps her jaws around the snorkel's mouthpiece. Her ankles are shocked by the coldness of the water; her socks had kept them warm, the walking had heated them.

Her hands are always cold. Not even exertion warms them up and so the water doesn't seem so shocking against her fingers, but her ankles are cut to the bone. They turn pink, then red, then purple and then they go numb. The boating lake is filthy; she feels the soft slime of the bottom oozing between her toes.

God only knows what it is: mouldy bread and duck faeces, most likely, with a smattering of old fish bones for good measure.

She can feel herself sinking, and she shifts lest she should be sucked under. Sinking-sands and quagmires are beastly things. Who can forget the young worm-digger who ventured out onto the River Plym Estuary one misty morning seeking ragworm? He took one false step, entered the dangerous flats and he sank like the Mary Rose. The tide was out and he shouted, but it was a Sunday dawn and all were in the Land of Nod. By the time they were awake, the tide had come in.

The next day, when the tide receded, they saw his purple head sticking out of the mud and all were horrified, for what a way to die! The water slowly getting higher and higher, and no-one answering the desperate calls. The men who found him said crabs ate his eyes, but she never believed that, for what would crabs find so appealing about a pair of blue eyes?

Still, sea creatures work by their own subterranean laws; they might well have been waiting a long time for a fool to take the wrong path.

It's so cold! It's so hatefully cold. Her knees are submerged and the goose bumps run all the way up her thighs. The water laps at them and leaves a faint grubby tidemark, like the tea-stained legs of stocking-deprived wartime women.

She goes deeper and she goes under, walking on her hands and kicking her feet out behind her. There is nothing down here but gloom: cold clinging gloom.

She feels for objects along the bottom, making her way across the lake, and vines of pondweed ensnare her legs.

She sees the faint glimmer of a rusted supermarket trolley, and beneath it there is a dark object – a severed human head. She nudges the trolley away and goes deeper. Her hands grasp something soft but it is entangled by the swarthy flora.

In the entrancement of the moment she has forgotten about breathing, and so she surfaces gasping. She screams in frustration and she goes under again, using the might of her body weight to pull the object free. She clasps it in her hands and brings it to the surface, removing her mask and holding it aloft.

It is the decomposing remains of a male Mallard, its eyes absent, its bright jade head sparsely-feathered and diminished with greyness.

She drops it. It sinks slowly to the bottom and she screams once more, and for the first time she perceives that a small gathering has amassed on the banks of the lake and on the waves of the wind she hears the voices of her neighbours.

Eight

He inserts his mahogany-tinted contact lenses and blinks. He raises his hands to his eyes and squeezes them, gently popping lenses between thumb and forefinger, feeling them bubble, then settle back onto his conjunctivas – an action he finds peaceful. He fills his palm with a squirt of abrasive grey salt scrub and pummels his skin and there is relief as he sloughs away the old dead scales, revealing something softer, something new. Grey-faced, he steps into the fast stream of the shower and blasts the crystals away and there is relaxation as his turgid body is engulfed in warm water.

He distracts himself with shaving his legs to kill some time, although his legs were amply shaved yesterday. He rinses his right leg, forgets he's already shaved it, lathers it up again and shaves it once more. He does not think about the old person deteriorating in his cellar; instead, as is his habit whilst naked and vulnerable, he thinks of his mother. A deeply pathological woman; a woman with a Jocasta Complex so intense that she would not be content to just fondle, she would not be content to just bring him to his knees, she must fully consummate a moment of incest.

There is no obvious reason for his mother's deficiencies: it's just the way she is. When he was young he thought he was the trigger, but now he sees that her strange moods weren't triggered by anything: they were utterly random, aleatory, as if she threw a die throughout the day – a smiley-faced five: the solicitous Mum. A solitary one: molestation.

He never knew the why of her moods, but even as an infant he was able to sense the when: the moment of transition. One second he had something at least resembling a mother, the next she was gone: she'd morphed, lignified, hardened into old timber, unbending and unscalable. But worse than this was his mum's unfailing righteousness: she was immune to all criticism. Not even the local battleaxes could chip her resolve. He heard their comments, for couldn't little boys be silent without being deaf?

Well, I never! Licentious, that's what she is: a libertine of a woman! We shan't say a mum, because the day she notices she has a little lad will likely be the day she dies of shock. Poor mite, not a penny to scratch his nose with and a mum who goes courting. Men friends indeed, over for tea and biscuits! I'd like to see what my Gerry said if I brought men friends back to the house! And I bet it's a damn sight more than tea they get to dunk their biscuits in. Nearly forty years old, but seventeen she is, in her mind. Marilyn Monroe, she says she looks like: her figure's for flaunting, not housework. That woman needs to learn the meaning of responsibility; wake up and smell her fancy coffee.

Smell was never his mum's favourite sense. She wasn't hot on audio-visual stimuli either, yet she wasn't adverse to taste – oh no, she was good with her tongue in all areas, but her strongest sense was haptic: touch. Eyes closed, deaf to criticism, hands outstretched, his mum, good time girl Gloria, she felt her way through life. Sometimes late at night when she was lonesome, she would crawl into his bed and put those raw hands on him.

If only he'd had a father to shield him, things might have been different; but perhaps a father would have been a double-edged sword, for who knew who his dad was anyway? Which one of her suitors was it – or was it just some rapist that knocked her up in a back alley?

It would fit with her hatred of men, with her belligerence, with all of the years that she silently waged war on him.

She told him she'd wanted an abortion, that she'd even tried a home one: filled a bathtub with boiling water, drank a lot of brandy and got the weapons out – she picked apart wire coat-hangers for foetus-prodding.

What chance did he ever have, with her for guidance?

She was a thief, his mother; she went into people's houses under the guise of cleaning them and stole their small stashes of cash. She closed her eyes, her powdered turquoise lids shuttering her vision, and then there was a wicked pause before the orbs reappeared – the same eyes, but different: an orphic light reluming them. And she would tell him how to do it: 'Just using your eyes is a mug's game. You have to picture the money in your head, fill your mind with its texture, its smell, the rustle of crumpled notes. Clear your mind of everything else, every other thought and eventually, your hands will lead you there.'

She was definite, no hesitation, no deliberation; she went straight to the money as if by some satanic intuition, and he would watch her bending over, black pencil skirt stretched tight over her callipygian bottom.

Withdrawing scrunched notes from a stuffed sock secreted in a saucepan, from the back of a paisley settee, from amongst the dirty duds in a laundry basket. She'd hold the notes aloft, victorious, all a-bubble with success and he would feel queasy.

She had no shame, that was the rub; she couldn't steal silently, querulously, apologetically. Her stealing was a gift, not a sin to be ashamed of; it was magic, prestidigitation for the court. 'Look, son; look at that, now! Twenty quid, they've hid! How about that!'

Those soft probing hands even led her to The Good Book on one occasion – he watched as her hands scrabbled on top of an ornate bookcase and fixed on a large dusty volume. Gripping it by the spine, she shook banknotes out of the Bible and all she expressed was contempt. 'The Bible, indeed. Lord knows what goes through these people's heads!' she jeered, turning her red waxy smile upon him.

It was diabolical, unnatural, he felt; communication with inanimate objects was surely never a good thing. 'The gift isn't mind reading,' she said. 'Now don't be silly. As if anyone could read a toff's mind! No, it's nothing like that; I can just sense money.'

As innocent as that: she could sense it. 'I sniff it out good as any bloodhound. Just a matter of opening the mind.'

He knew then that he would come to no good, for how could he with a mother like that, with such poison running through his veins?

He has spent many hours thinking of his mother, but here under the stream of the cold shower they still don't seem enough; they don't stick, because at the heart of his mother is a void. Underneath the makeup, the ebullience, there is a wasteland. 'Mum,' he tells himself, grimacing, 'is positively adiabatic. No warmth enters or leaves her territories.'

His be-furred and mini-skirted mother, ladders stretching up to her thighs – she was a whore. He saw those thighs disappearing and reappearing on the stairs as he sat at the kitchen table drawing, his mum's laugh mingling with the laughs of men he didn't recognise.

Yet she hated men, a fact her clients always failed to perceive. She had a repertoire of insults: she would say to him that men's brains were like the prison system, desperately lacking in cells; or that men were like public toilets: all the nice ones were engaged and the rest were full of shit; or that men were like mascara: they would run at the first sign of emotion.

And she would ask him what he thought the difference was between a forty-year-old woman and a forty-year-old man? He'd shake his head, at a loss, and she would reply sadistically that a forty-year-old woman thinks of having children; a forty-year-old man thinks of fucking them.

His mum was the bitterest hooker in town; it must have appalled her that her body had the effrontery to become fat and pregnant and then bring another man into the world.

He has killed his mother so many times in his head. Not in the flesh, but he can kill her through other flesh. Every time he kills one of them, he kills her. He has killed her at every stage of her life; he has killed all of her ages, and now he's onto the nonagenarians. It is her face that he sees when he yields the knife; it is her face that he will always see.

She didn't care enough; is that it?

It was surely more than that, he thinks; it was more. It wasn't just the absence of love, it was the abscess of hate.

It was the other men she brought into the house. It was the fact that she allowed him to be violated. It was the fact that she probed his body with varnished fingers. It was the fact that she allowed the world to treat him like waste.

Or was it simply that she wouldn't allow him to have what she considered to be a deviant lifestyle?

Either way, he hates her with absolute finality; he hates her more than all of his victims put together; and really, he only hates them because of her.

Yet strangely, although he is a killer, he cannot kill her in reality, for the two of them, for better or worse, are adnate – they are joined through having grown together like coppiced trees – and how can he unpick those bonds and disentwine himself from her?

Perhaps, though, it all comes down to the fact that he kills only because he wants to, because that want is so powerful that it overwrites all that tells him he shouldn't.

He kills to find personal peace, to find calm.

Sexual awakening comes in the planning; extreme ecstasy comes in the moment of penetration – the penetration of the phallus, the penetration of the stabbing implement and later the fine penetration of razor blade and meat cleaver – but it is the spreading of warmth through his limbs – through his very being – in the aftermath that he wants to achieve.

'Fitting in' is a miracle to all but the elite few, he feels; but in this act of extreme horror, the ultimate antisocialism, he finds that he ascends the vileness created by his mother. He finds that he slots into place, for in becoming the necessary dark underbelly that every society demands, he becomes an entity.

As a bonus, he has found that there is nothing more alluring than that which should not be done. For every day he doesn't wreak his desire upon a victim there is a struggle, a longing that has to be overcome, and this procrastination makes the finale so much more extreme. It is hard, though, to defer the fulfilment of his most basic urges.

The mutilation of female cats is one way to overcome this.

It is not always necessary to take the queen's life; the insertion of a long slit into the hind leg can be enough, or a red jag running along the back of the head and down to the collar bone might suffice.

The mutilation of horses is another way of indulging himself: mares he doggedly disfigures with his sharpened weaponry, shearing away their genitals with surgical precision, and through this infliction of pain he stays his hand from letting blood of a different sort: the blood of little girls and old women or whomever else should take his fancy.

He has no desire for boys.

Of course, he works with an awareness that inevitably he will fail, that one day he will take a child or a grandmother – in the way that a serial dieter knows that one day their lust for chocolate will end in sordid orgiastic gluttony – but at some level he tries to keep himself from murdering, and at least, during the destruction-droughts, he has his glass to occupy him.

Nine

On the cliffs, Mary sits on a denuded hillside. Soon there will be sea aster here; a carpet of thrift, lavender, campion, yellow horned poppies, scarlet and blue pimpernels will clothe this barren scrub. The only trees are gnarled, wind-battered, charred, where tourists have attempted to set them alight.

When the kidney vetch arrives she will pull bloody petal shards, one after another, from the vermillion mother plant to fathom if her mother is alive or not; she will gorge herself on destruction until there are only empty spaces where colour once blazed. The petals will break into jagged fragments so it will be impossible to decide the answer to her question, but she will ask it all the same.

When she looks down from this vertiginous promontory, sea laps against sea. A blue frothing sea mixes with another sea: one of pink and brown bodies. The brisk air does not deter the hoards and there is so much flesh on display that is sickens her. They are almost nude, and in their skins they're just another species of animal. This realisation chills her; it chills her because she's never let herself see it before.

There is the possibility that her mother has been poisoned and left to die somewhere remote. A quick blast of arsenic or strychnine, or a long slow poisoning with tapeworm eggs, like the preening Victorian ladies who consumed them by the pound to stay thin, overlooking the drawback that eventually they'd die.

Anyone could have had access to her mother's food. Perhaps the contaminant was in the disgusting dyed-black olives she used to eat? – she would pick them out of a stone jar, swirl around them her mouth and spit the slimy stone into a saucer.

Now that she thinks of it, she is sure that a customer brought her mother these very olives as a gift.

Think of a joke, she tells herself; think of a joke. That's what other people do to cheer themselves up. *A man is standing by his car with the bonnet open when a tramp approaches. 'Piston broke,' explains the man. 'Ah,' says the tramp, 'me too.'*

But the joke doesn't help, because the idea of being broke isn't funny any more. It isn't palatable, because she is broke, and because out there somewhere, her mother is broke.

Being pissed would be a blessing, but she can't be pissed, on account of her abstemious palate which refuses toxins entry.

She looks into this dead sea and there's nothing: not a whale, not a shark, not a seal to be seen. If she slips and falls now, she'll probably die; or if she's unlucky, she'll be paralysed from the chin down.

The scene in front of her should be cheering. Cobalt blue seas. Patchwork of miscellaneous fields. Pink pub high on the hill, its vast sign vaunting sea views and home-cooked food. Bright specks dotting the car park. Hedges snaking down to sea. Elderly residents pruning cottage gardens. A skylark ascending to sing, its wary eye searching for sparrowhawks. Brown farm buildings in the far distance. A green lifeguard hut bedecked with red and yellow flags. Tub-of-lard woman waddling across the sands with a ragtag assortment of children.

It should be cheering but it is not – it is merely an example of continuance; evidence of the world going on its merry way and not caring.

The wind changes almost imperceptibly, but Mary senses it and pulls on her raincoat. Loud in her ears, like the crackle of power lines or the wind through leaf-laden trees, is the buzz of rushing water.

She sits on a bench devoted to the memory of Timothy Brown, who loved this place. The inscription bids her to *Relax. See beauty.* Beneath this inscription there's another, much larger inscription, carved in white letters, too neat to be crafted by key: a knife has been used here and it says:

FUCK TIMMY
WE R ERE
E IS DEAD BUT WE R ERE
DAZ N CAIN

Strangely, her first thought is: are parents now calling their sons Cain, and is that wise? Is there another son named Abel who quakes in his boots?

She is stunned by this abhorrent graffiti and yet it is a sign of the times. The entropy of this nation is as clear to Mary as her morning reflection. The steady decline is everywhere; no wonder they can't see her uniqueness, appreciate her vision.

Taking her serrated knife from her pocket, she slices her foam pad into bite-sized cuneiform segments and pushes them into her bumbag where they'll be safe from prying fingers. A ghastly brood of tourist-spawn fidgets past, turning air that was previously pure to blue, and Mary feels a transient relief that she has never succumbed to the societal pressure that prods women into begetting children – although she supposes that her children would have been superior to others.

Still, as she reminds herself, it's no coincidence that 'lies' sits neatly at the end of 'families,' for the basis of a family is a veritable nest of untruths, and anyway, hardly any of the breeders would consider befriending their own relatives if they weren't shackled to them by blood. Beloved family members would just be like any other badly-dressed sour-faced strangers in the street, taking up space, guzzling air. She knows it. The Lord knows it.

There are two types of women, Mary feels: Mary and everybody else. Everybody else views Mary as some sort of witch. They don't care for her loss because they don't know of her loss, and they don't know of her loss because they don't care for any loss of hers. She is an evil magus to be cast down and branked, a metal tongue thrust down her throat to stop her speaking.

She hates them. Their sybaritic lives are arranged solely around the pursuit of their pleasures. Wilfully ignoring the credo that *luxury enervates and destroys nations*, they vaunt the satiation of their base desires, waving aloft their brazen trophies.

Indolent lotus-eaters, the lot of them; and even worse than their perpetual self-gratification is the sense of entitlement that they feel. They deserve new cars, designer clothes, semi-detached houses – and if they can't afford them they get loans and credit cards, and when all else fails (and even the Citizens Advice Bureau has washed its hands of them) they go bankrupt. Just like that.

It stupefies her.

When she was young she expected nothing, hoped for nothing, and what she did spend was earned through hours of tedious shop floor labour. And she expected nothing less, because what's bought must be paid for, and what's paid for must be earned.

Have it now, and then when it's old, buy new is a mantra totally alien to Mary.

Mend and make do is what she says, but her principles fall on deaf ears.

So where is assistance to be found in this selfish world, where even memorial benches are graffitied with curses? Who has she to turn to? They are so full of their own woes and wants that they do not give a thought to anybody else's; they do not make enquiries or offers of help: they are fully absorbed with themselves.

Everything in its place and a place for everything, her neighbours tell their children. The problem with this fatuous mantra is that it doesn't hold true for people – *everyone in their place and a place for everyone?*

Mary knows she's grimacing and she hopes the wind doesn't change, but it's been a long time since she belonged – to a place, to a time, to a family. It was as if one day she just fell out of the loop, out of phase with the rest of mankind, just a few seconds behind or ahead – but a crucial few seconds that consigned her to a different realm, like limbo: not quite here, not quite there, not quite anywhere. Humanity goes on about its daily business; no-one notices a change – but to Mary, the world is so very different. She exists in a realm which blurs away from the normal world, which stretches away into the distance and back into the past. Fish rings in a river.

She has found a curious artefact: a rock, smooth in the hand but misshapen, bedecked with orange and cream wanderings: a baked potato of striped marble. In her palm she clasps this primeval metamorphic rock and she feels strangely privileged. It's cold against her hand and the coldness is invigorating; she's strangely elated by this stone which is almost too big for her. It's heavy and she's shot through with energy when holding this beautiful thing, this weapon.

Her hand itches to throw it – at children, at mothers, through the window of the lifeguards' hut, through every single pane of glass – but most of all she wishes to use it to crush the life out of the man who has filched her mother. For it is undoubtedly a man.

Reality is a curse and she knows that she mustn't, but she so desperately wishes to escape to her numinous dream-world, her ethereal pied-a-terre, the different kind of consciousness she can fly to in times of spiritual privation.

Flee to the world of topsy-turvy, where those who fly, rule.

She'll be a harpy. She doesn't care. Give her the head and trunk of a woman and the tail, wings and talons of a bird. She doesn't care. She can be queen there, if nowhere else, and when the quadrupeds come, she'll beat her wings and soar.

Ten

It is at the Crystillery that he encounters his very first victim. He is twenty-four years old, and three years have passed since he graduated *magna cum laude* from a venerable art college.

The woman who catches his eye is an assistant blower. Her image is burned into his memory. She is brand new and she stands, young and fresh, minding her own business, guarding the furnace.

He can remember it exactly, every detail, like a cine film playing in his mind, slowed down, the camera zooming in upon her face.

She is grindstoning her nose like a good little assistant and then she looks up and sees him hovering: the talented artist who has been fast-tracked to senior designer, a man that she is desperate to impress and yet someone whose personal repugnance alarms her. Someone who sets her woman's intuition to red alert. A man unattractive and yet so enthusiastic; a gangly greyhound falling over its own feet. So paltry that she takes pity on him, and so when he offers her a tour of his lair after hours she accepts, enthusing at his craft and praying that one day she will be as proficient in the art of glassmaking as he.

She sweats as she stands in front of the furnace – but he's used to it by now; he hardly feels the burn and is his usual pale self – but she reddens; cool beads of sweat run off her face, which she mops at furtively with a sheet torn from the newspaper pad, and she shuffles backwards out of the flow of heat.

She notices a small ginger mole on his cheek as he offers to demonstrate the construction of one of his more avant-garde pieces.

He instructs her to begin, indicating that he'll guide her through the tricky parts, so she drops the gather of molten glass into a pool of water and they watch it solidify into a long teardrop. She picks up this fragment and hands it to him and he holds it up to the light to examine.

His grip must be too tight because she feels a change and instinctively she turns away. The drop explodes with a crack and when she looks back she sees that fragments of glass powder are embedded in his face, in his hands. His face begins to ooze blood from tiny pinpricks and his skewed countenance is pocked. He's wounded, and her heart's in her mouth; he's her boss and she's hurt him and that isn't going to go down well on her appraisal.

The glass is ominous. Silent, fragile, yes: but potentially lethal. Their work, their pretentious art, can maim. Thank God, she thinks; thank God the teardrop was only small, for if they'd made a sizeable one it might have taken his eye out or his head off.

Prince Rupert's Drop: a bubble, a 'gather' on the end of a long thin nose; molten glass dropped from a height into water. Strong glass – the head can take a blow with a hammer – but unbearable stress within this structure: a stress so immense that the tiniest scratch to the nose can cause detonation.

'Sorry. I'm normally so careful,' he says, coolly. 'I don't know what happened. I've never had one of mine explode before.'

'It's my fault, I'm so sorry.' She wonders how long it will take to get promoted now she's mutilated the boss.

'It's okay. My passion fingers are to blame.'

'Passion fingers?' she enquires, her eyebrows raised.

'Everything I touch, I fuck,' he quips smoothly, and it seems then that he focuses on the minutiae of her face: the small golden chairs on her cheek, the tiny blue thread vein on the bridge of her nose, the tiny open pores on her chin. He looks at her microscopically and yet he is not deterred, he's engaged. Engaged in some kind of communication with her face which she feels she is not part of.

She laughs, but she's mortified. Is this what she does to men, injure them? Is she that dangerous? No wonder they keep their distance, keep their heads down when they pass her. Like that snaky-headed Medusa: they should avoid her at all costs.

On that first night they go to bed. She drugs her doubt with vodka and there is a strange transformation: she begins to find him bewitching. Odylic force exudes from him, mesmerising her, momentarily alarming her, but ultimately inciting her. She is inconsequential in the shadow of his sexual aura, his feral magnetism and the thought of him unzipping her skirt, running his hands over her thighs is enough to make her blush. Her stomach contracts when he's near, a deep visceral reaction to the smell of him.

She reclines on the bed beneath him and her eyes strip away his skin. She sees red muscle and blood vessels and white fat, and somewhere within this red and white soup, he is there.

She will offer herself on a platter, fall to her knees and kiss his feet; she will surrender; she will be his personal odalisque.

She's disgusted at herself for this; her strident inner feminist wants to cut her throat for such apostasy. But she can't help it; he fills her with a desire that overwrites everything else. It's galling. It's warming. She doesn't usually go for complicated men, men with problems that need solving. But he seems different: there's something hidden that is alluring, and it's something she wants to find.

And so she falls headlong for the charisma of a killer. As she lies beside him this first night in post-coital torpor, her hands seek out his sleeping face; she touches his hot brow and she feels she's done a good thing in giving herself to him: he is in need and she has provided. His immersion within his art world is avoidance: it's born of pain. She senses this absolutely, and she wonders if she has it in her to heal him.

She watches him; flushed and hot, he throws the quilt aside and he lies naked, twisted, one arm protecting his head. She watches him dream, eyes flashing, teeth bared. In dreams this quiet, unobtrusive man fights; he stands his ground and kills, and she's happy for him. She watches him for hours, noting the ultradian rhythms of REM sleep and night erections – even in nightmares his deep, flickering eyes are somehow beautiful, old in his young face.

He is bathed in candlelight and the milky luminescence of his skin is quite astounding – the radiance of that blemishless countenance in the soft smooth light is almost monstrous, almost inhuman, more like the carefully mixed oils of the Renaissance super-realist painters than the face of a flesh and blood man.

The perfect skin hue that's too perfect: so perfect it betrays its artificiality.

The more she watches, the more she can see the white aura rising from his skin, strong around his throat and around the perimeter of his still head. Growing, flailing out of him, a quarter of an inch, half an inch, a whole inch, coming from his skin, then more, until it almost seems that he's aflame with white light.

Then, all of a sudden, it's gone.

With a guilty jolt, she realises that it's depraved to watch someone sleep, voyeuristic to stare when they're so deeply unaware, and she turns away and tries to read the pristine copy of *Bleak House* that is sitting on his nightstand. She stares at the typescript in the soft light thrown from the lamp, but she just can't get at it; the words on the page blur and she turns back to him.

Time makes a leap and a gory dawn stains the sky.

She rises and pads quietly to the bathroom and when she returns he's awake and smiling at her, so peaceful, so unaware of the violence of his sleep and she knows at this moment that the man watching her has been through something. It's written in the patina of lines etched across his brow.

'Ready?' he asks, throwing his arms casually behind his head, revealing gingery sproutings of underarm hair that make her feel guiltily queasy.

'Ready for breakfast. I'm starving,' she answers, embarrassed. But he's looking at her oddly: looking through her as if she is not even really there, as if she is a ghost.

'Come here, please.' He beckons her with an autocratic index finger and begrudgingly, she approaches him.

He pulls her across to him violently and nudges the straps from her shoulders, pulling the daffodil silk of her slip down around her waist. She resists, questioning her situation in the cold light of day, and so she does not lift her hips collaboratively and let her slip slither to the bedroom floor, but instead she remonstrates and holds it firm.

His hand struggles with hers and his kisses are urgent and primal and within twenty-four hours she will be dead.

On the final night of her life, after giving him a second chance (in response to his abject apology and plaintive mewing) they are together in the Crystillery and he is showing her just how good he is and just how much she has left to learn.

She's watching the moonlight flood through the glass shrouding the Crystillery, alighting eerily on his vast army of sculptures which he calls *The Viscera*. They are crafted in hues of ruby, emerald, sapphire and amethyst. They're rigid and they stand autonomously, but they're shaped like human organs. These are the prototypes; these will go on to grace houses the world over; these will be bestsellers.

'Thermal shock.' He turns back to her, wiping ash across his forehead. 'Extremes of hot and cold. If the piece changes too quickly there's no rescuing it. Bang! It's slow work, you can't rush it. Little by little. You know you'll make it in the end; it's just a case of perseverance.'

'You need another beer,' she says grumpily.

'You never touch it, mind. No touching allowed. It's a strange thing: you fashion her by hand, but you never actually get your hands around her.'

'A bit like the Lord making Eve, then? So really, what you're saying is that you're a god?' She laughs, gently.

'Exactly,' he says and she smiles, but she's not really listening. She's watching him. He's a different person when he's blowing: distracted, a mad glint in his eyes, the same glint that other men get when faced with naked breasts.

'Prince Rupert's Drop. What is it? Chop, chop! You can't have forgotten already. Tell me,' he orders.

'That stupid thing that exploded in our faces yesterday,' she answers joylessly.

'Don't forget her. That wee curvy bit of glass may be called Rupert, but she's female, definitely female, and she's a ticking time bomb just waiting to go off. Under too much stress, you see; any little thing could set her off. Just you remember that.' He grins and she notices that he already has crow's feet and laughter lines around his mouth, and she catches a glimpse of the old man he'll one day become.

'I'll be sure to remember Rupert's a woman,' she responds, and reaches for his hand.

He pulls away. 'It's going to be hard to replace you,' he says, brow furrowing.

'I'm not going anywhere.'

'You will. Do you know, it's my mother's birthday today?'

'I never had you down as a Mummy's boy,' she teases.

'I'm not: my mother demitted the office of mother during labour.'

'You were adopted?' she asks, wary of opening an emotional Pandora's Box.

'I wish,' he says, with such a hangdog expression that for a moment, despite his morning aggression, despite his sexual insistence, her heart goes out to him.

'All families are a mess; it's supposed to be like that. The trick is to not let them get to you.'

'My mother made Mr Hyde look jolly.'

'Well, we're all a bit funny. Best to think of her as dichroic.'

'Is it, now?'

'You know, she probably has a lot of sides to her, like most people. Like when you were showing me the dichroic crystal: look at it from different angles, and different colours show. So sometimes maybe a person reflects, say, buttercup yellow; sometimes sky-blue. What you see is more to do with you, the onlooker, than the crystal itself. It's about your point of view; where you're looking from.'

'Well, her colours were not the colours of the rainbow; they were the colours of purulence: snot green and mustard. Thankfully I don't have to look at her any more. She's dead.'

'I'm sorry to hear that.'

'When she was alive and kicking she was nothing like glass, and so *crystalline* and *dichroic* are the last words I'd use to describe her. *Scabrous* was more like it: rough and covered in scabs. Infectious, she was: pestilent. Like bubonic plague.'

'You really shouldn't speak ill of the dead like that.' She is uncomfortable now; he has gone beyond acceptable levels of moroseness; he is bordering upon the despicable.

'Why? In case she can hear me? She can't hear a thing where she is. It's noisier than a pneumatic drill in Hell.'

'How can you say that?' she asks, appalled.

'Because I believe in calling a spade a spade. Men paid to stick their dicks in her. She charmed them; they were feeling the soft hand tickling their chin and didn't notice the other hand rooting through the lining of their pocket looking for cash. She was a prostitute, a cheap penny hooker who'd sleep with a geriatric for a crumpled tenner. She hated the way she looked through my eyes, and so she hated me. It's funny: she thought that it didn't matter what she did in her life, because if she was on her knees, palms together, praying to God when she died, she'd go straight to heaven.'

She is stunned by this, which seems so over-the-top, so incongruous with her small experience of other men.

'She might have gone to heaven.'

'She didn't,' he asserts confidently.

'How can you know that?' She is on precarious ground here, and if she continues she feels that her questions will bring answers that she does not actually want.

'Firstly, because whores and thieves aren't welcome in Paradise, and secondly, because she wasn't praying when she died because she was drugged up to her eyeballs, and also because her hands were cut off at the time. And so were her knees, come to think of it.'

'Stop it,' she implores, fear percolating through her body.

'You weren't saying *stop it* last night,' he says coolly, conversationally.

'I wish you'd calm down.' She is not desperate, she is not defiant; instead she is overcome with submissiveness. She is pitiful, weak.

'Don't you ever tell me what to do,' he rages, egging himself on, working himself up, and she knows as he bears down upon her what will happen now, because there is nothing she can do to stop it, because an enraged man, no matter how short, will always win in a fight with a woman; because this terrifying man's will to hurt her is stronger than any defence she can muster.

He kills her on the stone floor of the Crystillery. Amongst the glass dust, the broken crystal fragments, the burned newspaper ashes, the smouldering fruitwoods. The murder is tentative, exploratory; he uses his bare hands to drain her life away. It is an exercise in the mechanics of life-taking. He feels what it is to hold a torch and extinguish it, and he is pleased.

However, after this first killing he is stuck, for without premeditation there is no plan in place, there is no destination for the body. He stuffs her awkwardly into a wooden crate that is normally used for vase storage, and after he has blanketed her in newspaper, he considers what to do. Twenty minutes pass before it occurs to him to use the furnace – the furnace that is hotter than a crematorium.

The furnace that leaves ash that can be disposed of by blending it with molten glass.

Eleven

More and more, Mary has been watching the world from the confines of her bedroom. She has sat in her window seat beneath cold lazuline skies streaked with white, and certain previously nebulous things have become clear. For instance: the only outcome of calling the police would be her own arrest, for the police are prejudiced against those with certain *black marks* on their medical records.

Yet Dr Rice – Old Pubic Lice – has scuppered her voluntary incarceration. He has sent a letter insisting it is in Mary's best interest to have an 'assessment at her earliest convenience,' and although Mary has sent her own letter insisting that it is in her best interest to resist all offensive judgements made against her person, that would-be Aesculapian demonstrated a certain shrewdness by using the promise of further sick notes as a bargaining chip. And so she has found herself out of the house for the first time in a week.

A broad-in-the-beam nurse waddles over and begins her irksome ministrations, prodding and poking where she is not welcome.

'How is your mother, Miss Sibly?'

'My mother is fine. She is on holiday with her foreign family in America at present. I do not notice her absence, particularly.'

'She's a foreigner, you say?'

'A displaced person, an asylum seeker, an immigrant. A refugee. She left Armenia – well, Turkey really; she may say those lands were Armenian, but they're within Turkey's borders, whatever she says – and fled to Jerusalem when the Turks began the genocide, the slaughter. Millions murdered, she said: babies, granddads, everyone. What to believe, though? What to believe, because how did a five-year-old keep her head when all about her were losing theirs? How did she hold on when there was nothing in her except the will which said to her: *hold on*?

'Yes, my eyes are open to mendacity, and yet she maintains that it was organised chaos, organised genocide, and she blames the world for it. She says Hitler only decided to go ahead with killing off the Jews because he knew that in Europe you could get away with mass extermination if you timed it correctly, since it happened

88

to the Armenians and nobody lifted a finger.'

'Awful,' the nurse says, with the indulgent air of a nanny addressing a five-year-old. Her patronising tone enrages Mary.

'Yes, it is awful, isn't it?'

'Well, we won't talk about that any more, will we? Now, one thing I do need to know is if there was a full moon the night before your final shift at Bodwicks? It's for a survey I'm doing for my Master's degree, you see.'

'You mean the night before I lost my mind? A full moon? I don't remember, but it is entirely possible that there was a full moon,' and Mary listens agog as the nurse finds it necessary to inform her – in her thick Scottish brogue – that the wards of psychiatric hospitals fill with the putative insane two days before the full moon until two days afterwards when it seems that 'things calm down again.' She sails on to explain that the origin of the word lunatic is from the Latin word *luna*, meaning moon.

'Very interesting,' Mary replies, 'but since I am not myself a werewolf, why are you telling me this?'

'I'm sorry, dear; it's just for the survey, and I just thought you might be interested.'

'Are you calling me a lunatic?' The nurse's sanctimonious tone continues to fire Mary's mettle.

'Of course not, love. Not lunatic, no. You just have some ... life difficulties.'

'Life difficulties?' she repeats with mordant astonishment.

'I mean – no offence, dear. I only speak as I see.'

'Dear? *Dear?* Do I look like an old dear to you?'

'Well ... yes,' says the nurse.

'Look here, Miss Butterball: I am here solely because my general practitioner is holding certain sick notes hostage. I'm not, however, required to listen to some Roly-Poly's extraneous thoughts on the universe. Thank you.'

'There's no need to be getting personal, Mary.'

'Miss Sibly, to you. Where do they find you people? Do they scour poor houses and asylums? It's almost as if they actively seek out the most dim-witted, the most unfeeling persons available.'

The ward manager approaches.

'What's all this racket?' she asks.

'That Scots doughnut has been insinuating I'm some sort of

mooncalf, influenced by a far-off lump of rock. It beggars belief. I know the NHS are having recruitment difficulties, but really! I shall write a letter voicing my concerns. One expects to meet these tartan shrews in Scotland, but never in Plymouth.'

'That's a racist slur, Miss Sibly; I take offence at that.'

'Well, you can take your offence back to Ben Nevis. Anyway, I thought the Scots hated the English. What's that Braveheart trash you people peddle? The BBC were playing it. Some Australian actor masquerading as a Scot, daubed in blue face-paint and effluence. Unkempt chap, uncombable skeins of hair flying behind him in the wind. I had dreams of flea-bitten crackpots for a week.'

'You're talking about William Wallace there, Mary,' she says, as if Mary has been blaspheming.

'Miss bastard Sibly, to you! Well, I shall send up a prayer that all Scottish termagants return to their homeland forthwith, taking their viperous insinuations with them.'

'I think that's quite enough for today,' the manager intervenes. 'You're free to leave now, Miss Sibly. This way.'

As Mary walks home she slashes furiously at bushes with a stick she filched from a passing Alsatian. At least the tiresome assessment will yield a ream of sick notes, and that's something. That will free her up, give her time to investigate. She will not give up on this mission; she owes it to her mother to find her. Her mother endured seventeen agonising hours of labour in order to squeeze Mary out of her uterus, and those were the days before epidurals.

Those were also the days before MRSA, as luck would have it, because otherwise her mother would have been a goner before the sun was up.

It was Mary's fault; she was too big. Two weeks overdue and fat as hell, a whopping twelve pounds of lard and she almost split her mother up the middle. She severed her back to front. Stitches were required to sew her mother's bottom back into place – as her mother was fond of pointing out – as if bottom-stitches were a testament of maternal love, as if somehow those intimate knots tied Mary to gratitude forever.

At least that was the plan, but how could Mary be expected to apologise for events that occurred before she was even born?

Could she help receiving the nutrients provided to her through the placenta? She could not. Anyway, wasn't it her mother's duty to stick to a harsh regime of fiery paprika dishes to kick her uterus into spasm? Or take the course that one of the neighbours chose for her brood: that is to say, sitting at the foot of the park's slide and allowing the children to use her belly as a bumper, gleeful feet hitting the foetus until contractions set in?

Mary sighs.

The answer to the riddle of her mother's disappearance must hinge on the actions of a secondary person.

But who, exactly, would have reason to abduct an elderly woman with the intelligence quotient of a peanut?

A disgruntled customer? An ex-lover? An illegitimate child? A marrow-munching elderly-collecting psychopath who's cut her mother open and is storing her in a bath packed with ice and using her for his own sadistic pleasures – taking freezing showers next to her mother's body every day so as not to melt the ice?

Then she must also consider such things as suicide, alien abduction, death by exposure to the elements, accidental drowning, attack by the Beast of Bodmin and temporary amnesia.

It might, of course, have been a religious enemy who took her mother; perhaps a Muslim or a Sikh or a Protestant. Her mother was devout, as all Armenians are. Mary's not exactly sure what she was devout in; she seemed to be a strange mix. It would have originally been the Armenian Apostolic Church, but the nuns in the Jerusalem orphanage must've inserted splinters of Roman Catholicism, and her years in England undoubtedly left smears of Church of England. She must have compromised on her faith many times, and come the end she probably didn't know where Catholicism ended and Protestantism began.

However, although she nibbled from a pick 'n' mix of faiths, she was addicted to the rosary: Hail Mary, full of grace, the Lord is with thee. Blessed art thou amongst women, and blessed is the fruit of thy womb, Jesus. Holy Mary, Mother of God, pray for us sinners now, and at the hour of death. Amen.

How many times did Mary hear this? A million, a billion?

It felt like more.

O My Jesus, forgive us our sins; save us from the fires of Hell and lead all souls to Heaven, especially those most in need of thy mercy. Glory be to the Father, and the son, and to the Holy Ghost. As it was in the beginning, is now, and ever shall be, world without end. In the name of the Father and of the son and of the Holy Ghost. Amen.

How a woman her mother's age found time to sin, Mary never knew, though perhaps she begged forgiveness for old sins. However, while she adhered to some Roman Catholic traditions, she didn't adhere to them all: the Lord only knew the last time she went to a priest to confess, though Mary often heard her praying solicitously to the *Anima Sola*, that lonely female soul imprisoned in the flames of purgatory. Her mother prayed to the *Anima Sola* that Turks (all of them, presumably) would burn in purgatory forever. When Mary suggested that Turks would be ascending to Allah and were likely to bypass Catholic torture grounds, Meghranoush feigned incomprehension.

Her mother also prayed to mysterious saints who answered to names along the lines of Sarkis the Warrior, Hripsime, Gayane and the Christian maidens, Gregory the Enlightener, Nersess the Great, Mesrop Mashtots, Vartan Mamkonian, Leontius the Priest, and Helena.

Saints, thinks Mary. That might ensure her safe return.

She asked her once, 'Is it true that the Armenian Church has two heads of state?'

'Not head of state, they are catholicos.'

'Yes, yes, well – how can you have two heads of the same Church?'

'One is Catholicos of all Armenian, and other one is Catholicos of … well, is reason. Reason is history reason,' was her Delphic reply.

'So you don't know?'

'I just say!'

'Calm down.'

'So what do they do, these catholicoses?'

'One go around world and see big men, and he see Pope, and he bring money for charity, he give speech, and medal to people that give money to Church.'

'And what does the other one do?'

'Same.'

'Well, what's the point of having two?'

'Second one do same, but he do bit later. If they not see first one, there second one to come.'

'But you don't need two catholicoses for that, you could just make the first one more efficient and then there would be no need for a second. It's ridiculous; it's like having two Popes.'

Her mother pleated her lips and snorted.

'It way it is.'

'It's stupid.'

'You stupid, you not see anything. I know why.'

'Tell me, then.'

'No.'

'Tell me, if you know so much,' Mary goaded her.

'I say no.'

'Because you don't know anything.'

'Stupid girl. Two catholicos keep down money for wedding and funeral. If only one catholicos, what if he triple money for funeral – what you do when you die?'

'Competition? You don't trust one enough, so you have another to keep an eye on things, in case one gets out of hand? Is that what you're saying?' She tried unsuccessfully to hide her glee.

'No. I no care what you say. I know. It make sense. It way always been.'

'Piffle.'

'What is piffle?' her mother asked suspiciously.

'You are.'

Mary couldn't help taunting her; she was exhaustingly illogical and stubborn as a goat. A person had more chance of extracting an informed opinion from a snowman.

Religious enemies are possible and yet they seem so out-of-place, too extraordinary for suburbia. In Plymouth people disappear, but they are not murdered; they just get fed up of their families and do a bunk; they start new lives with new people and never look back. Yet what would be the point of starting anew in the final months of life?

It is only as she nears her front door that Mary considers that her mother is not dead. Perhaps she is captive somewhere, tortured and abused on a daily basis. And this thought is worst of all.

Mary wanders empty-handed into the kitchen, puts the kettle on and refolds the tea towels. She kneels and taps her head softly against the cold floor.

Twelve

Summer has arrived, the sky a dazzle of deep blue, the finest cobweb of cloud stretched high across the heavens and still the house awaits her mother's return.

She tries to carry on as normal; tries not to think of her mother being tortured; tries not to see a faceless man stabbing her mother's nether regions with a penis; tries not to think of her mother weeping; tries not to think of her mother calling out for her. She closes her mind to all of this and carries on, because what else can she do with only tenuous leads, except look for concrete ones?

She pulls herself up a bosomy slope, struggling with the steep acclivity and trying to catch her breath. She notes that the air temperature is tolerable; not cold, not humid, just right and she dreads such sinister conditions, for they create perfect game-playing weather.

What she'd do for a nice icy wind, a brattle of thunder, sheet-lightning. She rounds the corner and there they are, muted for a second, eyes slewed from skateboards and footballs. Temporarily frozen but now slinking together, staring all the while. Her nemeses: the neighbours' kids. It's the ceasing of play that really irks her; the way they move out of the car park and onto the grass verge, purely to eye her. Completely unaware of the pain they inflict. So sure of themselves, such insouciance, such unerring faith in themselves, such offensive smirking, and when she's near enough they start to call:

'Got an itchy bum, 'ave ya, Mary?'

So she's different, so she has a few nervous ticks. So what? Can she help it if her skin itches? Should a legitimate case of pruritus make her a pariah? And so what if from time to time she blinks her right eye? So what if every thirty seconds she takes a long moist tight blink of that oculus? Is one blinking eye really so grotesque? Should it be censored when it brings the blinker such satisfaction? Why should she not follow the lusty blink with a good crick of the neck, which entails no more than the inoffensive little gesture of raising her right shoulder to meet her tightening neck muscles and a sharp head loll to the right?

Her blink/crick combination brings such relief to her; why can't they just give her a break? Just for once, in her hour of need, won't they stop bullying her?

'Maybe she didn't wipe it.'

'She can't wipe her own bum yet.'

It's the sun. The sun brings them out, like insects: like wasps. There's no fighting them, and she's tried. The more she tries to flick them off, the more they sting and it only brings out the queens: interfering bulbous matrons with craggy faces.

What these kids need is a good smoking out to make them dizzy; obtunding the little hoodlums is the only way to go. Maybe she should walk with a flailing fire brand, befogging the street ahead; priest-like, swinging a thurible of incense. Thankfully, Mary reminds herself, these mini-thugs will soon take to smoking of their own accord. All of these do-gooder politicians forever hectoring the kids to get off ciggies – they should just let them be. The sugar-crazed hellions need the smokes to calm them down. Mary personally will relish the sight of their carcinogenic activities and will avail herself of every opportunity to report the reprobates' behaviour back to their proud parents.

'A stale old biddy,' the last mother called her, in full earshot of her hyena children. 'A stale old biddy with frizzy hair and no tits.' And Mary wondered at great length why it is that women are so cruel to other women, because don't women have it hard enough already? Shouldn't they club together?

Yet they don't, and there are no darts like those blown from the lips of one woman to another, and no antidotes either.

The word that hurt most was neither 'biddy' nor the allusion to her less than ample cleavage. No, the word that stung her was 'stale.'

The rest could be overlooked, for women of a certain age are beginning to reclaim the word *biddy*; it's not the scourge of the elderly that it used to be. Her generation reclaimed it, just as they reclaimed *bitch*, just as the younger generation of women were currently reclaiming *slag*.

But *staleness* is hideous. Nobody wants to be *stale*, nobody would think to reclaim a word that is usually aimed at light refreshments left out on the worktop for too long.

The more she thinks about it, the more it seems that staleness is not generic; staleness is specific to who you are.

If, for instance, you are a biscuit, then the worktop treatment will make you soft and crumbly, slightly sickening in your staleness. But if you happen to be a baguette, overnight exposure to the elements will make you rock-hard in your staleness, unyielding: a murder weapon in the wrong hands. Some older women are categorically soggy digestives, Garibaldis and custard creams. Mary, however, would far rather be of the second camp, toughening past her use-by date, not weakening and turning to mulch.

'Don't mind us, you keep at it. We don't mind if you want to itch yourself. It's them fleas, isn't it?'

She tells herself that she's used to it, that their voices are no more important than the gusts agitating the wind-charms of the neighbours, charms that rang with every breath of wind until she took them and buried them in the woods.

'Come and talk to us, Mary. Come and be friends.'

'Go away.'

'We're not going anywhere until you tell us where she is.'

'Where who is?'

'Your mum. We haven't seen her in ages – what you done to her?'

'I haven't done anything to her; she's in hospital, if you must know. Her heart is playing up.'

'My dad wants his jeans back.'

'Well, he'll just have to wait, won't he?'

She continues the fraught journey back to her homely domicile, avoiding the flightpaths of seagulls which swoop low overhead. She can only guess what these birds are eating; they become larger and more menacing by the day. God's Seabirds have been tampered with by something unholy: in Mary's day seabirds stayed out to sea, but something, or someone, has lured them in. Sometimes, she's afraid to step out of her own front door. If it's not the scallywags, or abductors, it's the poop hawks.

She's had to cancel her order with the Rosedown Eggman as these modern pterodactyls have run amok with her doorstep half-a-dozen, cracking shells and licking yolks. Is this the nature of evolution? – she muses. Are these yellow-beaked, egg-guzzling monsters destined to rule the world?

She addressed her complaints to the local councilman, advising a swift program of shooting, egg-pricking, and egg-oiling, guaranteed to effect the immediate extirpation of the entire seagull population. He, however, responded with a sharp letter consisting mostly of desultory and unfathomable legalese concerning the Wildlife and Countryside Act of 1981, which purports to protect the raptorial seabirds (which have become so brazen that they don't even move when she approaches. Which, on the plus side, makes it that much easier to stick the boot in).

Of course, the twittering mothers who are so insanely hortatory in their feeding of ducks take offence at such rebellion and shoot her excoriating glares before steering their hooligans away.

Everybody hates her. She's losing it – she's losing it all. She's invisible. None of them ever smiles at her any more, even when bonhomie positively radiates from her face and she deigns to wish them a 'good morning.' They pass her by with blinkered eyes focused on the great beyond.

Now her mother's gone, it's as if she's been stitched into a chameleon skin and there's nothing she can do except blend into the background. She's so staggeringly alone. She lived a solitary enough life before, she thought, but this is worse. This unbearable solitude will kill her.

She has had no partner and she is chaste, despite her advancing years. She knows the Lord is supposed to approve of marriage, but she's a gentle soul who would bruise with too much handling.

She never thought she would ever feel lonely.

She has never given herself to any man because she'd rather keep herself. She is unashamed to admit that she's frightened of men, deathly frightened, and now it seems that she has made a mistake: she has underestimated the extent to which her mother's ongoing presence precluded real loneliness.

If only she had a man now, the burden would be easier to bear, but men are clueless when it comes to Mary. Men have a disconcerting habit of popping up from shady corners when she least expects them to, and saying things that only vaguely resemble words. She vowed many years ago that she'd live an untouched life and she's never broken that vow. Until this point she had considered herself lucky: her fears have meant that her quiescent quim has been entirely undisturbed by the phallus, safe from that fearsome purple-headed womb-ferret.

She has always thought that her grave stone would read: *Mary Sibly, born a virgin, lived a virgin, died a virgin* and that she would be proud of this. Now it seems ridiculous: she might as well have 'Returned Unopened' inscribed on her memorial and be done with it.

Yet, even if the thought of dying as a virgin does finally perturb her, it is too late to change now. She must accept her antisexuality. Who knows what punishment would be apportioned to her if she abandoned her vow of celibacy? Who could categorically say that she wouldn't be buried in an underground chamber and left to starve or suffocate like the Vestal Virgins when they were interfered with by the Lusty Pious? It is her destiny to remain innocent, and after all, the Virgin Mary has a certain age-old ring to it.

Vetoing men is one thing, but she's at a loss to explain what has made her avoid female friendship. The hostility between Mary and other women has always been entirely intentional on her part, and she dislikes them far sooner than they ever think to dislike her, but now she needs someone to help her and they are unwilling. She needs something to keep her afloat; even a carelessly thrown grin from a housewife would be a life ring. But there's nothing.

She's burned all of her bridges and nobody will help her, not even if she asks them on bended knee.

She has made her lonely bed and she must lie in it.

But it is not her fault. It's her disposition, and she can't help her nature.

Even as a girl, she found physical contact with females as distasteful as with males. Her natural flintiness irked the shop women and paved the way for her alienation, but if one is asked for an opinion, one should not lie. They would beg for comment on their sexual misadventures, and she'd far rather have kept silent. But to her utter chagrin, the lewd sorority continued to demand answer from her.

She's no fool; she already knew what went on in the top stockroom. It was a regular brothel up there. Menswear and Home Entertainment paid visits during the supposed stocktaking sessions undertaken by Women's Fashion, and it wasn't just the youngest and prettiest women who were involved in these scandalous liaisons: some of the women whose heavy grunts and small screams she was forced to hear weren't much younger than Mary, but were far more married.

Sometimes she could correctly identify the sounds of four or five different individuals participating in an orgiastic episode. On one memorable occasion she witnessed – from behind a sky-high stack of clothes rails – the naked White Goods manager, busy servicing the nether regions of a new and rather young-looking female employee, whose two thick braids of stramineous hair had perhaps caught his attention. So wrapped up was he in his gustatory delights that he failed to notice that the vagina in question had a very uninterested body attached – so uninterested, in fact, that it repeatedly sighed and consulted its watch.

At long last Mary grew sick of silence, but her animadversions were drawn from her without any real intention of divulging the fullness of her opinions. She notes again how odd it is that once the tongue achieves full wag, there's little hope of censoring it: it must have its minute in the sun. At the moment that she sailed forth with her opinions, they hated her more than they hated themselves. A feat indeed.

She was modest, yet capable; never thrust herself into the limelight, never tried to shimmy her way up the greasy pole. She comported herself with quiet dignity, always meeting sales targets and never showing signs of anxiety under pressure, and her visits to the stockroom were strictly business only.

Perhaps this coolness of head, combined with her moral fortitude and artistic talent, saved her from the axe-sweep of redundancies in which the often-interfered-with often fell. And perhaps this coolness, this aloofness, stood in the way of friendships.

Oh yes, it is all horrifyingly clear in the rear view. They all despised her, everyone of them. It doesn't matter who scorned who to begin with, they all ended up loathing her. They wished she would vanish. Her ongoing employment foxed all of them, and they must have attributed her presence in their midst as testament to the immunity of long-term employees: they must have been so pleased when she flipped, when she lost her marbles in front of all and sundry. They must have been laughing their socks off.

Thirteen

A hot night; scarlet curtains fly inwards on a scalding breeze and billow above him. A web of sweat criss-crosses his exposed belly and flashes of lightning illuminate him, rendering him unearthly.

He's waiting; a roar has penetrated the black air, an abnormal sound for his house: a thunderous clap that does not belong to this place of gentle sighs and groans.

He feels the wind on his bare skin as he lumbers to the window, and as the sky flickers he sees that the skeletal lightning tree has accepted another strike: it steams in the centre of the field where the paddock's motley assortment of horses are normally to be found vying for shade.

His house is being painted, and as he stands at the window he can smell the fumes in the air and the lightning illuminates careless spatters on the old flagstones below.

They have cleansed his house. He sat in his kitchen engulfed upon all sides by the issue of hoses, dissolving years of grime from his old walls. They splashed away the grey and revealed newness, an uncanny brightness of papery white and he was surprised to perceive that the whiteness had been there all along – not damaged, not stained, just hidden by the mould that fed on the sea wind.

The white has been obliterated now. Persons unknown and unloved have netted his beloved house with scaffolding, an exoskeleton to protect its essence from the world enveloping it.

So many sickly mornings of late he's listened to these new sounds, as they've banged and hammered and peeled tiles from the roof, as the painters have sprayed and brushed until the house sweated under their touch. He has sipped peppermint tea and inhaled its soothing vapours, trying to chase the nausea away, trying to ignore the quiet presence of the fading old woman in the cellar as they smothered his white walls in Kernow pink – that traditional shade of vomit, of first blood; layer upon layer of period paint to hide the tired, anaemic bricks.

He felt such perfect calm and now, as the killing day looms, in the depths of this warm flashing night, protected by his house, he loosens and lightens.

He smiles as the fledgling rain begins, dropping down tentatively, a pitter-patter of tiny feet. There, now: it is fully unleashed and it comes down in sheaves.

He is adept; he has served his apprenticeship and has graduated to grand dragon, and it is a given that by now that he has killed many times – dozens of times, but not too many times to remember because he remembers them all, and his memories are daubed in vivid primaries. And he dreams of them, he bestows his dreams equally, remembering them all in egalitarian revolutions, none favoured more than the other, each a favourite in her own way.

It is a perk of his job that the continual grinding of glass against the rasping diamond-coated discs also engenders the grinding away of his fingerprints. A happy coincidence that led him to believe for a long time – certainly in the days before DNA databases – that he was invincible, untouchable, a shadow man leaving no mark, invisible as an airborne virus – unseen but not unfelt.

But now he must be careful: he knows this with certitude. He has been a dedicated follower of science fashion, reading dull journals with relish, because ignorance is not bliss: ignorance is a prison cell and this is his life at stake. Or, rather, his life as he knows it; because whatever happens, however many useless lives he takes, he will not meet with the death penalty, not in this country of liberal high-mindedness. Slaves of statistics know that such a distasteful practice is not a deterrent. Just look at America. And, more than this: capital punishment legitimises life-taking, because if the government can take a life with premeditation and cold blood, why shouldn't anybody else? – and this rationale works in his favour.

Anyway, perhaps prison wouldn't be so bad. True, he'd be without his arts, both of them; but on the other hand, he'd be a legend on the violent offenders' wing. He'd top their tallies by tens, and if there were but world enough and time, he'd top their tallies by tens of hundreds.

He is an apex predator, and he won't stop until his arms and legs are cut off, and even then, he'd tear out their throats with his teeth.

A dazzling flare that cauterizes his eyes.

Hot on its heels, a clap of thunder, with an epicentre just above his roof.

He wonders what the old lady is making of this storm. Is she awake? Or has her deafness allowed her to sleep through it?

Thunder has always frightened him, but not tonight. Tonight it doesn't seem possible that it can hurt him.

Wet walls bring the stench of paint to him even more strongly. He shuts the rattling window.

He stretches back on the bed, focuses on the rain; hypnotised by the tapping of large raindrops, he floats.

Fourteen

She must search, that much is clear. Sitting and waiting is no good; the sheer force of her will is not enough to bring her mother back. She has waited too long already, for don't statistics show that most murders happen in the first three hours after kidnapping?

She must find her, wherever she is; she must go to her and set her free.

Her hope leads her to Bovisand, that mysterious beach where lost things are miraculously said to be returned. She leaves early, takes two night buses and follows the cliff path to the beach. The sun rises and once again the daybreak sweats scarlet as Eve's apple, its soft opal light touching all surfaces of hedge and stone with gentleness.

Dawn brings such emptiness to the world, she thinks, as she stands in the long expanse of golden sand that is utterly unblemished by tourists – there is only herself, and a beach full of foxes.

She doesn't know what she expects to find here, but she has a feeling that something will happen. Perhaps her mother is here already, awaiting her arrival in this special place where so many summer days were spent happily picnicking. Or perhaps her mother's body will wash in with the high tide, bloated and crab-eaten. At least the discovery of a body would be an ending, would preclude any further hope from tormenting her. She would grieve and mourn and eventually she would come to terms with it.

So she is here on these peculiar sands that are legendary for returning the lost, and she knows every shade of them, for didn't her young self make daily pilgrimages to this very spot? Her mother told her not to sit in the wet sand, but she liked to feel the wetness soaking through to her skin, seeping into her underpants. She dug herself a swimming pool and lounged in tepid water, keeping an eye out for ragworms, watching the waveline push nearer and nearer.

She saw that the beach had a new face every day. The lines in the sand would look different; rings around boulders and cliffs waved this way, then that way, but never the same way twice. She waited each day for the new work of the tide, lamenting always the footprints that her small feet cast in the sand. Sometimes the beach was flat as a pancake and cut a wall into the dunes; sometimes it was a gradual sloping descent down to the water line.

Mostly the sand was set like shells, rows and rows of clam outlines, semicircle upon semicircle scoring the sand. Cuttlefish were bountiful one day and gone the next; driftwood washed around, high up the beach, then lower, then higher, then claimed again by the tide. One day a shoal of barnacles washed up, glued together like everlasting gobstoppers.

Her eyes scour every inch of the beach but she cannot see her mother anywhere.

She searches the debris for clues. The tide has brought in a load of bric-a-brac: bucketfuls of flotsam and jetsam. And there are shells: she finds a mother-of-pearl, a beauty. And three dead crabs and the remains of four more and a purple jellyfish, but there are no headscarves, no embroidered handkerchiefs, no severed fingers.

She sifts through the detritus and she feels useful. She is doing something proactive; she is looking and she enjoys this feeling of energy. She searches enthusiastically, paying scant attention to the vile things: the unsanitary towels and old rubbers and the waves that are crowned with brown froth – which she tells herself is the effect of natural surfactants. She searches through rock pools, expecting with every new pool to see her mother lying in the water, small fishes darting about her face, anemones entangled in her hair, pale eyes staring at the sky.

But there is nothing other than a slit beach ball, some fishing wire and an elaborate rig of hooks. She cannot take the suspense any longer, so she runs along the wave line just a few times as the sun rises higher in the sky, before the dog walkers come out. And then she sits and watches a geriatric battleship on its way to the Devonport Docks. It is followed by the black square of a submarine which courses through the waves – past the solemn old breakwater that brandishes its impressive white tower – emerging only at the very last minute.

The strangest things can happen in life: anything is possible. The strangest thing happened once on that very breakwater. A bride and groom went there on their wedding day, she in her big white gown and he in top-hat and tails. But somehow, while they were taking the photos, she lost her engagement ring. It fell clear into the sea. It was an antique and worth a fortune, they said; it used to belong to the grandmother of the groom. It was in the paper on and off for weeks with colour photographs of the bleary-eyed bride snivelling into her hanky. The groom was compelled to offer a reward of two thousand pounds, then five thousand pounds, for anyone who could return it to his beloved.

The town came out en masse. Divers scoured the water, but there was no sign of the precious circlet. It was all doom and gloom – ruined her wedding day, apparently, since she took it for a symbol that they weren't meant to be together. Jinxed, she said they were.

Yet they stuck at it all the same and the next summer they went to Bovisand Beach and as that bride lay flat-backed on the sand her fingers touched something cold. When she opened her hand, lo and behold, she saw her engagement band.

Of all the people on that beach. Of all the days.

Therefore, there is order and meaning to world, even if it seems that there is not.

It is chaos theory. Which is no more than a case of simple things generating complex outcomes, like a shoal of fish, or a flock of birds, swirling together in their thousands. She once thought there was a lead animal organising the others. She later learned better; the complex patterns were simply achieved by each member of the group maintaining a certain distance between itself and its neighbours, and travelling roughly in the same direction.

Ergo, the foggy set of events that led to her mother's disappearance will become clear if she can discern which rules are in play.

The bride found her ring because she was meant to, just as Mary is meant to find her mother.

Of course, certain misanthropic persons said the bride made up the whole thing; others said she dropped it in her handbag by mistake and found it later, but couldn't say so after she had the whole city out in a treasure-hunting frenzy. But Mary believed the girl absolutely, because she had a look in her eyes which could not be faked. She looked as if she had been struck by lightning, picked out of a million others at the whim of providence.

Tabloids speculated that the odds were billions to one. After all, Plymouth folk will stoop for anything that glisters, bottle tops included, so the ring must have washed up on the day she found it, or else it would have vanished onto another lady's hand.

If a lost ring can be returned, then so can a lost mother.

Mary suddenly notices something large sitting in the small frill of waves lapping at the water's edge. The tide is far out and she walks nearer. Didn't she know the beach would provide if only she was patient?

She approaches and sees that it is a body, but it is alive. It is a young woman, and she is ensconced in the waves in her wetsuit. She looks to be in her late teens or early twenties and she is just sitting there.

Mary doesn't know what to make of it. Is she in some difficulty? Should she rush to help her? People take such offence these days though, if they don't want help. She once threw some coppers at a dishevelled young man dressed in the garb of a vagrant, languishing on the street outside Macdonalds. He was furious: his jeans were intentionally ripped, it transpired, and he *chose* to wear his hair in his face. Apparently he was just waiting for some friends.

This young woman appears to be in some difficulties, though; her breathing is laboured and she is exhausted. She slumps and allows the exposed skin of her throat to soak in the water, rubbing her head into the sand and letting her hair merge with wet grains. Amongst the clamour of the waves and the gurgle of water rushing through sand, Mary approaches. Scenting danger, she calls tentatively,

'Excuse me, young lady. Are you quite all right?' Her voice sends a jolt through the young girl, who turns her face towards Mary.

'I'm fine, thanks.'

'Are you sure you don't need assistance?' Mary continues, stepping into the swash and allowing the brine to soak her socks.

'I'm sure.'

Mary is unconvinced. She is certain that people who are fine do not allow their bodies to be rocked left and right by incoming waves.

'If you're sure, then.'

'Honestly, I'm just relaxing.' The girl flashes her a dismissive smile.

'Well, perhaps you can help me. I don't suppose you've seen any little old ladies on your travels today?'

'I've seen loads, actually.'

'In the water?'

'At the bus stop.' She turns again and casts a look of amusement at Mary, who tries to make her face benevolent.

'None on the beach? She would seem very old to you: in her nineties, smallish, long white hair, foreign?'

'No, but if I do, I'll be sure to let you know. Now, if you don't mind, I have a lot of thinking to do.'

Mary can only imagine how she must appear to this young person; she must seem very old herself, and maybe more than a bit eccentric.

'All right, then; but if you see her, please tell her I'm waiting for her and tell her I'm sorry I hit her.'

'You hit an old lady?' The girl's curiosity is piqued now, and perhaps she will be interested enough to remember and look out for her mother.

'It was an accident,' Mary explains.

'Okay. Whatever, love.' The girl turns away from her and swishes water over her knees in a gesture that clearly conveys her distaste for Mary.

'You don't understand,' Mary persists.

'Look, I just want some privacy. I'll keep an eye out for your friend.'

'She's my mother, not my friend.'

'They are allowed to be both, you know.' Mary reddens and retraces her steps back up the beach, but she's too anxious to return home, so she finds a place in the rocks where she can sit as if looking at the view. Surreptitiously she watches the girl, who continues to sit there in the small waves. She must be freezing, is Mary's recurring thought, when suddenly all becomes clear as a frumpy woman pushing a wheelchair strides past.

Mary's astounded.

Isn't the girl afraid of freak waves?

She must have been a surfer or some such thing before her paralysis, she supposes. She watches both woman and wheelchair diminish until they reach her. Mary expects some pulling and pushing to ensue as the woman hoists the girl back into the chair, but she's wrong. There is a prolonged moment of what appears to be argument as the elder woman stands over her, brandishing the wheelchair – when suddenly she gives up, exasperated, and walks away, pushing the chair in front of her, and the girl emerges from the waves through her own efforts.

Facing the sea and using her arms, she drags her deadened legs over the sand ripples and slowly advances backwards up the beach. Rather than be seen to be pushed, she chooses to suffer the indignity of hauling herself along. The noise, the loud dragging scraping noise of dead limbs. It must be a quarter of a mile that she drags herself, the tide at its furthest ebb.

A few walkers come past and avert their gaze. As she progresses past Mary's position in the rocks, Mary hears her gasp painfully, as if her lungs will pop.

The woman stands some distance off, hand on cocked hip, embarrassed, as if the entire world were blaming her for letting a crippled girl suffer thus. But she keeps her place and when the girl reaches her, she pulls herself up into the chair. Her face is purple, sweat running from her blonde hair, and Mary notes that the black of her wetsuit is entirely slathered in sand. Mary watches as the girl waves her guardian away and begins to wheel herself across the ripples towards her own position.

She can't believe the stubbornness, the ferocity in thwarting her mother, and Mary wonders for a second if she would have done the same.

No. If her legs didn't work, she'd cut them off; she'd halve the weight she had to heave. What's the point of something if it serves no purpose? As she passes by, Mary feels drawn to know more of this girl, and she emerges from her nook in the rocks to converse with her.

'Why don't you let your mother help you?' Mary asks interestedly.

'She's my aunt, not my mother: my mother's dead.' The girl seems unsurprised to see Mary appearing so abruptly before her.

'Cancer?' asks Mary uncertainly.

'No, it wasn't fucking cancer,' she replies.

'What then?'

'She was murdered, if you must know.'

Can this be a coincidence? Another daughter whose mother has been stolen from her?

'How was she killed?' Mary persists while attempting to enact cool disinterest.

'We don't know. The police still haven't found the body and it's been twenty years.' Mary's heart stops and she is trapped, caught in the fine sticky filaments of a spider's web.

'How do you know she's dead, without a body?'

'Because of the blood loss.'

This is turgid; these are abnormal answers; this is all wrong. Mary cannot believe this is happening here at Bovisand. The girl laughs violently.

'I bet you wish you never asked.'

Mary tilts her head sympathetically and wrings her hands.

'I'm sorry for your loss, but what happened to you, Miss?'

For a moment they look at each other mutely until the silence becomes oppressive, heavy with the weight of things unspoken.

'I was in a collision.'

This is more bad luck than any one person can be expected to shoulder, surely?

'With what, a lorry?'

'With an iron rod.'

'Somebody did this to you?'

'The rod didn't swing itself.'

She glances at Mary with a wry smile and Mary feels the blood drain from her face as she allows herself to understand the meaning of this revelation. Maybe the attack was more than an opportunist encounter, more than the casual rage of a drunkard?

'Who did it?'

The girl reacts with puzzlement as if this is an utterly stupid question.

'If I knew who he was, I'd have killed him by now.' She means it and Mary nods impatiently.

'I understand that, but I mean what kind of person was he?'

'Well, firstly and foremostly he was a complete bastard.'

'Agreed,' says Mary appeasingly, 'but more specifically?'

'A man I've never seen before. I'd say he'd better pray he never runs into me again, but I suppose that's *my* bloody prayer.'

'What did he look like, in detail?' Mary asks.

'I wasn't making notes.' The girl speaks so hoarsely now that Mary almost regrets her invasive questioning, but she has to know, she has to follow this lead.

'You must remember something about him.'

'He had big eyebrows and he was old. In his fifties, I'd say. He had big hands too, fingers like pigs' tits, but he was shorter than me, and thin. I might have been able to take him if it wasn't for his metal fucking bar.'

This mindless paralyser is the same individual that has her mother. This is it – this is what the beach has to show her: this broken, dauntless girl.

'They didn't catch him?'

'No. Not yet. I don't think they ever will,' she says, raking her hands through the sand.

'How did he get you?'

'I don't fucking know.'

'You don't?'

'No. I thought about it and I still don't know what happened. One minute I was walking home through the park, and the next, this man comes out of the bushes and he's hitting me and then he just stops and goes on his merry fucking way.'

Mary is chastened by the coolness with which this girl recounts such a terrifying moment of her life. However, she must plunge on.

'What park?'

'Just across the Tamar Bridge, in Saltash. But it doesn't matter; he's no local. I'm sure he's not: he didn't have the face. I think he was just passing through the area, maybe on holiday. He was dark. He looked Polish or Bulgarian, maybe. Something Eastern European.'

'Tell me, do you think he was the same person who murdered your mother?' Mary asks gently, apologetically.

'How the fuck would I know?' Mary is stung by the angst in this girl's voice and by the note of accusation, her finger pointed at Mary for making her relive her pain.

'I'm sorry. He'll be caught, I promise.'

The girl laughs. 'The police never catch people like that.'

'I'm not talking about the police. I'll catch him and I'll kill him. I'll commit him to the whims of the perfidious gusts. I'll trice him up with hawser and leave him hanging from a cherry tree. I'll watch his fragile body flailing until his neck snaps. I'll watch him spin like a fly in gossamer webbing.'

She's concentrating on her now, Mary can see it in her eyes: they are animated with the suspicion that Mary's words are the febrile ramblings of a diseased mind.

'You're crazy, love.'

'You don't understand,' Mary says, bordering upon exasperation. 'He has my mother.'

A look of bemusement appears in the girl's eyes; Mary registers this look and is saddened by it.

'How do you work that out?' she says, frowning.

'I just know it.'

'You can't know that.'

'I've spent every day of my fifty-eight years with my mother. We have a link. When I hear the description of her abductor, I know it.'

'Well, don't go hanging anybody on my account, but thanks for the solidarity.'

Mary holds this new information in her heart all day and she is strengthened by it. She imagines this man's dark face in minute detail and she knows that now she has a definitive lead, for though she hasn't seen his face herself, in meeting one of his victims she's as good as seen his portrait.

Fifteen

Her eyes are hurting. It is still dark out there, dawn is hours away and the minutes are dragging. She's had no sleep – not a wink, not even five minutes of shut-eye: no sleep whatsoever. She was just on the brink, when the hideous clanking of the milkmaid reverberated through the entire neighbourhood, and then there was a car alarm, and then the rooks started crowing.

She needs sleep – she must sleep – but there's no sleep to be had. It's not her fault; new sounds are keeping her awake, noises creaking on and on, strange susurrations, whispers, groans, bangs, whimpers. Not normal noises: worse noises than ever before. How can one sleep when the walls are talking? But the walls can't be making noises – that's ridiculous. No: it's Next Door. There are noises coming from those covetous people with intrusive noses.

Instead of fighting the noises, instead of tossing and turning and using a pillow to smother her head, she stops and listens. Definitely Next Door. She can hear them from her bed. They keep moving; she can hear breathing – loud breathing. The more she listens, the louder it gets until it is suffocating, until it fills the room and closes in on her like a ticking timepiece.

If only she could get up and make some noise of her own to counteract their relentless onslaught of sound, then she could redress the balance. If only the wireless had not begun to call, she could have played some music to drown out their sounds, but it did, so she buried it at the base of the blanket box and smothered it in moth-eaten woollens.

The broom has been confiscated by persons unknown, so she doesn't even have the satisfaction of banging. The neighbours say they haven't touched the broom, but the broom lived under the stairs and more recently in the wardrobe, and now it's gone altogether.

It's been taken.

It wouldn't be so bad if she'd noticed and had the time to purchase a new one, but she didn't notice until nightfall and now it's too late.

However, in the grand scheme of things, the broom is inconsequential; the point is that she can't bang on the wall. The sort of dull (barely audible) thud she could achieve with her hands is not worth the exertion, and besides, her digits are already inflamed from wringing her hands, the knuckles sickeningly pink.

She has called the police on a regular basis to report the neighbours' activities. They have tormented her in a thousand ways; they have gossiped about her and fed the rumour mill, they have trespassed on her property, and they have knocked at her door to demand that she keep down her singing. On some occasions they have even sent their husbands around in the early hours of the morning with their banal requests to 'Put a sock in it.'

Always the same whinges: 'You're keeping the children awake. They have school; we have work.' As if she cares. She has more important things to worry about: matters of life and death, and she doesn't complain to them when they host their obnoxious children's parties out in the back garden. She doesn't complain when the walls bang rhythmically late at night after kissing and shrieking.

Only yesterday they were flaunting their families at her, rubbing salt into the wound of her mother's loss. They can't just have a birthday with an extra cup of tea and a cream cake; they have to have balloons pinned outside their front door and banners stuck onto the pedestrian bridge for all to see, and party poppers and sparklers too.

It's a given: the moment she closes her eyes for a desperately needed afternoon snooze they mow the lawn, or their truculent kids have a scrap; and the second Mary puts out her clean tea towels to dry on the washing line they strike up a barbecue so that she has to wash her tea towels twice.

She has enough to worry about without having to wash her tea towels twice.

These most offensive neighbours are always burning things; there are always plumes of smoke dispersing into the air from the end of their garden. As Mary informed the police, it's like living in a village perpetually pillaged by the Vikings. She listened, once, to find out what they were doing and it seemed that it was a ceremonial bonfire: children burned the intellectual fruits of their year; the mother burned fat photos of herself on the beach during their summer jaunt to Tenerife; her husband burned his work appraisals. All seemed to take great comfort from the cathartic inferno; they warmed their hands on the flames of their unhappy moments, but thought nothing

113

of the pollution they sent up into the clear skies, thought nothing of the ash falling down on Mary's mother's roses.

Supremely irresponsible, she screeched to the police. People should bear their own misery without forcing it onto the rest of the world, without forcing innocent bystanders to inhale it into their lungs.

At one of these eventide bonfires she sneezed – a natural reaction to the ash raining down – and they *Yoo-hoo*ed her.

'Hello, is anybody there?' She remained, standing stiff as a board in the dark, but they guessed. 'Mary, are you there? Why are you lurking in the dark?'

'I am not lurking.'

'Come and have a beer.'

'No, thank you.'

'Come and get yourself some wiener.'

Laughing. Jeering.

'I have never enjoyed wienerwürst. It is said to have been Hitler's favourite,' she replied haughtily.

They knew she wouldn't join them; they just wanted to make her uncomfortable, wanted everybody to know that she'd been standing there in the dark, listening. They couldn't just harbour suspicions; they wanted to make them fact. It still surprises her how she's ended up here, with the dregs, with the riffraff.

She must confront them. It's intolerable: the noises, the sighing, the bed-creaking. They have to stop, it's insufferable. They have to stop. She mustn't be afraid. She must put on her dressing-gown and go to them. She must tell them; she must tell them to stop.

She locates her dressing-gown – which is crafted from the finest chartreuse green silk – and she steps into her old faithful slippers, which have been with her through everything. As she walks through the silent house, she suppresses a shudder. What if the person who has taken her mother is one of the next-door mob? What if her mother is being kept hostage by them?

It's probable; they're certainly perverse enough to steal a mother.

Maybe that's what she can hear – the breathing sounds are her mother's and the banging is her mother attempting to communicate with her through Morse Code.

She cautiously opens the front door, alert to the possibility of her mother's abductor lurking in wait on the doorstep with a wad of chloroformed cotton.

The doorstep is vacant except for a solitary white milk bottle, luminous and refulgent in the yellow glare of the street-lamps.

She's shocked at the coldness of the air. It takes her breath away and stings her damp cheeks.

There is silence out here: absolute quiet. The air itself is still; not so much as a puff of wind. Gathering her dressing-gown tightly around her, she navigates the path. Her peripheral vision spasms into overdrive: to her left, an ominous scurrying in the hedge. The undergrowth's moving.

It's big, whatever it is. It could be her mother, half-dead, crawling on hands and knees towards the house.

She reaches gently into the hedgerow and flinches at the hiss. Her eyes pick out a patch of puffed-up black fur which slinks deeper into the undergrowth: it is one of the triumvirate of swarthy toms that haunt her property, three creatures betokening perpetual bad luck. She shivers as the rustling continues and calls quietly, just to be sure: 'Mother? Mother, are you there?'

Her enquiry is met with a hostile *meow*.

If only that cat was her mother. If only her mother were tucked up in bed.

The doubt is driving her to insanity. For a second, she even considers luring the sooty animal into the house for some company, and she despises cats: there's something about cats that makes her want to whip them. They are innately shifty – it's the yellow eyes and long, thin fangs; the way they lick a person's nose and take a savage nip when one least expects it; those wafer-thin translucent ears just begging to be snipped at with sharpened scissors. She finds it impossible to fathom how anybody can find these bloodthirsty creatures lovable – these decimators of the native songbird population – and she is quite sure that the only reason the pusillanimous Egyptians worshipped them was because they were afraid of them. Slinking mouse-munchers. And yet, she is so *thrown* that she would take one in, just to fend off the loneliness.

The rustling has stopped; whichever of the three lurks there, it is watching Mary at this very moment through bright eyes.

Trying to clear her thoughts of cats, she resists the urge to turn back and she proceeds out of the gate and onto the path. At the bottom of the hill, the boating lake shines onyx.

She approaches Valerie's front door and hears another noise. A thudding. A strange whine. She remains silent; the soft pad of feet. Something jumps up against the door and she narrowly escapes a severed tongue. A small clawing and growling. Valerie doesn't have a dog, but this is a dog. Has she somehow come to the wrong house? No, poppycock: this is it all right. What to do? – if she knocks, this dog will surely bark and awaken everybody. But she can't go back to her bedroom only to endure more ear-shattering noise. Suddenly, she hears the creak of Valerie's bedroom window opening overhead.

'Who's there?' asks a voice loaded with malice.

Mary presses her belly against the door, so that the porch shields her from Valerie's fierce gaze. The dog begins an onslaught of barking.

'I can hear your muttering. Who's there?'

She's shielded by the porch. She must not panic. They can't see her if she remains calm and still. Unless they come to the door. Lord help her.

'Come on, Val; there's no-one there,' says a deep male voice.

'I heard voices. The dog heard it,' comes Val's shriek.

'Well, if the dog heard it...! Don't be stupid, doll; you were probably dreaming, or something. Come back to bed. The mutt's got to get used to sleeping downstairs. He's not coming up here again. He pisses on the quilt.'

'If you won't go and look, I will.'

The window slams. Descending footsteps on stairs.

There's not time enough to get back to the house. With a burst of speed, Mary runs to the short privet hedge that lines the path and leaps over it, crouching so they can't see her. Thanks her lucky stars that her chartreuse dressing-gown will provide such good camouflage.

She can hear Valerie's voice, shrill in the soft night. The air lights up as the door swings open.

'Go on, Ty: find 'em. You sniff 'em out; we didn't pay six hundred quid for you for nothing. Out. Out you go. I said OUT.'

A bang. Scratching ensues as the dog attempts, ineffectually, to re-enter the warm house. A woof of reproof, but he at last submits to the finality of a closed door. Sniffing. Dog-steps. Slosh of streaming water from the urogenous critter and a slight twang of piss in the air. Loud snuffling; snout appears, followed by compact body. A small blob of dog. It's tiny: a boxer, by the looks of it, although not much of one. Reddish-brown with a white stripe down its face, its head not more than eight inches off the ground.

Mary scoffs to think that Val thought a snippet of a dog like this could maul a potential burglar. She reaches out and proffers her hand for it to sniff, and it licks her, a slow slimy lick smelling of tripe and onions. It chases its tail, which thankfully has not been docked.

It can't be much more than eight weeks old; it probably shouldn't even be out, but Val's thick as two short planks and lazy to boot: this dog will only ever take itself for walks. Yet it's surprisingly muscular for such a little dog; a small but thundering barrel.

A slight gust of wind sends him tumbling down the path after litter.

Mary meditates on the prospect of making a run for it, when the blasted door opens again and she is forced to duck. Through the lattice of privet she can see Val in a lacy negligée, holding a steaming mug in one hand and in the other, the red glow of a cigarette. Noisome smoke assaults Mary's nostrils.

'Come on, Ty. Get in here. They'll have gone now. Good dog – you showed them.' Without so much as a backwards glance, the little dog bounds up the path and through the doorway, struggling slightly with the doorstep. Opting for the safe side, Mary crouches in the foliage for a further twenty minutes until she's positive they're not lying in wait, spying from the window. When she's sure the danger has abated, she moves cautiously to the pavement and makes a run for her front door, which is worryingly wide open.

Why hadn't she thought to bring her key? What if a gust had slammed it shut with her still outside? The slam would have awakened people. People who would then want to know exactly what she was doing outside in her best green dressing-gown at four o'clock in the morning.

The consequences of her mistake could have been disastrous. Adrenalin courses through her veins but she shan't admit defeat. She'll write a note asking for the return of her mother. Talking to them is out of the question: there's no talking to such people. Val is a gobby fishwife and her husband is a nonpareil no-hoper. In a note, she can remain anonymous. Although there's the question of handwriting to consider…

Rummaging through the potato cupboard, she retrieves an old copy of *The Extra*. Using her mother's best sewing scissors, she snips a miscellany of vowels and consonants, and in the absence of glue she cellotapes them to some notepaper.

The note is simple, for brevity is the soul of wit. It says:

GIVE HER BACK

She slinks out into the cold night once more. She doesn't want to rouse the mutt by using the letterbox, so picks up the milk bottle sitting on her doorstep, pours the milk into the hedge, and tucks her note snugly inside. She leaves it sitting squarely in the centre of Val's garden path and enters her door for the second time this night, returning to the kitchen to clear up the newspaper carnage.

Above her, in her mother's room, she hears a noise. It sounds distinctly like her mother's bedroom door closing, the click of its lock, and then the footsteps of someone who doesn't want their footsteps heard. Slow and delicate. Almost imperceptibly, she hears – she's almost sure she hears – the creak of her mother's bed. But of course there is no-one there. It is a physical impossibility, with her mother gone. Unless her mother is dead, and her ghost is now inhabiting the front bedroom.

She cautiously ascends the stairs and listens at her mother's bedroom door. The bed creaks again and she hears a sound like a window opening.

Paralysed with fear, she stands shaking. She can't breathe.

When she opens the door, she will find her mother. Or she will find her mother's abductor.

She plunges down the handle.

Emptiness.

The room is dark and as vacant as ever. The old photographs hang undisturbed on the walls, her mother's tiny dresses are hung neatly in the wardrobe, and her embroidery sits unfinished on the nightstand.

But there is a smell. A smell like burning; a smell of burnt wood.

Applewood, or cherry. Something ashy; something strong. As

she turns to leave, she notices that the window is shut: a window she was sure she'd earlier left ajar to prevent fustiness.

She approaches it to open it a crack, and she sees in the distance the small figure of a man standing nonchalantly beneath a street-lamp. He has dressed for the cold in a black fur hat and matching full-length coat, and he reaches into his pocket and withdraws something that Mary has seen before, for even from this distance she recognises the shape.

He rests the object on the pavement and walks rapidly away.

Mary runs barefoot from the house and collects what he has left her.

She stops a few feet away from it, wracked with a chilling sense of foreboding.

She can see it quite clearly now.

It is another glass bird, akin to the one her mother mysteriously acquired the day before her disappearance.

But it is not a robin: it is a raven.

As soon as her hands touch this cold object, she feels her mother's presence, she smells her mother's talcum, she hears her mother trying to tell her something.

She holds the black ornament to her eyes and for a split second, she sees her mother's face reflected in ebony wings.

Sixteen

Someone has told someone else something of potentially great importance, and another soul has passed on this precious information to another nameless link in the chain, who has in turn spread it so far and so wide that it has winged its way to Mary's ears.

'How's your mum?' asks the postman as he stands on her doorstep, making it look untidy. 'Haven't seen her much, lately. I hope she's well?'

Mary inclines her head in assent. 'Yes, but she's hardly ever in the house.' She regrets having to tell these white lies, yet she is astute enough to understand the pernicious nature of the apocryphal rumours that abound in regard to her mental health.

'She's lucky to be so agile at her age,' he rumbles on. 'So many of these old people are kept cooped up like chickens all day long, wrapped in cotton wool, not allowed to do anything without asking permission. When we was young we respected our elders and betters. It's not the same nowadays. It's a disgrace.'

'I should say so,' Mary agrees politely.

'Some poor old lady has been spotted banging on a window in a house near Carkeel. Come to stay with her son, they say. Perhaps she's too weak to live on her own no more, and he probably don't want her in a nursing home. Comes out for half an hour every morning at first light, stares out the window, eyes like saucers and she bangs on the window, bangs like she's been locked up in a jail.

'Very frail they say she is: very frail. Lost her mind as well, most likely, but it's terrible to hear of an old dear being treated like that. I never did see the point of prolonging life if you can't prolong health. Freedom gone. Suffering, is what it is. I suppose the son won't have her going out because he's worried she'll do herself damage, fall over and break her hip or something, but it's no life that, no life at all.'

Mary's heart freezes as the postman reports this information, her thoughts flickering over various ghastly scenarios.

'Carkeel is over the water, in Cornwall, yes? Near Saltash, is it

120

not?' she asks sharply, shearing through the persiflage.

'That's right.'

'What part of Carkeel?'

'I don't know, exactly.'

'Please, think.'

'An old house, I think was mentioned. I might have got it wrong, but I think they said there was horses nearby.'

'Who told you this?'

He scratches his head protractedly, ruffling fine ashy hair.

'I dunno.'

'I must prevail upon you to try to remember. It's very important.'

'It's only a bit of gossip.'

'Please. You must have some idea who told you?'

'Sorry, love. I come across so many housewives during my day. I can't remember all of them. To be honest, they blur into one.'

Mary takes her letters into the house, closes her eyes, and sees her mother's face.

Does she have the abductor within her grasp? Is this trapped old person her own mother? Is Carkeel where she has ended up, just a stone's throw from where the beach girl was attacked with an iron bar? Is this where the collector of glass birds lives?

Her poor mother might be a prisoner shrouded in a straitjacket by day, and released for one half-hour at dawn to gaze through the window.

It could be just one man working alone, or she could be some kind of sexual slave, prostituted to the insane: perverts who dream of elderly genitals and incontinence pads awash with piss.

She knows that there are such people out there; one only has to read the newspaper to find accounts of molestors who prey solely upon the elderly. She remembers that one such criminal has been operating in the Home Counties for over a decade now, without detection – for who would make it their business to investigate the claims of aged ladies whose nether regions had received so little attention in the preceding years as to have quite grown over?

Sympathy is not lavished upon aged rape victims. No, sympathy is the sole preserve of the perpetrator, who needed help, surely: psychological evaluation and ongoing medication to deal with his errant sexuality and evident disregard of common decency.

If such a rapist can exist in the Home Counties, then why not in Plymouth, home of nefarious seamen? Plymouth, that port in a storm open to all; yobs, murderers and rapists traditionally welcome, as long as they drink hard and tip harder.

There is only one course of action to be taken: she must go to Carkeel. And watch, and wait, and see what the breeze blows in. If it is nothing, it doesn't matter; at least she will have looked, and her mother is worth more than a day in the cold; her mother's retrieval must come before everything.

Once upon a time, Mary had no purpose, but now that has changed: she has a quest. And if she fails, all is lost and she'll never be able to recover from such losing.

Many years ago, she vowed to kill herself if she wasn't married by the time she was twenty-five – for what purpose did she have if no man wanted her? She has oftentimes regretted the fact that she was too cowardly to kick away the chair – but now she is glad. Because it doesn't matter what kind of sociopath has taken her mother: she is strong enough to track him down and fight him.

And she is strong enough to win.

Seventeen

Mary sits, cowed, on a Carkeel hill, beneath the fierce heavenly dawn that goldens vast swathes of watercolour sky. Her face is turned toward a pink house where a face like her mother's has been seen.

As yet, there has been no movement, but Mary is in it for the long haul. She will be patient.

Minutes tick by and still there is no sign.

Perhaps her mother has been moved elsewhere, in the time it took for news of her entrapment to whisper its way to her door.

She turns away from the window and looks down to the Tamar below: the sweep of the valley, curve of the river – blue as the sea, bluer – and down to Ernesettle Creek, where a bridge constructed from slender arches genuflects its way across the flood.

A white sailboat glides nearer, and she wonders if her mother knows she's looking.

She hopes she does know; she hopes her mother feels it in her soul.

The lure of the empty window is great but Mary will not keep staring, because a watched kettle never boils and a watched window never yields mothers. So she keeps her eyes on the view. Fields of green, yellow and orange, bright in Mary's eyes. Ancient slate walls stacked by long-dead farmhands. A blasted copse atop a shagreen hill, where perchance another soul sits, like she. Someone who could understand the despair of the interminable wait.

Where are the animals? – she distracts herself. Where are they all on this bright morning?

Ah, they are gathered under trees, standing shoulder-to-shoulder, like Antarctic penguins sharing out the cold. Sheep, cows, goats, the beast of Bodmin, perhaps – they say that puma likes to day-trip.

For a minute, she forgets that this is a city; it seems too beautiful to be such. The moors smoke blue in the distance: Sheep's Tor, Little Mis and Great Mis Tor; Princetown and Brentor, echoes of a long-gone age, relics of pools of molten magma that surged up from the planet's crust and solidified under the surface; future land forming deep beneath the earth while those up top were ignorant.

Those were the days when the land was so much higher, when there was a volcano at Torquay, when dinosaurs roamed the lands.

Yet underneath all the chaos, all the mess, the future was forming. It was only when the softer rocks eroded away that the tors came into being: dense masses that wouldn't be worn down. They'd been there all the time, lingering beneath the earth where nobody could see them; but eventually, when enough time passed, they came into their own.

Mary understands that Dartmoor is wild in a way that people don't like to accept: they build their roads and their cafés and their visitor centres and they demand an ice-cream man in every lay-by – but the moor is wild; it can change as quick as a flash, and the tourists, with their tans and Raybans, find themselves shivering in mists that come in a rolling wave from the sea.

That's the thing about the moor: just like a sociopath, there's no predicting its moods. A bystander doesn't even see it coming, and then it's on them, and suddenly it's too late.

The worst thing about Dartmoor, in Mary's opinion, is its lizards. Picking them up to look them in the eye is no good; they don't avert their gaze like cats. They stare back and they are capricious critters: they shed their tail and then slither off to grow a new one.

As far as defence mechanisms go, it's effective – she concedes that much – for ravens may peck to their heart's content at flicking tails, when the former owner is long gone.

Mary curses as she realises that her mind has worked its way back to ravens, and to the glass ornament that her tormentor left behind.

He wants to confuse her, to enrage her, to play cat-and-mouse. She knows all of this; but he will not win. He will not win.

The hedgerow in front of her is alive with birds and moths and rodents, and an elegant tabby cat emerges with a wriggling grass snake in her jaws. The snake's mouth is open and its tongue tastes the wind.

Mary can bear it no more; she turns to look at the house, but there is no figure in the window. She screams, a moment of luxuriant release, a scream loud enough to wake the dead. Tears cut tracks into her cheeks and she lets them wash her mind away.

She inhales deeply. The sun is on her hair and neck, but her hands are cold. She rocks herself, disturbing pooling blood, and she blows stale breath into her fingers. There's a scent of sap and decay in the air, signalling fields and woody detritus. A brisk wind has crossed the line from cool to uncomfortable and she knows it's time to move.

She reaches up to a stunted tree and plucks some unripe apples. Her fitted silk blouse doesn't make an adequate apple apron, so she unbuttons it and slips it off.

Lord, the blazing whiteness of her arms. Her blouse is usefully employed as an impromptu handbag, and soon she has a baker's dozen of compact fruitlets.

The paddock holds three patchwork horses standing together. She holds out a small bitter offering and the largest of the three – a skewbald colt – approaches, eyeing her suspiciously.

It stops short of the white knicker-elastic fence.

Palm flat, fingers outstretched.

He takes the apple gently; snorts and chews, spraying her hand with cider and saliva. She offers another, which he takes eagerly, and another, until she is dazed by the feeding ceremony. She's wary of horses: it's not so much the bacteria they're embalmed in – Mary's hands have a habit of washing themselves – it's the worry that she'll hurt them.

Like the time she encouraged herself to feed a black stallion a Jammy Dodger, thinking that the muscular beast looked hungry. And in the absence of carrots or apples she prompted herself to offer a biscuit, which the moronic horse took.

Coughing ensued, foaming of the mouth, and wild bucking. She scarpered, sure she'd killed it, but jammy dodger indeed, it survived. And when she hesitantly returned weeks later, the stallion had an impressive array of stitches adorning his handsome throat.

Suddenly there are three horses, not two, and Mary feels very short. Two of these towering creatures vie for prime position, shouldering and nipping each other. Necks extend further into Mary's territory and she steps backwards. A sneaky bite gives way to savagery. Chasing, kicking and butting.

The remaining beast, a small bay mare, takes a tentative step forward. Mary offers a mottled apple which, to her frustration, the mare takes but doesn't swallow, and loses it in the grass.

Mary berates herself: she's out of apples and it's not fair that this docile beast should miss out. She plucks another apple from the tree and bites this one into three manageable pieces. The mare accepts the first two fragments without mishap, but on moving forward for the final third, her chest brushes the fence and she's repelled backwards violently, unleashed like a coiled spring.

Mary's heart is in her mouth.

Recriminating stares excoriate her heart, and she realises that the knicker-elastic fence is an electric fence, put there to keep quadrupeds out of flowerbeds. Further investigations reveal that it is powered by two car batteries, which are swiftly disengaged.

After a guilty frenzy of picking, she pelts the field with apples for the beasts to feast upon. One bounces off the grey and white muzzle of the Appaloosa and there is a startled shake of the head.

A curtain opens in the pink dwelling, and then a window.

A middle-aged head that is streaked with peroxide thrusts through.

'Oy,' it bellows. 'Leave them horses alone.'

'Who are you?' Mary asks sharply, squinting through the morning sunshine at the odd-looking man, whose face is obscured with thick glasses.

'I'm the owner of that field, for starters, and I said leave them alone.'

'I'm feeding them,' Mary informs him. There is no need for this man to be taking such great umbrage at her actions: it is a distinct overreaction.

'You're trespassing. That field's private property.'

'Oh, shut up,' Mary responds, bored by the man's proprietary stance.

'You shut up, and get yourself some clothes, you bloody weirdo,' he counters.

'I've got plenty of clothes, thank you. What I don't have is a bag. So I'm using my blouse as one.'

'Ugghh, don't do that. Cover yourself up, for chrissakes.'

'Not until you let me see your mother.'

'My mother's been dead twenty years.'

'An elderly woman has been seen in your property, banging on a window.'

'That was my aunt. She's in the hospital now, she had a stroke. Hospital's the best place for her.'

'I don't believe you.'

'I don't give a shit what you believe; you can believe I'm an orang-utan if you like.'

'An orang-utan would have nicer hair,' says Mary, sneeringly.

'Swivel,' he says, raising a finger.

'You seem very keen to be rid of me. Very suspicious, I find that; very suspicious.' Mary scratches her nose and lets her breasts oscillate freely.

'Who the hell would want you hanging around their property?' he asks, covering his eyes in disgust.

'Tell me this: do you have a collection of glass birds?'

'What's that, a bloody riddle? A secret password? This is not James Bond,' he says vehemently between his fingers.

'Answer me. But be warned: I can spot a liar a mile off.'

'You are really starting to grit my shit.'

'Answer.'

'No, I do not have any glass birdies. Now sod off.'

She throws the remaining apples into the field and puts on her blouse, carefully brushing traces of apple leaf from the fabric.

'Go away, I said,' he reiterates, exasperated.

'You go away.'

'I'll call the police on you, if you're not gone in two seconds.'

'Good, and I'll tell them you're harassing an innocent woman.'

'What? You're starkers in my field, lobbing stones at my horses!'

'Apples.'

'Pardon me?' he asks with mocking politeness.

'Lobbing apples at your horses.'

'You just admitted it!' he says, celebratory, as if he has won a game of chess with Kasparov.

'I was feeding them, as I said.'

'They've got plenty of food, all right. Now piss off, missus.'

'I'll piss on you.'

'What did you say to me?'

'I said I'll piss on you.'

Mary leaves Carkeel and walks through the woods until she comes to the river. Somewhere she can think; somewhere she can breathe.

Her eyes rejoice at the sight of a moss-drenched weir, aglint with diamond water. A man with such simian manners could surely not be an abductor; he didn't have the intelligence for it, and her mother would never have accompanied such an uncouth person. No, whomever has taken her mother is charming, flattering, unctuous. Someone wheedling and sly; someone who could make her mother take leave of her senses.

In the shallows, she paddles ankle-deep upon slimy slates and she holds her arms outstretched to find her balance. A narrow underwater path is raised three feet above the riverbed and leads to the salmon leap. It's covered in rotting leaves – one slip and she'll be up to her eyes in green – but she'll not be deterred by mere danger. She walks carefully, arms above her head like a ballerina, and meets no misadventure until the path ceases midway.

She ponders the edge, turns tail and takes this slippery tightrope back to land, where she sits on a grassy bank and dangles her feet in the water.

Gold shimmers in the shallows and catches her greedy eye.

She tucks her skirt into her waistband and slips in, roiling the river, stirring up sediment as she plunges her hand into the water. When she finds her ingot and holds it to the sun, this pyrite is just a brassy rock. FeS_2: an iron ore, and nothing more.

She throws it backs into the water and wades deeper, thinking of that infamous grey-muzzled Cocker who went into this very stretch of river to retrieve a stick, and turned about. No yelps, no growls, just a flinch. A pool of red amassed; vibrant drops trailed at his rear. A pike swam away with his paw.

Her legs are numbing and in this deeper water there's something else to catch her eye.

A fish. Unmoving, except where it undulates in the waves from her thighs. It's silvery pink: a salmon, a dead salmon.

Not killed, no brains hanging out. Both eyes intact.

She would like to go under, pierce the liquid film, scoop it out and hold it aloft in the sun, but she's repulsed by its death.

An egg at the source of the river is where it all began. On hatching, the parr stayed put for years and one day it morphed into a smolt, which somehow knew it was time. The journey began. It swam downstream, avoiding the nets and hooks of the hinterland until it ran out of river. A v-sign tail-flicked to the estuary and it headed across the Atlantic to feed near Greenland, where it stayed for a year or two before turning tail and coming home as a grilse. It found the river of its birth: the exact river; and leapt upstream through rapids to the spot where it was spawned. It procreated.

There's no happy family, though. Proud parents do not shelter their offspring; these eggs will be orphans and latch-key fish.

Once the oldies entered the home river to spawn, they stopped eating, and now they're weak. Only a minute fraction survive procreation, and these leave the dead to begin again.

Mary's no vegetarian, but she lost her relish for slivers of salmon on rice cakes a long time ago. It would be like eating Ellen McArthur. Let them find their homeland; let them spawn, and die, in peace.

Eat trout, she thinks; or better still: eat pike.

Just as she is turning away something else catches her eye: something smaller, something familiar, something silver.

Mary swoops down and retrieves the misshaped thimble, and she knows by the scratches, by the bends that have accrued over eighty-years of wear, and finally by the engraved *M Z*, that it is her mother's.

Her abductor has thrown it in the river and something has brought it to Mary.

It is her mother. Her mother is showing her; her mother is telling her not to give up.

Eighteen

There's been time to think, and rethink, and she's found that nothing is the same. With her mother gone and unaccounted for, everything is in question. Everything.

When Mary looks up into the night sky, she considers the object that might be the moon. People say there is a moon, but she does not know it for sure, and if she doesn't know it for sure, why does she believe it?

Because science says so, or because she can see it? Well, science is renowned for being wrong, and so too are eyes. Never believe teachers or eyes, is Mary's mantra – they are simply there to make a person accept their version of reality.

Hence, just because the moon looks as if it's there, it doesn't mean that it is. Because seeing is only believing – seeing is not knowledge.

Has Mary been to the moon?

No.

Has anyone?

Doubtful. She doesn't believe any of this hippy moon-walking guff for a second. All of those shadow irregularities in the photos; the fact that the clever dicks don't think they can get back there for another twenty years. It's too fishy for Mary to swallow, and even if she did personally go to the moon, there is nothing to say that it wouldn't disappear or transform into something else, the second she departed.

Her mother's disappearance is the most recent in a long line of incidents that make no sense. Sometimes the Lord talks through the television and the wireless. Mary can hear Him quite distinctly, articulating truisms behind the programmes. People with her sort of intuition can open their minds and listen. Really listen – and there He is. He is aware that if He transmits through the television then He will attract attention. When His voice becomes too interfering, the swift appliance of tinfoil around the television screen and wireless provides an adequate method of drowning Him out. After all, Mary reasons, when one turns the television off, one expects it to stop talking. Human beings have to sleep, even if the Lord does not.

An experimental knife-delving has slit her eye.

Her hand mirror reports her whites to be a parchment of bloody runes. Capillaries bursting left, right and centre. The consultation of medical volumes yields nothing, and the only treatment to be had awaits at the doctor's surgery.

Damn and blast, she berates herself; she should have known better than to insert a sliver of kitchen knife to gauge its suitability.

She ventures outside and the sky is silver-grey sky – a thick film of cloud veiling sunlight. She plods onward, trekking across the muddy playing field. There is a treacherous moment shy of the cricket pitch and her flip-flop is lost in the quagmire. She retrieves it and wipes it in her skirt.

She arrives at a whitewashed school building streaked with the red of roof tile. She looks through the window; the backs of small heads confront her, as does her own face, grotesquely reflected, frighteningly near.

On she goes, until she smells the surgery. She enters to the sound of flip-flop slapping on the floor, and she is accosted by the stench of TCP and the elderly. A harassed matronly receptionist grunts a greeting.

Mary waits for her name to be called. There is a cacophony of coughs and a symphony of sniffles, as an angry Hun student in a university sweatshirt attempts to register, to no avail.

Murmurs and gurgles as mothers and babies converse.

A quondam teetotaller – perfectly inebriated – recites poetry in the corner.

A spotty youth scratches below the belt, paying for sexual peccadilloes.

Finally there is a buzz, and a light illuminates the name of her venerable physician.

'Miss Sibly!' An ear-shattering hiss from the north.

'Announce my marital status to the entire waiting room, why don't you?'

A maze of corridors. Unpronounceable foreign names are printed on squares of card and pinned to doors. Mary sidesteps a black rubber bat hanging outside the nurse's station, and locates her GP's room. She opens the door without knocking, clutches the cold knob in her palm, and surveys the back of her humourless doctor. Sepia print curtains ripple in the breeze.

There is a brisk eye examination; some talk of trauma and infection.

Excoriating drops stain her whites yellow, and she is ordered to cry as little as possible.

A searchlight aimed at her shrivelled pupil causes the doctor to lament that the stain has settled in a trauma. A deep scratch in the eye-tissue has been invaded by bacteria.

Her examiner tittles at the spookiness of orange eyes, but assures her that the saffron dye will disperse in the fullness of time.

Mary fights the temptation to slap him.

Penetrating questions regarding her mental heath go unanswered. She parries these clinical questions with the rationale that none of the answers constitute his business and she explains, for good measure, that she will agree to smears, breast examinations and fancy medicines … never. The doctor circles a contentious abyss and Mary counters with vehement negatives. He offers a line about chemical imbalances in the brain and her roman candle of execrations rain down around them until finally he is rebuffed and she is offered a prescription for antibiotic eye-drops and nothing more.

'How did you scratch your eye so deeply?' he asks.

'I was seeing if my knife was sharp enough,' she replies with a hint of impatience. This is all she needs: more interfering busybodies thrusting themselves into her life, demanding answers and explanations.

'And you're adamant that you're well?' he asks, stroking his Adam's apple.

'I am fine, thank you. I have a quest, a mission. I must not allow tablets to dim my mental lights. I have human rights; you cannot force me to swallow your offerings.'

'Very well,' he sighs. 'But if you feel any worse, you must come to me immediately. Just for now, we'll see how things go.'

As she departs, he casually asks, 'How is your mother?'

'Same as ever,' Mary replies carefully, cautious of arousing suspicion.

'Her legs, are they still swollen?'

'No, I don't think so.'

'Good.'

There is a beat.

'Tell her she can come and see me whenever she wants to.'

'I'll tell her, when I see her.'

'Mary, are you sure everything is normal?'

'Strike a light! I'm fine; I just had an accident.'

As she leaves, the words of the Scots nurse come back to her: schizophrenics are affected by the moon.

There was indeed a full moon on the night preceding her mother's disappearance, and so, Mary surmises, if the moon had not been full, maybe her mother would still be safely in her armchair, nodding as the heat from the twin-bar electric fire infused its way up veined legs.

If someone has taken her mother, they might be schizophrenic: someone liable to flip in the light of that white face; someone liable to murder in the tug of that vast monolith.

She is unravelling more by the day.

Nonetheless, she feels she would know her quarry if she passed him in the street. Like the bride who found her ring on the beach, it is meant; and it is merely a matter of right place, right time.

Nineteen

The sun is not shining when she peers out today. Purple clouds in the east overshadow the land, but she doesn't take it as an omen because she's exhilarated: she has worked her fingers to the bone this night, she worked at it all through the dark hours and when she achieved the climax, the completion, she was flabbergasted at the rush.

Such glorious exertion! The buzz, the sense of worth, the high that she has had on her own in the dead of night is unknowable to all but the initiated. She cannot let herself care what the neighbours think – although she's sure they must have heard – but she doesn't give a hoot.

It needed to be done, it needed attending to: ecstasy does not come in a tablet.

She started in the kitchen. She filled deep buckets to wash the kitchen floor, which must have a preliminary mopping, a deep cleansing, a drying with her mother's hairdryer, and a final buffing to polish the tiles to burnished black.

She moved into the front room, removed all of the cushions from the settee, and hoovered beneath. She took a pan and brush and half beat, half swept the upholstery, which removed such a quantity of dust and dirt that she still feels quite wheezy.

She stripped the settee covers and proceeded to the kitchen where she scrubbed them by hand, one after another, until the scalding water and detergent made the skin on her fingers crack.

Now, at last, the house is ready for her mother's return. Everything is ship-shape and Bristol Fashion. All that remains is to track down the errant man, kill him and retrieve her mother.

It must be a man that has taken her mother. It must be, because as Mary imagines it, women just aren't interested in dealing out abduction or mutilation or suffering. Because they have traditionally been the victims of such acts. Because in England and Wales there are seventy-five thousand prisoners and hardly any of them are female. Because women know better, as exemplified by the fact that, although women account for six percent of prisoners, they account for twenty percent of cell suicides.

Women feel; women empathise. The turning off of sympathy is a peculiar male attribute; it is a sex-linked trait; it comes with testicles and anal furring.

Men are interested in fulfilling their desires; they use blandishment, they cajole and wheedle, and they play on women's sympathies. Like Ted Bundy: so charming, so needy as he dropped his glasses on the floor accidentally-on-purpose and requisitioned eager women to find them. He would walk with a cane and feign the seductive odour of helplessness, and women would gallop to his rescue.

She knows it is a man who has her mother. And since it is a man, it is probably the man who crippled the girl in the waves at Bovisand. Because Plymouth could not harbour two such sociopaths at any one time. It is only a small pond, and consequently there are only fish enough for one rod.

Furthermore, she is convinced that this man is a serial killer. It was not long ago that ITN reported a case in which a policeman broke into an abandoned house in Somerset to find a veritable nursing home's worth of female pensioners, strapped and gagged and frightened witless. The Force remained undercover, waiting for the perpetrator to return. But, alas, the devil incarnate caught the whiff of pork on the air and skedaddled.

Mary thinks that perhaps *skedaddled* is too flippant a term for a man that systematically abused thirteen grandmothers on a rotational basis, day and night, for nigh on a year; but she is damned if she can find a better verb. *Scurried* is a possibility, she acknowledges; most people would sanction the allusion to vermin. Rats scurry, mice scurry, even children are said to scurry.

This person who has her mother is a professional, an apex predator. He knows all the tricks; he knows when to lure, and when to grab and smash.

Her mother would be like a kitten to such a person. She wouldn't have known the basics; she wouldn't have known that, should she be locked into a car boot, she should kick out the rear brake lights and use the holes to alert the attention of passing motorists. Of course she wouldn't. And even if she did know, she probably wouldn't be strong enough to do so, with only seven stone of weight propelling her bound feet.

There are men with a desire for small-handed girls, or for women who rub themselves with olive oil. Some men like them young. Mary remembers reading about a study in which a couple of researchers attached a group of Czech soldiers to 'penile responsivity' meters: devices capable of detecting sexual excitement. They showed them a variety of photographs. Women and men, girls and boys, all of varying ages and in varying states of undress. A large number of these soldiers experienced a sexual response to the innocuous photographs of the female under-tens: pictures of small girls playing with dolls, smiling on their bicycles, that sort of thing. Some soldiers had far stronger sexual reactions to the photographs of little girls than to the raunchy images of beautiful women.

It occurs to Mary that the doctors who spend so much time discussing the so-called 'threat' that she might pose would be better employed in castrating the male *homo-sapiens*.

In the Czech tests, twenty-eight out of forty-eight soldiers showed a penile response to girls aged between four and ten.

She has also heard about a study in which two psychologists discovered that in a sample of nearly two hundred university men, twenty-one percent described sexual fantasies involving children. Five percent admitted to having masturbated to sexual fantasies of children. Seven percent indicated they might have sex with a child if not caught. The psychologists remarked that, given the probable undesirability of such admissions, it could be hypothesized that the actual rates were higher.

So, thinks Mary, if some men like them young, then perhaps some men like them old. Although, of course, psychologists wouldn't think to test for an affinity for the elderly. The elderly are unworthy of research, because they are grotesque and unappealing.

Yet are they? – wonders Mary. For isn't it true that old women get raped all the time? Isn't it constantly on the news? A teenager breaks into a house in London, and thinks – as he's rifling through the ancestral jewellery box – that perhaps there is another box, of sorts, worth rifling through. The house is quiet, the old lady is tied ... why not stay for a screw? A faint notch on the bedpost and even if it's crap, even if a warm haddock would have given more in the way of satisfaction, how many of his mates can say they've done a nonagenarian? Except he won't use the word nonagenarian, because he won't know that ninety-somethings have a term denoting their age in the same way that teenagers do. He won't know, because he doesn't think they deserve labels. Because they are all old and past it, and because this applies to anyone over forty.

It is a sad world, thinks Mary. It is sad world indeed when the youth of today are simultaneously the rapists and murderers of today.

In her day, she's sure it was different: rapists were desperate men in their thirties who hadn't had sexual relations in a long time – maybe years; maybe never. But now, rapists could be fourteen-year-old paper-boys or 58-year-old doctors with degrees from Cambridge. It makes things so much more complicated. It is no longer enough to fear the characters, the eccentrics and the oddbods; now she has to fear everybody of the male gender equally, because the ones she doesn't fear – the ones she suspects of being merely boring – are the ones who have the secret stash of anile pornography and who fantasise over the red image of old ladies penetrated with kitchen knives, of blood oozing from bright slits in bloated legs.

There was a case she read about in America, in which a deranged man entered a college dormitory and killed every woman with dark hair that was parted in the middle, and it occurred to her just how much of murder is fetish. And as in all fetishes, there are rules. It is an exclusive club and some are welcome, some are overlooked. Blondes and side-partings were not part of that particular nutter's fantasy, and he left them to life.

But every girl that fit his description was throttled.

When the blondes woke up, perhaps they cried and prayed to their peroxide bottles as if they were magic shields, masking them from the gimlet eyes of murderers.

And if, Mary surmises, a man can murder on the basis of hair colour and style and nothing more, what is to say he can't murder on the basis of creed? Nationality? Number of years lived? What could be more satisfying than the idea of killing the aged – murdering people who have faced all that life could throw at them and yet survived? The ones who lived, the ones who made it to dotage without being killed, who managed to repel the sweet seduction of suicide; these outwardly frail beings are the tough ones, the survivors. These could yield the maximum pleasure. It worked for Harold Shipman; he killed hundreds of them. Maybe her mother's abductor was of the same ilk.

And then Mary's thoughts turn to people-smuggling: to the white slave trade; to exotic lawless countries where people are taken against their will and lost forever.

Thoughts of her mother, trapped in a harem in some dusty corner of Mauritania, haunt her.

Hundreds of thousands of women live in slavery as sexual playthings for the wealthy and disturbed. And what if her mother is one of them? What then? What can be done in countries where even mentioning the word slavery is illegal? Where talking to journalists is tantamount to committing a crime? What then?

Perhaps it is her mother's thinness which delights the head honcho. Her smallness, her four-foot-nothingness in a world full of six-foot amazons. Or perhaps it is the translucent skin that gathers, age-spotted and parched, at the wrists?

Perhaps it is none of these things; not even a grandmother fetish. Perhaps it is something else entirely, something that can't be imagined by anyone other than the man who abducted her.

Mary is trying not to panic.

She is wading her way through despair and looking for a bank of rationale.

Her mother might have gone away. She might be on a holiday; she might have a secret lover; she might have checked herself into a nursing home – all these things are possible; they should not be overlooked. There is nothing to say she is dead. There is no evidence, no suggestion; only the absence of contact, only the lack of fiscal means, only the fact that absence is so out of character.

Mary's mother told her the story several years ago of a region in Armenia called Karabagh. From what Mary could gather from her mother's inarticulate mumblings, Karabagh is a green and rolling land, like wrinkled baize. The skies are a pale blue and the sun hangs low over mountains – but this sun is a different sun; it's blanched of its yellow so that it's almost silver.

So perhaps her lost mother is ensconced in the Elysian plains of Karabagh, land of the undying, because beneath this foreign sun there's a village, the quondam home of Mary's grandmother and her mother before her where, Meghranoush maintained, everybody lives forever.

Well – far beyond their three-score and ten.

There's a church that can be visited, with gravestones in the dozens, showing people who lived until they were a hundred and twenty years old. Even more extreme, there are marital gravestones where only the husband has two dates – a birth date and a death date – and apparently to this very day there's one such stone where the wife (a teacher, by all accounts) has a birth date of 1880 and no death date, as yet.

Her mother said that this superannuated pedagogue still lived in a remote Karabagh village, and when Mary heard of this woman who lived out there somewhere, still – fettering her elderly children, demanding succour, sucking on the life force – she was sickened.

It was to do with the sour yoghurt they ate, her mother thought; or perhaps it was something else. Perhaps it was the original site of Eden, and that explained the longevity. Whatever: Mary found it horrifying. But now things have changed.

If her mother has gone to Karabagh to be enfranchised, to be with long-lost family, then there is hope. And anyway, Karabagh should be the site of her mother's twilight years, not Plymouth, which is just a pale imitation of a city. Not Plymouth, where even the children plan incapacity as a career.

But how could her mother make a journey of two thousand miles, unaided and unfunded? – and if she was planning such a trip, wouldn't Mary have caught wind of it?

Her mother has always wanted a cat, but Mary forbade it, on the grounds that she abhors them. Her mother might have gone somewhere with a cat. Her mother might now spend hour after hour sitting in a warm conservatory, surrounded by potted orchids, with a pomegranate and a cat on her lap.

Cats. Could cats be the reason for the defection?

Cats: squinty-eyed and scratchy even when happy. Mary knows that a pregnant female cat – if left undisturbed and in decent surroundings – could in seven short years beget enough kittens to overrun Devon. She and her progeny would have produced four hundred thousand new cats.

Cats are a virus that plague the British Isles, thinks Mary. They are convinced they are gods and that humans are stupid, fat and lazy, and should the ready supply of Whiskas dry up they would, without a second's hesitation, tear strips from the face of a stricken owner. Because cats, like humans, are predators; smaller, softer and furrier, but predators all the same – and what's more, predators with slashing claws.

Predation is a factor that can not be overcome by any amount of domesticity, because a cat, by any other name – Gypsy, Misty, Sooty – is still a cat; and though it might eat cat meat and cat treats, it will always find warm blood just as sweet.

Yes, maybe her mother would leave her for a cat, and perhaps the cat is only an emblem of a greater problem.

Who has been overbearing? Has Mary really been dominated, or is that the wrong way around? Has she silently controlled every nuance of her mother's life, to the point where her mother has screamed and bolted?

Because whilst her mother was verbally dominant – caustically and constantly so – isn't it almost always the submissive who holds the real power? Has she, for all these years, been misreading the situation?

It is unbearable.

Can it be?

The light that such an idea would cast over her past is too torturous to bear further inquiry. She is locked – *locked* in a situation that will yield no answers. Unless she finds the truth, her already dislocated mind will fracture.

She is so desperate for these answers that she grabs rumour and transmutes it into illusion and thereon into fact.

She is going mad, she suspects; but her madness is born of grief, it is not born of paranoia.

It is not all in her mind; it cannot be in her mind. People don't just disappear.

Has she been abducted by aliens? Has she spontaneously combusted somewhere?

Who are the suspects, apart from herself?

Perhaps she has just died somewhere and has not been found yet.

Mary is constricted by fear. Panic grips her. Her heart throbs in her mouth as she looks ceaselessly for that familiar face, but she cannot see it. She paces from lounge to kitchen, to hall, to bedroom, to lounge again and on. The smell of her mother is here: talcum powder, and wash-in/wash-out dyes, and olives – but she is gone and there is no knowing where she is or if Mary is capable of finding her.

If her mother is simply lost, she might have had a stroke. Whatever has happened, it can't be good for her mum's heart to have such stress thrust upon it. Especially now she's had her pacemaker taken out, Mary thinks, guilt tight around her jugular.

The old lady was blissfully ignorant of the fact that her pacemaker was powered by plutonium-238.

'Oh yes,' Mary explained. 'That fancy pacemaker you picked up whilst jaunting around America with your precious Armenian relatives is powered by a radioactive power source, which means you have a toxic heart.'

'What you say?'

'Nuclear-powered.'

'Not nuclear, is battery!'

'No, it's plutonium-238. The heat from the radioactive decay is what keeps your ticker tocking. You should consider yourself lucky: they only made a few hundred, and they cost two hundred thousand dollars a pop. Good job you had insurance.'

'Plutonium?'

'Plutonium – the stuff in your heart – is what blew up Nagasaki and killed hundreds of thousands of innocent people.'

'No ... why they put bomb in heart?'

'It's not a bomb. The radioactive decay gives heat to power the pacemaker. All this is in your paperwork. You should have read it; it's no good moaning now.'

'Why not put battery?'

'Plutonium is better than any battery. Plutonium has a half-life of just over eighty-seven years, which means it can keep providing power until the end of someone's life without ever having to be replaced.'

Her mother paled, her lips tightening and whitening with horror.

'But it make me poison? Make me go bang?'

'No, I'm sure it'll be fine. Except, if someone shot you in the heart then the plutonium might start mixing with your blood. Although, if you were shot in the heart, you'd probably be a goner, anyway.

'And of course, there will be a slight problem when we come to cremate you. Since plutonium has a relatively low melting-point, the crematorium will suddenly become a bit, well, radioactive.'

'What?'

'Oh, I'm sure I'll remember to mention it to the crematorium staff.'

After this, her mother swore the pacemaker hurt her chest. She kept going on for months, complaining of the pain. Mary tried to get her to retain it, but she was adamant she didn't want it.

She had it removed on the advice of an unscrupulous doctor. Posh, he seemed; he had a patrician swagger and a moustache, an air of aristocracy about him.

In hindsight Mary concedes he was indeed a scam artist of the highest calibre.

Mary was with her mother when that slimy elver spun her his line. They sat in his plush office and he set to work:

'Mrs Sibly, I've looked at the paperwork and you can be totally reassured that in my extensive medical expertise, you really don't need this pacemaker. It's thousands of pounds of useless wires for you. Your holiday insurance paid for it, you say? When you fell ill in America? Oh, Hollywood, how lovely. Do you know my wife has an Armenian father? My poor wife is terribly ill, Mrs Sibly. With heart irregularities. Would you consider donating your pacemaker to my wife?'

'I no need stupid pacemaker, I no even ill. Give your wife: make her better. I old lady. What I need all wires sticking in my chest, hurting me for?'

'Marvellous! That's fantastic! We can operate immediately! How about Wednesday?'

It was a performance of great élan and sophistication, Mary must allow that much, and they swallowed each hook, each line and each sinker. Her mother signed over the toxic hardware protecting her heart and she wouldn't let Mary breathe a word of it to anyone. Recalcitrant as ever, she went through with it all on her own.

There were certain complications during the removal procedure, and then an infection took hold of the wound, and she was in hospital for some weeks.

Their own general practitioner, who had been absent, holidaying somewhere mountainous and pure of air, was furious with Mary for allowing her mother to take such drastic action, but her mother wouldn't be gainsaid and once it was done it was too late to change.

The GP made belated enquiries, but by the time her mum told him the venal doctor's name, the grifter had set up a new practice on the continent.

A policeman investigated, announcing that the illustrious force 'just followed the money trail, because there's always a money trail,' and it transpired that her mother's pacemaker was not given to the doctor's wife. It was sold for $125,000 on the black market to a Belarusian.

The doctor's wife was not Armenian; the doctor's wife was twenty-five.

Mary grimaces as she remembers this painful story and she is more adamant than ever that, after all she has done to her mother, after all the pain she has put her through, she will not give up on her now.

The house is ready for her mother; she must bring her home.

Twenty

He can hear the old lady crying down there: soft stifled sobs, and he goes down to check on her.

He unlocks the armoire and she is there, slumped against the back of the old wardrobe, a glass of water and some olives untouched at her feet; her once-sanguine complexion is pale and wan and she looks up at him with pleading eyes.

She doesn't talk to him. Her mouth is dry and ashy; her lips are cracked and sore.

'Why are you crying, Meghranoush?' he asks her gently.

She shudders and he can see she is cold, she is shivering and so he brings her a thick red tartan blanket that is so large that it encircles her twice.

It is wrong to keep her here like this, he thinks. He has grown nonchalant, improvident; this is the longest he's ever kept one of his victims after snatching them.

He picks her up and takes her gently upstairs and places her at the window so she can get some light on her face, and so that she can watch the horses.

He leaves her there and returns to his sitting room where he thinks about his own mother, who is alive, despite his fervent fantasizing that she is dead. He is eight. The bitter taste of early morning plants forces itself past his teeth and into his locked lungs; he looks down and sees them, fluorescent, hung with wet jewels.

He wanders away from the hum of his mother's voice. She is talking to a strange man she has just met on the cycle path that used to be an old railway line for the slate quarry. Before he knows what he's done, he's cycling fast down the gravel path and the trees close in on either side.

A feeling of freedom and solitude buffets him; he absorbs it into his skin and he feels it tingle as it creeps among his tissues. He wishes he was a wild animal in these woods: maybe a bear running fast to find some honey. (He later finds out that bears eat pets and sometimes people.) He picks up speed and strands of coarse ginger hair whip past his ears and then back again to scratch his eyes. Turreted pedals dig into the flesh of his sunburned feet and leather

144

strains against his thighs. Sunlight jabs at his eyes and makes them water until, relief: the sun passes behind a cloud and the light blinks out. The strange twitters of hidden avians cease, and a river wind picks up, stinging his ears, crushing his head; it mouths strange words at him and the base of his neck answers with a searing pain. Silence surrounds him.

He skids to a stop on the gravel of an ancient viaduct; the woods spread beneath him for miles. He bites his lip and ponders the sweat icicles hanging from his hot limbs; they fall to the ground, turning inside out as they fly. He sniffs his wrist and smells the sun.

His mother came to his bedroom for the first time last night; she crept in beside him. She was cold and she warmed herself on him.

He cocks his head and listens again, but hearing nothing, he drags his body with infinitesimal movements towards the bridge's gridded viewing panel.

He spits off the side and watches it fly amongst the leaves until it turns invisible.

His mother rested her cold hands on the warmth of his private places in a way that she shouldn't have, and she whispered to him like she whispered to her man-friends.

He pulls at the flowery weeds tangled around the flaky metal bars and rips them up. He stands on his toes, and then on his heels. He peels the flakes off the bars, barely noticing the metallic splinters that settle under his nails.

She smelled of old ladies' perfume; she smelled of sweat.

For the first time, he senses how wonderful it would be to stand on this thick bridge wall.

He clambers up, wobbles for a moment, then stands up straight; he elevates himself onto tiptoes; he spreads his wings.

Her make-up was thick, smeared around her eyes and mouth, black and red crayon rubbed into skin. She turned her mouth to his and there was a stink of chemicals, a stench of drink. Her lips were thick. Her tongue was fat.

He doesn't look down; looking down makes him feel as if he's falling. He looks up; he looks up into the sky. He tries to decide which cloud is heaven.

She made noises, rubbing her body against him and she disappeared beneath the covers, where her head shook as she touched him with her mouth where she shouldn't have. When

145

she came back up, she sobbed and told him to forget it, told him she loved him, told him she loved him more than anything in the world, told him she would make it up to him with a bike ride in the woods. When he awoke the next morning he thought he had dreamed it, a night terror; but there were marks on his pants: there were smudges of red, like crayon.

A noise – an electric shock of noise – jars him: the noise of tyres on gravel – and he almost falls from the bridge. He sways, but regains his balance, and with eyes painfully wide, he looks down the path made into a tunnel by trees, and he searches for his breath.

His mum's contorted face, as she flies around the bend on her red, basketed bike. Her look of terror hits him like a saucepan of acid and peels his child-skin off. She scoops him up, hits him hard across the mouth and she cries.

He sighs, and turns off the memory tap while he still has the power to do so.

He looks at his watch. He's allowed the old lady thirty minutes at the window. This should be enough to cheer her up. He returns.

She flinches when she sees him; she is too deaf to hear his approach and she shakes her head at him vehemently, beginning to cry again, and he knows he cannot let this continue. It is inhumane; it is torture to prolong this.

He must put her out of her misery, and he must do it in a way that is befitting. He must not let Meghranoush become just another missing person; he must consign her to history.

Her death must make her famous.

Twenty-one

Time is ticking onward, and Mary has necessarily become more proactive in her approach to tracking down her mother. Indeed, she questioned an exceptionally tall Special Constable – who doffed his hat to her – this very day. 'Where's my mother?' she asked him.

'Pardon me?' he said, his eyebrows shooting upward.

'My mother. Do you know where she is?'

'Trick question, is it?' he ventured, smilingly.

'No. It's just that I lost her … some months ago.'

'Well, I suppose … heaven,' he said, patting her hand.

Mary wanted to hoot with laughter.

'No! Wherever she is now, it's not heaven.'

'You shouldn't say stuff like that.'

Mary looked around her and surveyed the leafy avenues of old houses.

'Do you know, a serial killer used to live in this village? I refer to it as a village because once, a long time ago, before the sprawl of the lardy city consumed it, this neighbourhood was an entity in its own right: a couple of hamlets linked by a Roman road. Not that this impressed the maniac who came to settle here. He had his reasons for choosing this place over any other to live; it's just that nobody knows what these reasons are, because nobody has ever worked out just who that serial killer was.'

'We don't have serial killers in Plymouth, love. This is Devon,' the Special Constable said, with a look of quiet pity. Mary looked at his thatch of fair hair, his clear blue eyes and nascent facial hair and deemed him old enough to be informed.

'We do, actually. This particular serial killer was at work when I was a young woman. Before your time. I doubt you were even born, young man. We know he existed, because he left a trail of bloodied bodies in his wake. But beyond that, we know nothing about him. I refer to him as a man, but in all honesty there is no foundation to support the assumption of our killer's gender, other than the premise that psychopaths tend, as a rule, to have penises.

'They say that men have emotional responses to murder that

women do not: sexual exhilaration being one of those responses. Women poison and feel remorse; men sever, and savour, and feel that they are the king of the world.'

The Special looked at his feet throughout this speech, uncomfortable with the drama of it.

'Well, I never heard of any serial killer.'

'He existed, I assure you. You know how they say the elbow is the strongest part of the body and should be used as a weapon in close combat? No? Well, it should, and this is why the killer had a selection of elbows, wired together and scrubbed clean, strung on string around walls, like Christmas cards.

'A gesture of religious defiance? A mocking of the rules of Tae Kwon Do? Or perhaps he viewed them as ornaments, an aesthetically pleasing alternative to etchings.'

'That's sick,' murmured the young man, blanching.

'Quite. The authorities would not believe that no-one knew who lived in that house, that no-one saw any comings or goings. How is it possible, they said, for someone to live for two years in an abandoned ramshackle house without anyone ever seeing or hearing anything?

'"It was a detached house," was the answer that the residents made. And how was it possible for the squatter to bring the bodies of so many victims into this house without anyone seeing him?

'"Maybe he didn't live there; maybe he brought them in bits," they answered; "and maybe he used the dark alleyway to transport them: it was only overlooked by box fir."

'"But this is the twentieth century!" – the police exclaimed. "Boo Radleys do not exist in the age of Neighbourhood Watch!" Well, Neighbourhood Watch might be fine for some folk, but we don't have the time to squander on it. And so he prospered in his game of calculated annihilation; he walked unseen under the noses of the nosy, and he ripped and stabbed and sliced his way into the record books. Seventeen, he stopped at, before disappearing and moving on somewhere new – God knows where, and God help those who live there.'

'Why weren't his victims reported missing?'

'They were reported missing, but many people go missing in Plymouth all the time. Most come back after a few weeks or months, but the long-term lost started to grow in numbers in the years that he was at work. Yet still suspicion was not aroused. In fact, it was only aroused after he left and the critters started returning with blood around their muzzles.

'He did it before he went: a parting gesture. He installed a cat-flap. And so he instigated the great game of cat and mouse, which he played so successfully with the police – with everybody – for years. If he'd not drawn the cats to the house, his crimes might have remained undetected.'

'Come on. Nobody murders in Plymouth: the only violent crime we have here is the fighting down Union Street. You must have got it wrong.'

Mary looked at this young man who aspired to be a real policeman, and although it seemed a shame to disillusion him, she felt that she must continue.

'I suppose we are all more accustomed to murderers yielding American passports and living in New York or Los Angeles, but remember that civilisation – in the form of the Founding Fathers – left for America from the Mayflower Steps in Plymouth in the seventeenth century, and thus the horrors that spawned from these first invaders were descendants of Janners.

'So one could surmise that it was Plymouth folk who set the wheels in motion for the ruin of that buffalo-ridden place. And so perhaps a serial killer coming to haunt us is not so unlikely, after all.'

'It's a bit of a stretch,' he said.

'Tell that to my mother.'

'Well, whatever. Now, is there anything else I can help you with?' His eyes darted around his environs, resting anywhere but on Mary's face.

'Yes. I would like you to tell me, in your professional opinion, how long it takes people to crack and become brainwashed. When, for instance, do sex slaves stop kicking? When do they give in to the whims of their tormentors and submit to their plungings and delvings? Does it take weeks, or is it a matter of days?'

'I honestly don't know, Miss Sibly. All I want you to do is to promise that you won't be calling us any more today. We know you're not very well, and we're sympathetic, but 999 is for emergencies. And only for emergencies; not because you think the neighbours are slandering you. Will you promise me?'

Mary consulted her palm studiously.

'Not until you give me an answer.'

'I don't know. Maybe a month, maybe less. I expect it depends on the person.'

'What if they were very stubborn?' Mary persisted.

'Blimey, I don't know. Maybe two months.'

'I think it's time you left,' Mary instructed, ushering him off the doorstep.

'You're right,' he said, as if this were a noteworthy event.

Faced with dead ends and delays, she finds she must get out of the house. She wants a cup of tea. She doesn't normally frequent tourist places – cafés, tearooms and the like – but today her gut is under attack and she finds solitude unbearable. She wants a cup of tea, so she has come to one of the better cafés.

It's busy in here, so she seats herself near the kitchen. The chemically floral aroma of an Airwick plug-in device embalms the air and she wrinkles her nose unappreciatively. The task of ordering should not be beyond her; she is, after all, a woman in her fifties, for heaven's sake. There's nothing to be anxious about. There's just the young cack-handed waitress to contend with. She flits around taking orders. She goes to the mothers with children, the young man with the dandruff-spattered suit, the teenage girls, the old lady emitting putrescent gases ... but although she tries repeatedly to catch her eye, the waitress doesn't come to Mary.

Ah, the relief, the unutterably pleasant pain of pulling a warm scab, found nestling deep beneath whorls of brittle hair. Mary slides this scab carefully along the hair shaft and extracts it for perusal.

When everybody else is served, the waitress reluctantly advances toward Mary and hails her with a perfunctory greeting, to which Mary doesn't respond.

All she wants now is a simple cup of peppermint tea to soothe her belly. She tries to normalise her voice as she orders this beverage, but the waitress looks at her oddly all the same, and with no other word of introduction she launches into a speech which Mary does not understand.

This insolent serving wench doesn't even smile; instead, she pouts and waits with her small hand on her hip before beginning again. Mary gathers at last that she's reading out a list of different cakes. Cakes with obtuse and frivolous names: Madagascar Bourbon Vanilla, Little Redcap's Basket, Death by Brown Bean, White Witch, Barbie's Boudoir, Choccy-Woccy Truffle, Peppermint Python and Staypuff's Log.

Mary says no to all with a wave of her hand. She needs only her tea, now; she needs it for her body; she needs it to calm her insides.

'What can I get you then, love?' asks the waitress, running out of patience.

'Tea. Peppermint. Hot.'

'Just that?'

'Just that.'

'Split cream pink-iced buns half-price all day,' she says, unnecessarily.

'Are they, indeed?'

'Yes.'

'Okay. I'll have all of your cloying cakes for my children, here.'

'But you don't have any kids,' says the waitress, looking around to make sure.

Mary shakes her head sagely.

'That was an example of sarcasm.'

The waitress consults her notepad.

'So. Just one cup of peppermint tea and nothing else?'

'Exactly.'

'Do you want milk with that?'

'No, I do not.'

'Sugar?'

'Just the tea, nothing else. Preferably today.'

'Keep your knickers on, love.'

She will definitely be keeping her knickers on, for there are worms crawling out of her bottom. Wriggling worms. They quieten for a day or two, but then they recrudesce.

This is a new thing; her body has gone topsy-turvy in the weeks since her mother's vanishing, and her belly is no longer continent. There have been upsets that have caught her by surprise and sent her running: attacks of laxity, of encopresis.

The sponges are no longer working; they're not binding her as they should be. Sometimes she's bound to the toilet, she refuses Kaolin and Morphine and she can't go to Doctor Rice because he

151

might want to examine her again and give her tablets – medicines that she doesn't know anything about. She can't trust unknown things; she can't let them enter her body. How does she know what he might be pushing inside her? No: her body is a temple that will remain unsullied by the pills and unguents of that quack.

The tea arrives in due course, but turns out not to be peppermint at all, but Earl Grey, which nobody really likes and which she positively abhors. In desperation she considers the milk, which fills half of a small metal jug; but for some reason, the breast juices of cows repel her. Small tongs draw a line to a pile of sugar lumps and she flirts with the idea of sugar – but disregards it, remembering her already decayed teeth. And so she takes her tea virgin and unadorned.

Out of nowhere the air in the café changes: the door opens and there is a blare of voices. A commotion of shapes disturbs the window, filling the café with darkness after darkness as the shadows pour through. There are at least twenty of them, from nesh striplings to hardened barbarians, and the noise that these rodomonts generate is staggering. They're wearing desert camouflage in shades of taupe and tapioca grey, and their enormous rucksacks make her bumbag look positively minute.

Their status as red-blooded virile soldiers is established instanter, and they position themselves so as to face the windows. They indulge in lecherous musings about various passing women, taking into account such factors as breast size, leg length and buttock roundness. Age and facial details seem unimportant; they ogle both a pinch-faced mother and her pretty daughter, who can't be older than twelve.

The waitress appears only after taking the time to utilise her eye-liner and lipstick – Mary watches her strain to apply these cosmetics in the reflective grill strip – and she takes their order without imposing the Cake List upon them. She is the picture of magnanimity, forgiving their impudent insinuations, their laughter; forgiving even their chorus of *Oy-oy*!

In the absence of an alcohol license they opt for milkshakes and pots of tea to accompany their Genuine Cornish Pasties, with sticky buns for pudding. They wolf-whistle when the waitress turns her back to take their chit to the kitchen. She turns, red-cheeked and flashes them a smile.

Talk turns to Action and A Tour In Iraq. They don't notice Mary, so she avails herself of the opportunity to eavesdrop; any distraction from the worms is welcome.

Tales of murder, of butchery, of despoliation, of villages torched, of rapine, etcetera – very much what Mary would expect from service gentlemen. The conversation meanders from action of one sort to action of a very different kind: from killing to sex in two sentences.

The marines are making the most of their shore leave and are planning multiple trips to that avenue of bestial depravity: Union Street. As if the string of nightclubs and public houses were not bad enough, the council has recently approved the addition of a de facto brothel, or so Mary read in *The Evening Herald*: a lap-dancing establishment boasting a number of obese and ugly Women Of The Night who declared that they would shed their sequin-strewn habiliments for a measly ten pounds a pop.

Gender traitors, thinks Mary, as she listens to the marines' enthusiastic musings regarding this place.

Several of the more senior ranks are animatedly discussing the chances of getting some poon-tang with the 'natives' – she assumes they mean female Plymothians – and these gentlemen are not young either. No: they must be in their forties at least, and though they are none of them wearing wedding rings, several third fingers of left hands bear definite white bands.

Mary wonders if they know that *poon-tang* is from the old French word, *putain*, which means prostitute, which comes from the Latin *putere* which means *filthy slash stinking*? Can they really regard their sexual conquests as stinking whores? Perhaps they do, she thinks; one never knows with military men.

The worms squirm. Stress winkles them out. Why don't any of these vermicides that she keeps taking ever work on her? The worming tablets she purchased from the pet shop in vast quantities have failed in efficacy. Pill after pill she takes, and still these vile parasites live in her gut. She wishes she'd left before these men entered. The worms are coming. She can't let them fall onto the floor.

She stands, and quick as she can, she pulls up her skirt and has an exploratory feel for them. She extracts her finger. There are no worms. At least, none she can feel.

153

The waitress drops a plate of split-cream pink-iced buns and the marines turn as a collective and look at her for the first time. They are agog, white-faced and jaw-dropped. They're more frightened of her than any renegade they met in Iraq, she thinks, but not one of them says a thing; they just stare at her. Before she's pilloried she clasps her bumbag, clips it around her waist, and walks slowly through the café. Tutankhamen's tomb was not more silent. Once outside, she's forced to walk past the café windows. As she does so, she hears clangourous peals of laughter, erupting volcano-like from the jaws of imbeciles.

Mary cocks a snook, finds her heels and runs. When she can run no more she ducks into an empty bus shelter. But she's not had any peppermint tea, and she doesn't want to go home because her mother is not there. She doesn't know what to do.

This is not the first time she's itched her undercarriage in public. It is the worms. They wriggle at the most inopportune moments. Anxiety dislodges them.

For instance, when she's lost track of time and the school bell peals loudly and floods of jostling teenagers appear from nowhere and swarm around her like sticky-fingered flies.

Or when she visits the supermarket belatedly and it's infested with vermin even more virulent than the worms: small children bedecked in full regalia, flying the flag for their schools, growling expletives at their mothers, raining punches on their three-foot sisters, helping themselves to stolen grapes, repetitively bouncing basketballs upon the heads of catatonic younger brothers, pulling random articles from shelves and leaving them for the unwary to trip upon.

Or when she has to deal with the infuriating elderly who stop dead in front of her and look surprised when she berates them and threatens them with an organic cucumber. It's stress that brings the worms, and she has been more stressed than ever in these last few weeks. The itch, the perpetual itch on skin and in bottom, the horror of bugs crawling out of her nether regions is ghastly – as is the deep need to scratch them into oblivion. And it is an itch that won't budge until it has been utterly attended to.

Vigorous scratching is the only calming measure. The doctor may say her itches are nervous ticks, but they're real, and they're torture.

She doesn't need the extra strain of a lost mother: she's had enough. She doesn't need adventure, she doesn't need drama, she doesn't need any more stress: it is time for her mother to return now. Enough is enough, the jig is up, the bell has tolled, it is home time.

The sky darkens; it begins to drizzle and Mary waits for the bus under the metal skeleton that once contained a fully waterproofed bus stop. Wet and hateful, because vandal-munchkins have smashed the glass.

The drizzle seeps into her soul like a soft and slimy death. What kind of council builds a bus-shelter out of glass, anyway? It should be wire-reinforced super-toughened Perspex or something. Glass cries out to be smashed and comminuted under heel.

If a person wanted to kill someone, an effective method would be to grind down glass and sprinkle it in the victim's food. Give it a good stir and they wouldn't even notice. A few months to take effect, and eventually it would grind away their digestive system. They would keel over and die and no-one would ever know why.

Glass is the answer. Glass is the key to success. The perfect murder is not being stabbed with an icicle (whoever heard of an icicle sturdy enough for stabbing? – and it would slip out of one's hand like a mucilaginous bar of Palmolive). No: the perfect murder is to poison an abductor with glass.

Twenty-two

The dark waters of the lake splay out before her on this bitter morning. The odour of rotting pondweed predominates and wafts of manure blow across from the stables, adding unpleasantly to the stench.

A restless kind of rage is upon her; she is not sure what has happened, but she is filled with an angst that will not remit. She is disgusted that she has found herself in such a place in such a state, her head aches from thinking, and all she wants to do is destroy.

'Lazy sluts,' she shouts, watching the fowls still sleeping under the shadow of the willow-folk. It disgusts her that they never spread themselves out, never opt for solitariness; instead, they conglobulate in cowardly collectives, they opt for safety in numbers. Mary picks up a stick and aims it at a large white duck with a red waxy cere.

'Oy, you bastard! Wake up!' she calls.

She'd never do serious harm to an animal; she just likes to motivate them. Ducks, she believes, are largely corrigible: she instructs them for their own good.

'Wake up, I said!'

Thwack. It misses the duck. She throws another and is treated to an echoing quack. The duck grumbles to its feet and eyes her evilly.

She used to bring her mother's best herbal granary to feed them, crusts carefully scissored into tiny brown squares, but now her mother has been taken she has only herself to offer. The fowls need no alms anyway: they're fat, stuffed with white tourist bread; not her carefully-severed bill-sized fragments, but huge hunks thrown for them to fight over.

The faded sign that declares "white bread harmful to fowls" is ignored. Sometimes, whole slices of white death are thrown into the lake – she watches them in disgust, gradually browning, then sinking, as the fleet of brown ducks silently approaches.

Often, they hit the island and large hungry rats come out to feed. A hail of gravel stones normally follows the bread when the rats appear (it appals Mary to note how people are happy to feed beady-eyed birds but not furry-coated rats).

Mary's conscience is clear, though, for she has always told the tourists that white bread causes stomach complications, explained patiently that it's fatal for ducks to fill up on white bread, but people just look at her oddly.

It's a strange expression, and one which many faces have cast at her lately. Not ridicule, as she'd first thought; no, it's something else. The same expression that passes over their faces when the rats come out. She can't credit the expression; she's sure she's done nothing to provoke it. Still, she can't be expected to account for the actions of moronic bystanders. Let them have their nasty glares: she doesn't care.

She walks towards the row of tethered boats: a handful of blue pedalos and old wooden rowers. These boats hardly ever bear passengers. The place was misnamed: there are rarely boats on the boating lake and anyway, it's more of a pond than a lake, barely deep enough to support ducks. The only people who hire the boats are the heathen: the tourists bored of beaches, eager for cool water and the shade of dark trees. At the cost of five pounds for half an hour, no local would be so extravagant. And a rower can never get twenty yards from the boat attendant, who gawps like a seagull scouting for Mr Whippy.

She's tried so fiercely to forget the day she herself hired a boat. She can't remember what possessed her to do it. Hormones or caffeine, she surmises, but she'll certainly never repeat the exercise. It was vile, the oars were out of sync and the boat attendant's teenage assistant laughed at her. He lounged on the jetty, his feet dangling in the water, and every now and then he tore his face from the *Radio Times* and smiled.

She disapproves of teenagers, and she especially disapproves of radios. There are quite enough voices filling the air without radios adding to the clamour, and as for television sets, who knows what might come through them? Anything could get into a house.

She tries to keep the television off as much as possible now. Her mother used to insist upon watching *Animal Park*, fascinated by stately houses and exotic animals, but now, even when the television's off, the blank grey screen is unnerving; it sits there in a ghastly state of readiness, just waiting to burst into life at the touch of an unseen button.

These days, since her mother has scarpered, she envelops the set with a bath towel.

She passes the boats and watches the ducks stir; she's glad they're awake, feeling the cold wind on their bills, the ice water beneath their bellies. The manner in which they sleep, with their heads swivelled onto their backs, is surely unnatural, and she turns to look at the far-off spires of the Crystillery instead: that vitreous property of hyaloid walls and refulgent roof. It resembles the Emerald City, but without the emeralds.

No, it's not exactly green – although green reflections from the cypress trees and Japanese oaks are cast over the eastern flank – and yet, despite the regrettable lack of green, it's magical in its countenance. She approves of its transparency: everything's on show; there's nowhere within for anything to hide.

The ducks begin quacking, loudly and gratingly.

'Stupid ducks. Be silent, ducks!' she commands, but they do not quieten.

She does not even have the power to stop a duck quacking.

She breaks her angry stride to pause in the rose garden. The lure of the boating lake is not the lake; it is certainly not the boats, nor the willow folk, nor the ducks: it is the rose garden. It's stuffed with splendid roses that fragrance the air with the scent of Eden – but people avoid it like the plague. More, now, in this time of plenty, than ever before. The garden houses the benches of the dead, and passers-by are wary: the brass plaques of the dearly departed are uncomfortable to rest against.

> ### THE ROSE GARDEN: DEVELOPED BY THE BOROUGH WITH ASSISTANCE FROM THE TOWN COUNCIL, ON THE SITE OF THE FORMER NURSERY, FOR THE USE AND ENJOYMENT OF RESIDENTS AND VISITORS TO THE CITY OF PLYMOUTH.

She reads the plaque for the thousandth time, resisting the urge to count the words, siphon them out and pair them in groups. There are thirty-four words, a propitious even number; but it's not good to divide too much, as it throws up seventeens: menacing numbers.

The rose garden's really something, despite the tourists who

mumble that it's oppressive. Mary finds it calming to admire the
trellises of climbing roses in every shade of pink, peach, yellow,
red. Bedded roses, climbers, ramblers, hybrid teas, floribundas,
old English bourbon: a thousand eyeless faces. Some of the roses
are wilting, half are browning with decay, petals wrinkling and
shrinking into death, while others on the same branch bloom in
the full insouciant beauty of youth: perfect form, exquisite scent.
They don't even notice those who rot beside them.

'Who'll leave me a bench?' she asks them.

She smiles; there'll be no commemorative bench for a dead Mary.
Her mother is absent, she has no friends, and the rest of the heathen
barely notice her now, whilst she's alive and kicking. What chance
does she have of being noticed when she's kicked the bucket?

If she is killed by the man with the glass birds and if she is found
floating face down in the sluice, then there might be a chance of a
bench – but even then, she'd only be news for a week before they
forgot her, and what are the odds that they could procure one in
a mere week?

She approaches a bird-spattered bench and perches on the edge.
She'd like to slump back a little more, but the seagulls have been
busy spraying the seat.

People think it's turds, bird shit. But it's not: it's piss. Uric acid.

She breathes the stagnant morning air, trying not to think about
the bacteria multiplying in the microscopic smearages plastering the
bench beneath her bottom; trying not to think about this skinny,
short man who has wrecked her life.

For a moment, the foul vapours rising from the lake engulf her
and she coughs a wracking cough and drags her eyes over the roses
before her. Something odd is standing in the soil; something erect
and bright with definite edges. Reaching into the flower bed, she
withdraws a child's chalk stick: it is a cool, mint green. She rolls it
between her hands and considers the iridescent residue. It puts her
in mind of the thick peppermint sticks her mother used to buy her
from the sweetshop. Taking chalk between finger and thumb, she
extends her tongue and flicks the tip over the surface: dry and earthy,
not much like peppermint sticks after all. More like the Kaolin and
Morphine she was force-fed after she'd eaten too many peppermint
sticks and suffered the peppermint squits.

She bends and draws carefully around her shoes, leaving their

159

outline on the muddy tarmac. When she moves her feet she finds that she's left an incandescent green butterfly on the path beneath her, and underneath it she writes: Give her back or I'll kill you, and she knows without a shadow of a doubt that this message will be read, that this threat will be heard, because she knows, as she has known all along, that this man is following her, that this man is watching her every move, and that soon, when he deems the time right, he will strike.

In the distance a tiny duckling, yellow with blobs of brown, slides into the water and swims towards her. Expecting food, no doubt. It bobs on the water waiting for her gift, emitting small quacks as it paddles in a wobbly circle.

The birds breed all year. It's the abundance of food: it gives them lusty thoughts. This little birdie disturbs her; even for a duckling, its eyes are incredibly beady. She sits contemplating it until it hops out of the water and pecks around her feet.

The impudence of it astounds her; the cocksure greediness of the little pest. Before the bird can run, she has it in her hand. The coarseness of its down surprises her; the shrillness of its voice grates in her ears. It wriggles; it is surprisingly strong for such a little bag of bones.

All the fowl are awake now; quacking fills the air as, one after another, they launch into the water. A single brown duck heads the fleet, and squeals as it hastens to the chattering fledging. Rising, she holds the tiny bird tightly and walks to the water's edge.

It tries to peck her hands, straining its neck to reach her, but she evades it. She has thirty seconds before the fleet is upon her, so she uses her time wisely. She immerses her hands in the dark waters and the chick struggles beneath the lake, making funny noises – not quite a quack; more a cough. The lead duck arrives: the mother, quacking with outrage, the rest just behind.

She ignores Mother Ducky snapping fiercely at her arms and drawing fine pricks of purplish blood. When eventually she retracts her hands they're covered with a viridian film which shimmers in the morning light. Baby Duck bobs up on the surface.

It's ruffled, but quacking.

She knows that ducks can hold their breath; all they do in the warm months is bob upside down, fat bottoms in the air, heads underwater searching for whatever it is they eat – insects, probably, or mouldy old crusts of white bread.

She feels the briefest pang of guilt and plugs the pang by popping a fragment of sponge into her mouth and swallowing. She always keeps some for emergencies, and they calm her insides better than Kaolin and Morphine ever did. She didn't want to hurt the little ducky, but they have to learn: they have to be moulded. Greed is a sin; one of the Seven – she shudders – one of the Seven Deadly Sins. Greed should be obstructed at all costs, and fear of man is essential in a duck – especially nowadays, with all the ducks going missing, necks wrung, eaten by poor folks and mad people.

The ducks engulf the little one, protecting it; they shout at her, their bright bills cursing her, anger in their yellow eyes. 'Dirty bird,' she explains to the accusing animals. 'A hotbed of bacteria.'

They swim away, hoarding the duckling in their midst, whilst she holds her wet hands up to the morning sun and admires the tiny rainbows of oily film.

She is engaged in this activity when Mrs Kennings from number twelve passes on her way to the morning shift at the factory. After exchanging pleasantries, Mrs Kennings begins to ask questions.

'So your mother is in hospital, I hear?' she asks, tentatively.

'She is; it's her heart.'

'Which ward is she in? I'll pop in and see her.'

'Raven wing.'

'Raven Wing? I never heard of a Raven Wing at Derriford. They're all named after places on Dartmoor, I thought?'

'She's not in Derriford; she needed more specialist care than they could provide. She's in a hospital in London.'

'Oh, how terrible for you! How on earth are you managing without her?'

'Quite well, thank you.'

'We thought she'd run off with her fancy man when we didn't see her around!'

If only this intriguing and intoxicating thought were true; if only there had been a love affair in the extreme twilight of her mother's life – an affair that might have led her mother to a love nest in the Karabagh sun; to a land that was not grey, but blue and yellow.

'Fancy man? What fancy man is that?' Mary asks.

'Oh, it's just us being silly, but my aunt Emily noticed your mum talking to a foreign man in the street a few months ago. At least once; maybe twice. She said he was a gentleman who might have been a Jew, but who didn't have the nose and so who might have been a Bulgarian or a Hungarian, but who was definitely not a Frenchie or a Kraut. You've got to excuse her way of talking; she's very old.'

Mary knows that her mother would never have associated with a German or a Frenchman under any circumstances, so no surprises here; but on the other hand, she didn't think her mother knew any Bulgarians or Romanians either. And yet ... a nugget of information stirs in Mary's mind, and that is the fact that Bulgaria housed the lion's share of the Armenian diaspora. It is feasible that the man might have been a Bulgarian Armenian.

'Your aunt was eavesdropping, I presume?'

'She doesn't mean any harm; it's just that the days are long when you're that age, and she loves her gossip.'

'Did she eavesdrop a name?'

'Now, I think she heard a name. What was that? Oh yes. I remember it. It was a funny name. Mr Nowak, she thought he was called; she swore this was the name your mother called him. My auntie thought it sounded like "no work," and said it seemed to suit.'

'Why?'

'He seemed to her a feckless, shabby sort of person. Dirty, he was; had stains on his shirt.'

'And this person was dark, yes? With large eyebrows? Skinny, though, and short?'

'That's right. That's him exactly. So you do know who I'm talking about?'

'I've heard him mentioned, here and there.'

She is sure now; she is sure of the person who has her mother. It is the exact same person who attacked the paralysed girl. It is as she has feared all along; it is her worst nightmare come true. It is no longer speculation; it is fact.

She runs to the water and calls; she opens her lungs and bellows to her mother.

There is no answer and so she puts her fingers in her mouth and scratches away at the lining of her throat until every ounce of her bile is afloat on the lake.

A yapping dog runs past, and tempted as she is to kick it and teach it the valuable lesson of quietness – of being seen and not heard – she lets it be, for the owner is in sight.

Drying her hands with her handkerchief, she walks slowly back to her house, frowning as the dark façade enters her field of vision.

Her cold hands fumble for the key and the lock clicks very slightly as she enters.

The clock in the hallway chimes seven – she shivers at the seventh gong – and then she hears a sound in the garden. No; it is only the play of the north wind as it spins empty milk bottles around and around.

She must give up the hope. She knows it now in her belly: her mother is beyond her reach.

Before the sun comes up again her mother will be dead.

Twenty-three

Late sunbeams slant low under amethyst clouds; night is beginning to fall, and her mother is dead. Or if she is not, she soon will be, and her roses will not bloom this summer.

Dreams, she has, where her mother is still alive; torturous dreams that haunt her. Her mind, it seems, will not accept the mastery of death; it seeks to invent new scenarios in which her mother is still with her.

She misses her fingersmith – or rather, her fingermouse; and she would give anything to see that small person sit and sew. Not even to talk to her: just to see her, even deep in snoring; sleep would be enough. The old story: you never know what you have until you lose it.

All these people talk so of *discoveries* and yet she, who can see so much more than others, can't find her mother. She wants to kill herself; she wants to take a knife to her throat and do it.

The moil of her unceasing thoughts is too much. If there's a God, he'll kill her and stay her bloodthirsty hand.

She wants to kill herself; she wants to kill herself. This thought is the only medicine. Give her strength, whoever is listening, to kill herself: to jump in front of a train, or from a cliff.

She must go; she's stayed too long. There's nothing to love and nothing to hate and she's nothing.

There are noises; when she turns her back, she doesn't know who will be standing there when she turns around again. There are noises. She hears them. She's always listening.

She's frightened when she can't hear, when the vacuum is on, when she's blending her evening soup of broccoli and potato. Anything could creep in behind her, and she'd not be able to hear it. So she's stopped vacuuming; the carpets are filthy with dust and sand. She's stopped eating homemade broth and has resorted to cold Cup-a-Soup; the kettle screeches and so she's stopped drinking tea.

A hideous music came from the television today: strange accordion music, horror film music – so loud – from an advertisement, she thinks. She can't believe she thought comfort would come from switching on that box; she can't believe she thought loneliness could be dispensed with so easily.

She abhors this house. She is too alone; he could come in at any minute and nobody would be here to protect her. Her mother was only small, she was not strong: she wouldn't have been able to protect her, but she'd have been diversionary. There would've been two of them: one would have been reached first; she could have made her escape whilst he was occupied, but now there's only her.

There's only her and he has her mother already; she is the only part needed to complete the set.

So quiet, she can hear her own breathing and she can hear footsteps – she can hear her own footsteps even when she's not walking.

Things get knocked over – things she could explain if only she had a cat, but she doesn't have a cat. She doesn't have anything at all. She expects a figure to appear at the top of the stairs or on the landing when she's lying in bed. She expects the bedroom door to open at any minute, or a shadow to fall across her face, a dark outline to appear. At any time this might happen, and so her peripheral vision is growing sharper – it has to – so that she can watch in all directions without other people knowing.

She is defenceless against him; she is a toothless tiger. All she has is a bag of ineffectual feathers to throw, a handful of vile adjectives to shout, a stack of insubstantial threats to skim at him, and he knows it. He has her just where he wants her: she is frozen by despair.

She wants the lights on. She doesn't want dark spaces where things can hide. Lamps are no good; lamps cast shadows and make her think she's going crazy. Lamplight moves when she walks past it.

She thanks heaven for electricity, for artificial light which illuminates her darkness. She doesn't want to be in the dark any longer; she doesn't want to be alone in the dark. She'll keep the lights on: this long night – the night in which her mother will be killed – will be the worst of all nights.

She doesn't know where it will happen, but she has seen the sea fog coming in and she knows with rare prescience that tonight will be the night. If she calls the police, they will dismiss her as they always dismiss her. They'll talk calmly and try to rationalise, and then they'll hang up and hoot at Mad Mary, who seems to be getting worse by the day. So she'll keep the lights on in every room so that this night, at least, she will not have to walk into darkness.

A social worker came over earlier, wanting to know why the lights were on. 'Day and night,' she said. 'Day and night.' Mary categorically denied that they were always on but the lady said 'Well, turn them off now, and prove me wrong.'

She went to the switch, but she didn't want to turn the lights off; why should she? She didn't want to turn them off, and that was the end of it. The interfering madam threw up her hands and asked 'What's going on with you, Mary? Are you seeing things again?' and Mary replied curtly that 'Nothing is wrong, except your interfering,' and she left her; she slammed the door and then Mary was alone again.

It is too dark, even in day; not enough sunlight comes in. She needs brighter lights than even the bulbs can offer, but she won't use candles because she doesn't like the way they flicker.

There is a noise like footsteps coming to the door; a rustling outside the porch. It can't be, but it sounds as if something's there. She should've locked the front door, but she left it too late and then the porch was darkened and she couldn't go into a dark porch, not even for a second to switch the light on and lock the front door because he could be outside waiting, and the moment he saw her outline he could hurl open the door and grab her, and so now the door is unlocked and he could be in the house.

She might as well have left the door wide open, an invitation to that bar-wielding bastard to come in.

Maybe the wind has blown it open slowly. It could be swinging in the breeze – maybe that's what that noise is. Or maybe the ghost of her mother is trying to get in.

She's dead already. Mary felt her presence earlier as she sat in her armchair. She felt her mother's eyes on her. She was looking in from outside; she was looking at her through the crack in the curtains. She should have got up and closed the gap, she should have – but she couldn't and now she too is in the house. She can feel her.

'I'm sorry, Mother; I'm sorry. Go to heaven: be gone, be gone.' She smells her, she smells her hair-dye again, the talcum, the olives.

Her eyes hurt; they're dry. She's neglected to blink. Her eyes are mad. Her eyelashes have turned inward and they scratch the surface of her eye with every blink.

She must relax. Her mother is dead; her mother's passed on; she's in heaven.

She wouldn't come back to haunt her: she never did anything wrong. She never harmed a hair on her head except for that one time, but all mothers make their daughters angry and although she might've felt on the very odd occasion that she wanted her mother to die, all daughters feel such things about their mothers, surely? – and if she did touch her mother in anger, she should get some credit for all the times she wanted to knock her block off, but didn't. All the years she sat and listened to her moans and bitterness; all the times she was called stupid and ugly – she should get some credit for the times she held her tongue and took the hurt into herself.

She saw it – she's sure she saw it, just then, out of the corner of her eye: a translucent pink form moved across the hallway and back. Someone is in here; it has happened. Her mother's spirit has risen from her body and it is inside the house.

Twenty-four

The blood will come off his skin; it will come off because it always has. He steps in, and resists the urge to dive out. Liquid burns his ankles, constricting them like too-tight socks. His mum never had any conception of why he insisted, as a boy, on having his bath so hot.

She liked her bath water tepid, so that it grew steadily colder and colder, and consequently (she said) more cleansing. Hot water made sweat, and so left a person dirtier than before. He's different: he likes to be steamed; he likes to see just how hot he can bear it.

He dares his blood to boil.

He grits his teeth; his red feet turn purple. He drops to his knees and just shy of a scream he lets in a quick flood of cold. The iciness is orgasmic and he lets out an involuntary groan but soon the cold becomes too cold, becomes slippery and uneasy, inching its way into the warmth, so he turns it off and wrenches the tap tight to preclude any disconcerting drips.

He leans his head back against the comparatively icy enamel behind him. Fortunately, a veil of bubbles cushions him from the cold tub, and soon enough the enamel steals body heat and becomes as he is. He leans back into the water and knocks a bar of orange glycerine soap into the tub. He feels it slithering next to his thigh and he half-heartedly attempts to grasp it – to no avail, tricksy eel that it is. He abandons all further attempts to locate the soap, for the first time understanding the benefit of soap-on-a-rope outside of a prison-shower context.

Sliding down the warmed enamel, he reclines until the water slips over his features and pools in a still mass over his face. Beneath the surface he opens his eyes, but is stung by a concoction of scented pharmaceuticals. The muffled sounds down here are wonderful; they lend themselves to imagining.

It's a buffer against the world outside, as if he's travelling through some alternate plane of reality in which time is slow and movements are exaggerated, like astronauts traversing the surface of the moon. Every small movement he makes causes a huge ripple, oddly loud in his ears, and disturbing the perfect stillness of the water. His hair has lost its hue and is black now as it fans out around him, rising up toward the surface. All he needs are some floating flowers, and he'll be Ophelia or the Lady of Shalott.

He watches the bath water reaquify the droplets of her blood and he is suspended in pink juices, his hot body camouflaged and there is peace in this.

A few bubbles escape from his nose, and when his lungs reach the point of *pop* and he can hold his breath no longer, he gasps for ambrosial air.

He runs his hands lightly over his chest and sloshes soapy water around his legs, disturbing the delicate convection currents, redistributing the scalding with the hot. He surveys the water again: the fizz is gone. The soap killed it, and now the water is strawberry milkshake, a blood smoothie streaked with trails of dead bubbles. He allows his hand to wander to his groin.

It is now, in this moment, that he decides upon the construction of the vase that he will make from her.

He will commit her disconnected bones to his furnace, which he will crank up to sixteen hundred degrees to render her ashy. And he will use the carbon and calcium of her powdery remains to colour a *magnum opus*: a memento to enshrine her essence; the crowning jewel of his collection.

Twenty-five

It was on the news. Nobody could have survived the blood loss; the police felt they could be sure of this. Blood spilled everywhere, more blood than any of them had ever seen: red splashes bedecking the cenotaph.

Of all the places to kill, that white granite monument to the dead was the site he chose. A labyrinth of smooth ivory plinths; a perfect cutting surface. Butcher's blocks.

Perhaps he had not counted upon the splashing of arterial vessels, which threw red blood cells onto the walls twenty feet away until that straight milky monument was painted with lurid arcs.

Perhaps he had counted upon it, and had gloried in the effect. 'The colours of the English Flag,' the newspapers commented, with a morbid lingering on 'the body of a foreign immigrant, murdered in the land of the civil and reduced to that land's flag.'

The irony bubbled in their mouths and it had to come out. 'Red and white,' over and over. They would chew upon these colours and fathom new ways of reading them. 'A monstrous imitation of Smeaton's Tower,' one grey-eyed, ginger-browed reporter announced.

The analogy wasn't too much of a stretch – not really. The old red and white-striped lighthouse which overlooked the murder site was a stone's throw from the cenotaph, but the lighthouse cast no light over the site. It stood shrouded in sea mists, ponderous and ineffectual.

The one eye of Smeaton's Tower's was extinguished when it was brought, brick by brick, from far out to sea, and replaced by Douglass' Eddystone Lighthouse: too old to stay, too nice to throw away. Mary was fascinated with this ancient lighthouse, once so alone – fourteen miles out to sea and then rescued and erected in a prime position on the Hoe. An ornament: no longer a life saver.

Perhaps if there had been light, it would have saved her mother's life. Perhaps if there had been a good brisk wind to blow away the fog, the maniac would have chosen a different day for his butchery.

Perhaps, in fact, he had waited diligently for meteorological conditions to be perfect before executing his plan and victim.

How fitting, Mary sees, that in his warped mind – his misogynist mind – he should daub walls of dead men with the blood of a living woman. A mother, a woman whose womb had brought forth life. To cut that life out, to disembody a soul and send it floundering over the murky sea, to fade and disappear.

He walked her through the mists, along the promenade – was she fighting all the way? – past the statue of Sir Francis Drake – was she screaming for help? – a left turn just shy of the twin statues depicting the Spanish Armada and the Royal Air Force – or did she just mutely submit, knowing resistance was futile? Or perhaps thinking erroneously that he was letting her go? – and then down the steps into the bowels of the naval memorial – how alive was she at this point? – in the pink of health, or was she battered and abused and fit to drop? – he placed her on a wall – did she try to run? Did she? – and a few metres away from the towering line of eighteen flagpoles, he murdered her.

The television is covered with images of the kill site, a phalanx of policemen performing fingertip searches of turf; forensic officers taking swabs of blood from various clotted puddles, hoping that there was a struggle, that the victim drew a drop of the murderer's blood.

A blow to the nose is all it would take; a smidgen of haemoglobin and they'd have him. The public amasses in the background, laying flowers under Drake (which is as near as they could get) for an unknown person. They speak to the cameras: they speak of shock and disbelief and horror and then Mary watches as they walk away to climb the lighthouse for a pound, to swim in the revamped Lido, or to sit and admire the sparkling Sound, which is awash with bright vessels.

The police can't be sure, because they don't have a body, but they think, judging by the spatter and the 'cast-off' and the blood pools, that he cut her throat first. Then he cut off her limbs while her heart was still beating. There were no body parts left over – not a finger or scrap of buttock – but they have determined through genetic markers in the blood that the victim was female and Eastern European.

They are desperate for a pound of flesh which might yield evidence and some sort of timescale; they would sell their souls for a body which could be read forensically for hair and fibres and measured in terms of violaceous lividity.

Even a carelessly-misplaced weapon – one of the knives he used – would be something, but all they have is blood. He left no forensic evidence to betray his own identity, and this dismays the police. Because they know they are looking for a professional, because their perpetrator is good, because he understands how to 'work clean,' even though he acted in almost total darkness.

Mary knows exactly who the Hoe Victim is; she knows in her heart that it was her mother. Her mother who loved the Hoe more than any other place, save Armenia.

Shattered, but how can she go to the police? – she with a schizophrenic black mark upon her medical record? She who has not reported her mother missing for fear of being accused; she who is friendless and alone? She who is the daughter of a woman so unimportant that few remarked her absence?

Mary must find her mother's remains – such as they are – and bury them. She cannot rely upon the police to find the culprit; they will spend months scrabbling around in search of evidence that they will not find, by which time the murderer will have moved on geographically, or moved through his list of victims.

The horror of it all is almost too much … but *something* keeps her going; something keeps her breathing and eating and drinking, and that is the knowledge that she has failed. She has stood by and allowed her mother to be murdered. She will not do a 'Hamlet' any longer; she will not stand by and wait through five acts, crippled by fear and indecision. Now is the time to seek justice – by which she means revenge.

But first she must rid herself of her mother's morality. She must snuff out her light so that she may kill.

Twenty-six

She is on the cliffs in Cornwall, home of surfers and the elderly. The sunlight is fierce and unyielding; the sea's glitter needles her eyes.

The walk is taking it out of her. Her clothing is sensible but she is hot, deathly hot; she has a good strong pair of boots and thick orange walking socks that she has topped with a long burgundy dress. It's hewn from heavy cotton, blended with a smidgen of Lycra, and though it hangs beautifully – regally, even – it mummifies her. She thought the dress would be an adequate prophylactic against the coastal chill, but it is boiling her alive. There is an excess of unnecessary material, and it falls down to the soles of her muddy boots instead of being cut off at the mid-calf, which was the length her mother sanctioned.

Despite her red face, she feels that she looks imposing in this get-up: less 'batty old mare' and more 'noble old witch of the coven.' It's appropriate that she's wearing it today, of all days, for today is an auspicious day: today augurs the beginning of the end.

Over her shoulder is a battered leather satchel. Within it, a heavy object that weighs her down and hangs pensile under her left arm. If she lands awkwardly on the spongy turf and turns her heel even slightly, the bag crashes against her hip-bone unpleasantly.

It's strange how the eyes of other walkers have been drawn to this object; perhaps fearing it's a brick or two, with which to lash herself.

Walkers, she's noted, can't abide panic; they deplore any drama which might dispose of the serenity in their afternoon jaunt. She's ceased talking to them, seeing the alarm in their faces at the slightest mention of her recently-deceased, illegal-immigrant mother.

The brackish wind is in her mouth, alarming her taste buds and making her thirsty. The crest of the headland is in sight now, from where she'll have a panoramic view of the sea. To the south, the sheltered confines of the bay; to the north, the wildness of the Atlantic, sending powerful rollers crashing against the sharp rocks.

Turning her head, she can see both of these sights, but she wants them simultaneously in her field of vision. Up there at the central peak of the headland she'll be able to see it all beneath her, a theatre of animate water.

The burn in her legs is becoming unbearable, so she stops on a grassy knoll bedecked with piss-a-beds to watch the gulls soar overhead, feasting on invisible insects. A cormorant flaps low and slow across the bay, a fish bulging in its crop; the skylarks wheel in perfidious gusts that would smash them against the rocks with no consideration for their skeletons.

Memories reverberate through her brain and her embowed and embrittled mother looks down upon all.

Blank stretches of numbness. She blesses the numbness.

Unwelcome, unbidden thoughts slink into her mind, cleaving the water. *Tempus nascendi et tempus moriendi:* A time to be born and a time to die. She thinks about her mother because she can think of nothing else, and she rues the day her mother came to England, for even her mother's Homeland or Holy Land would have been safer than this Unfair and Unpleasant Land.

Her mother was sewing in the tailor's corner of a Palestinian Post Office when her English George came in, letters in hand, and spotted her. George, her father, was a policeman sent from Plymouth to keep the peace in Palestine. He didn't do a very good job, given the current state of affairs, but he was a respectable man – strong on theoretical principles, if nothing else.

Meghranoush was an old maid before George came along, thirty-two and beautiful, black hair and almond eyes. Back then she plucked her brows into high arches like Rita Hayworth. She was admired by many but vowed never to marry – unless, of course, that elusive foreign millionaire should enter her territory, bearing a diamond.

Her mother didn't realise that her father's precious offering was made from diamond chips. She had a habit of missing the obvious. So, consumed by her ambitions of wealth, she made her merry way to Blighty, land of the blighted.

She spoke not a word of English and he not a word of Armenian, yet apparently they fell in love. How did they fall in love without language? Mary has never fathomed this, yet George married the pretty Armenian lady and brought her back to England. They boarded a cheap and rusty tub that stank of vomit and effluence, along with a number of other scrofulous passengers too poor to board a better vessel.

She can just imagine her mother, who had hitherto only ever travelled by foot, donkey and cart, attempting to overcome seasickness and prejudice, hanging close to her new foreign man. Hopelessly counting down the hours until their landing, trying to disguise her pious disgust at the antics of carousing tars and Englishmen.

It was a regular Saturnalia – or so Mary gathered, from her mother's inarticulate grumblings.

No white cliffs for her mother: they arrived in Scotland in the dead of night, and that mountainous land loomed against the night sky. For some reason, they waded through freezing water to get ashore. Her first impression of the green and pleasant land? Black waves. Not exactly a great start. From Noah's playground at Ararat she had progressed to Jerusalem, where Jesus walked; and finally, aged thirty-two, she found herself on British shores.

They endured two days of back-crunching rail travel on a decrepit train which finally chuffed its way into a drizzly mid-winter Plymouth. Wreathed in a miasma of tobacco smoke for most of the way, due to a pipe-toting gentleman in the same carriage.

Her mother had unwisely unpacked many of her clothes and arranged them around her person to keep warm on this awful journey; consequently, the first thing she did upon arrival in her new home, before she even looked around, was to set to their immediate washing.

She never adjusted to the temperate climate; she worshipped the electric fire, even in summer. Whatever was she thinking as she juddered along on that cold train with her new husband? – not speaking, just smiles or frowns, unable to understand any of the strange words around her? What would she have thought if she had known she would survive the horrors of genocide only to be wiped out by a man masquerading as a good person, in her twilight years, in a quiet corner of suburbia?

Mary used to show her mother the stars; she did so the night before she disappeared. She held her mother's arm to steady her, and she pointed out a star called Capella. The sixth brightest star in the night sky; a yellow giant. She showed her Cassiopeia: a W-shaped constellation near the north of the celestial pole.

175

Mary and her mother looked upwards at the silver pin-pricks – 'needle bites,' her mother said – but Mary thought she was looking at the wrong stars: looking at Orion's Belt, or the moon, or something. They looked for satellites and shooting stars and Mary received the suggestion that her ancestors were up there somewhere, bathing in the astral rays. She could have stood there blithely watching all night, the passing of hours marked only by the motion of the stars. No watches and clocks: only the sidereal time.

She told her mother that there are a hundred billion stars in the galaxy, just in the Milky Way alone. And that the stars were alone: multitudinous, but millions of miles apart and getting further from each other each day. A hundred billion stars, but all so far away from each other that the others might as well not exist.

Her mother couldn't imagine a hundred billion; she couldn't wrap her mind around it. Mary told her that the easiest way to think about it was that the extent of the known universe was approximately the size of the Sahara desert and that in this scale, the earth would represent one grain of sand. But her mother still struggled to grasp this idea, stating that she had never been to the Sahara. Surely, Mary asked her sceptical mother: surely you must believe there's intelligent life out there somewhere?

'Must be somewhere,' her mother said.

Now there will be no more star-gazing. That much is certain. The ambiguity has dispersed, leaving only cold facts. Everything that has passed until now is annulled; he has erased her like an artist's smudge, and Mary must erase her again if she is going to kill him.

A skylark sings somewhere close at hand, but Mary can't raise her head to find it. She doesn't want to think any more. Something will engulf her, overtake her, and if it gets her she'll never breathe again.

There are fishermen beneath her on the rocks, slithers of silver glinting in the golden afternoon. They reel in mackerel after mackerel, cast after cast, thud after thud of the hammer, then a slosh into the bloody bucket.

Emetic smells of fish guts.

Omnium deliciarum et pomparum sacculi brevis finis. Mors, dolor, luctus et pavor invadit omnes. All the delights and pageants of a lifetime soon end. Death, pain, grief, and terror fall upon all.

Then the floats stop bobbing and the men stop catching. Something black in the water; a mammal is in the *eau de Nil* shallows: the head of a dog. Of course, a seal. Then another. Two of them together: Cecilia and Vasilli, she names them unthinkingly. She watches these seals looking at her, and she watches them turn and dive deep, and she sees their slick bodies at the seabed through the turquoise water. Warm rays touch her bare neck and the seals bob up again and return to looking at her. She's so hollow that they must see through her ears.

Bawdry morsels from the mouths of the fishermen waft up to her. They're cursing the seals for existing and eating their small fish, which they need for cutting up, and catching bigger fish.

A khaki welly-boot is thrown with gusto and misses the artful Cecilia by a good eight feet. Normally, Mary would go and explain that seals are not 'greedy fuckers.' She would explain that seals don't drink; that seals get all of their water from fish; that when captive seals are unwell, they must be fed fresh water from a bottle, otherwise they dehydrate and die very quickly. That seals have more right to fish than northern holidaying fishermen who have no possible use for them in their grubby pistachio-coloured hotel rooms.

She stands up and walks again, the thought of her mother propelling her far up the hill. And suddenly she's here; she's at the summit of this beautiful cliff.

She stands with bated breath at the edge, and the wind quickens and the whistling begins, eerily, as the rock oscillates.

A squall approaches: a dark patch hastening toward her, birds auguring the storm. She turns around and sees that far behind her other walkers ascend, following the wending pathway through the scrub. She must be quick, then: there's no time for dilly-dallying. She unpacks her father's satchel, retrieves an object and places it on the uneven rocky ground. Walking to the precipice, she's satisfied to note crashing waves and razor-edged rocks below.

Picking up the object with proprietary reverence, she steps backwards and runs, using the full extent of her small weight. She angles her body, shot-putter style, and hurls the photo album over the edge.

Winged pages flap in the air currents, spinning the large book end over end. The red dust-jacket disengages from the spine and

177

flies away, exposing the pale body that it has so successfully masked all these years.

Then it's over. The book is impotent, gone; to be consumed by the tides. It's not destroyed, though: it's not smashed. Memories can't be destroyed through brute force alone. Terminal falls will not do it; memories need more careful destruction – minute-by-minute annihilation – for them to die. And, even then, they have a nasty habit of living on in the subconscious mind.

Her mother filled the album with images of Mary. Images spanning every one of her fifty-eight years. Her mother was a consummate collector, and this album charted Mary's progression from innocent child to innocent older woman.

But she will be innocent no more. She'll soon spill the blood of another human being, and she can't look at her mother's album. She needs distance from her feelings of bewilderment, so that she can muster the necessary loathing.

Looking down, she is relieved to note there is only a mote of red; which might be a dust jacket and a speck of white; which might be an album; and she turns off the part of her brain concerned with empathy and allows a flood of vengeance of biblical proportions to enter her body.

Twenty-seven

Francis Drake stands there, sword at his side, shoulders back, hips cocked, groin thrust artfully towards the world, and he stands with his hand on the globe because, just like the man Mary seeks, Drake has conquered. He looks over the sea; he looks towards his island, which was once called St Nicholas Island, but which Drake usurped as a reward for killing.

He looks but he does not oversee all and he stood rigidly through everything, through every second of pain. Drake was undisturbed, his face turned away from the bloody frothing mess of fluid and flesh that stained the naval memorial so absolutely. He was deaf to the screams, he ignored the pleas; he stood proudly, and his face was composed as he surveyed the sea.

The police think the murderer paused here briefly, sat at the base of Drake and rested after his exertions. They found a smidgen of fibre and a sizeable blood stain.

The fractured segments of Mary's mother rested here on the marble steps and seeped through the bag, but this was the last bloodstain they would find. Perhaps, they surmised, he transferred her into a superior bag afterwards. Something watertight; something waxed, perhaps; something sturdier than the thin fibrous sacking she was originally poured into.

He felt contentment, Mary thinks, as he sat there beneath the great man, a woman he had fixated upon at his side, reduced to meat, drizzling her juices over the steps.

He cannot do without them, these old ladies; he would rather die than forego them. He loves them. He probably loves children too, enjoys dipping into both ends of the spectrum, looking for smallness, looking for vulnerability.

He challenges the accepted view that children and elderly ladies are not sexual, because to him they are the only territory in which sexuality is to be found. He fills himself up with them and delights in the unusualness of his inner life and the physical manifestation of that life, which is rape and death; and then, with time, the rush drains out of him and there must be more.

If sinning were not wrong, he would not find it appealing. It is

179

in the breaking of barriers that he delights. In the sinning that is so wonderfully wrong, so depraved, that he feels more alive.

Even if six billion stood against him he would stare back and feel the thrill.

He is not ashamed: he is a conqueror. He is ahead of his time, and great men do not achieve greatness by taking prisoners. A lengthy index of deaths bring victory, and history heralds the killers as kings. The more killed, the greater the payoff. Morality shifts in place and time and there's nothing but law to decree what morality should be, for wasn't cannibalism a respectable practice once? Wasn't murder ritualistic and condoned? Isn't it still? – thinks Mary, considering the United States' Death Rows – and wasn't the age of consent once ten?

Mary knows all of this. And she's spent so much time fixating upon her nemesis that she's sure of his make-up.

Yet children are bubbly and vibrant and teeming with life. There is attractiveness in all children, but what is the attraction of the elderly? Can it just be frailness, vulnerability? Is that all it takes to turn his head, or is it more? If she could decipher this, she could find him. She must unravel his strings and find the buttons.

Twenty-eight

L ambent moonlight flickers over the street; softness, stillness. She wants to walk; she must process what has happened. She wants to walk somewhere she'll feel small.

Her feet take her up the hill to the primary school.

She enters through the unlocked gate and all is deserted; the lights are on but nobody's home. She walks through the playground and sees herself reflected in black windows. The neighbours' children went to this school. They started when they were tiny, cried to leave their mama's knee and then grew boisterous and strong, eventually growing cynical of their mother, growing weary and ashamed of her long kisses and clinging hugs.

Thankfully, Mary has never had to suffer this: never had to endure the heartache of children who grow too big for their mothers. She's never had to leave a child at a school gate or worry when a little darling trotted home late. All the pain and pressure of motherhood has escaped her – or, rather, she's escaped it. Through living quietly and selflessly she's avoided some of the greatest pains in life.

She pauses for a moment on the concrete and walks towards the spidery structure which stands at the edge of the playground, overlooking the school field. The climbing frame is getting old: the blue paint flakes, revealing silver beneath; the world has worn it thin.

Too many children have clambered over it, and it suffers.

She perches on the lowest rung of the frame and her thin skirt rides up, exposing goose-bumped thighs. It's cold: deathly cold, a burn against her flesh. She fears that when she moves, her plucked-chicken skin will tear. She'll leave it behind on the bars.

She must get away from her thoughts. She reaches up above her head and grasps the bar. She lets her arms take the weight, and she dangles for a moment before changing her mind and climbing decisively to the top of the frame. The smooth slippery bars freeze her fingers and she might fall, but her thin arms have strength in them yet.

When there are no more bars left to climb and she's high, she takes a deep breath, a gasp: the reverse of a scream.

181

One at a time, she kicks off her slippers. Then her caramel pop-socks, and the wind is ready and runs away with them. The gust whips her skirt against her legs. It's so cold, her clothes do nothing to warm her; they flagellate her: they fight.

Delicately, so as not to snag, she unzips her skirt and pulls it down around her feet. She mustn't lose her balance. She can't fall here; she can't be caught.

Without her skirt she's inexplicably warmer: freedom – wind against her legs is exhilarating. The skirt in her hand flies like a windsock. The gale wants it.

At the zenith of a gust, she lets it go. Gently, gently, wheeling in the invisible wind, the flimsy fabric riding a rollercoaster of air.

Then, with no warning, it is stopped, caught by the prehensile claws of a holly bush.

Her thin purple blouse is all that remains between her and a criminal offence.

She mis-times the release and it lands on the tarmac of the play-area, thin and effulgent in the moonlight. For a moment, she's bilocated: she's here and yet she's not here as she watches her supine blouse, vividly heliotrope, but still untouched by the wind. Thank heavens, she sighs, as the wind returns and claims it. It rolls across the playground higgledy-piggledy, head-over-heels, down to the field and past the luminous sandpit in the far distance. By the light of the streetlamp, she sees it catch in the ancient Devon hedge of which the council is so proud.

Naked as the day she was born, she's calm. Even the road is quiet. She no longer feels the cold; she's hot. Her skin is aflame, it's burning.

If someone should see her naked on a climbing frame? – she wonders.

They'll admire her for her courage, they'll envy her for her innate armoury against the cold, they'll be jealous of her lithe figure.

She's tired – the wind stings her eyes. She should rest. She climbs back down to the playground and her clothes are all gone but she doesn't care. Why didn't he let her mother live?

The answer flies into her head: mastery. He could have let her live, but then there would have been unfinished business, loose ends to tie or cut.

When he knows his victims inside out there is only one thing

182

that can top that, and it is the taking of their lives: watching as their vitality and hope run out.

The killer has done this before, but he has only ever worked publicly on one site: the war memorial. Under those long lists of engineers and stokers and officers he sat and navigated her mother's body, judging it in terms of angles and breaking points, cutting tenaciously and unremittingly, and when he was done, he left with a bag of bones and offal, and that was the end of Meghranoush's body as a unit.

He did it to taunt Mary; he has become cocky. He's always been arrogant, but cockiness is a new acquisition. The ability to dare fate to do its worst is something he has hitherto abstained from, and this cockiness is what will unseat him. This cockiness, which brought him out into the open, will bring him to Mary's house and to his knees.

Twenty-nine

Her energy is drying up. It's been on the wane since her mother's decimation, slowly dripping out of her and now it's almost gone. She doesn't like to leave the house empty; doesn't like to come back to a property that is vacant and yet that potentially hides a villain, a murderer in wait, because locks are easy to pick and windows are easy to shimmy through and she knows that soon he'll be coming back for her.

Loveless it is, and sinister; more so than it has ever been before. The house has always been quiet, but now it's so very quiet. The afternoons are the worst. All of the small tasks have been done – the mopping, the polishing of thimbles, the opening of the post – and when there's nothing to do in the afternoon and the TV can't be trusted, only sleep remains.

Her hands are so cold but her bones yearn to relax into sleep. For a moment there's no getting comfortable, until she puts her hands between her thighs and feels them icy against her skin. They gradually warm and by the time they're as hot as the crevice, she's far into sleep and she dreams of kissing the man she hates, which is the worst dream – so much worse than the dreams of killing him.

She awakes and curses God with a litany of blasphemies.

Losing her religion was a blow, there's no denying it. There are no longer a quaternity of gospels to protect and guide her: she's alone, a wanderer in the wilderness, tumbling from one place to another with little hope of salvation. Her guiding light erased, her Biblical essence removed; she's left with a mouth full of vitriol and no religious weaponry at her side.

If she doesn't find the perpetrator then he'll get off scot-free because there's no hell awaiting him, only oblivion and the ignominy of being forgotten. She's ceased to feel faith because how can there be a God who would bestow such stomach-churning pain as an entrée and such a little skimpy measure of pleasure as a main course? – a God that has allowed her mother to be consumed by a pervert is a God not worth having.

A God so capricious or weedy that he couldn't even stop one murderer, let alone a worldful, is a joke. A God who the men

184

in robes would have her believe is omnipotent, omniscient and omnibenevolent is a lie, for how could her mother be murdered under the watch of such a God?

She finds a contradiction here that cannot be overcome: he is either not all-powerful or he is not all-knowing or he is not all-good, and compromising on any of these things is a deal-breaker for Mary. She only wonders how she never saw the inconsistency before.

She knows the Bible-wavers would cite the supposed existence of the Devil as a reason for evil deeds on earth, but the Devil doesn't prove a thing, because if God can't keep his Earth Devil-free; if he can't win a scrap with one fallen angel, then who is really Lord Almighty?

Her mother should have been safe; her mother should have been shrouded in the protective armour of old age; her mother should have been flying under a psychopath's radar.

How could he throw away a person with that kind of provenance? How could he reduce her to bits? Another piece of litter in the kitchen bin, just some foreign arms and ears mixed in with the vegetable peelings, the rotten flowers, the used tea-bags, the remains of yesterday's stew?

Suddenly, as she stares out of the window, she sees that a small man is outside her house. He is dark and heavy-browed and there is a knitted scarf about his throat and it covers his face almost up to his eye sockets. It is hard to gauge his age; he could be anywhere between thirty and fifty – he might easily be deceivingly old, like a Monet; he might look one thing from a distance, but that could all unravel up close. At a guess she would put him not far behind her own age, but his hair is not streaked with grey: it is black with an ominously red glow in the afternoon sunlight. The glow of dye.

He genuflects and fiddles with the laces of his polished brown shoes, but his head is turned towards the window.

Mary takes a step back from the window and stands in the shadows of the kitchen so that she can look at him unseen. He's not supposed to be here, this man who kneels looking at her house: he's a stranger.

He's dressed like a mannequin, shirt pressed and starched so rigidly that it hangs still. His hair is side-parted and there is a small bright dot in his earlobe – a recent addition, judging by the redness surrounding it – and it catches the light and glints like a diamond

185

in the bright light.

This earring seems at odd with the straight-laced, scrupulously clean man in front of her. He coughs and brings a blue handkerchief to his forehead, and his eyes dart again towards the house.

Mary walks through her front door and stands on her stoop.

'Yes? Can I help you?' she calls acrimoniously.

'I was just admiring the house.' His voice is odd. He sounds as if he might be suffering from a cold, his words are so hoarse.

'Who are you?'

'Just a passer-by with a compliment.'

'I don't want strangers staring at my property and I don't want their compliments either, thank you.'

'Is everything quite all right? Is there anything I can do for you?' he enquires in a tone of polite chivalry.

'Put a sock in it. I know who you are and I know why you're here. You've had a nice little canapé and you're after a meal, but you won't eat me. You think you can take whatever a shop assistant throws at you; well, it hasn't always been like this, you know. Once I was a different kettle of fish. I swam in another element: the balmy ocean of youthful optimism.'

'And you're not swimming in it any more?' he says, contumaciously.

'I never intended to stay at Bodwicks,' Mary continues, without really hearing him. 'Who in their right mind would want to work in a department store for decades on end, surrounded by the ignorant and unkind? No, it's been a sacrifice. Working in Bodwicks was a temporary phase that crept into permanence; sneaking up on me like middle-age, it gripped me too tight. I couldn't get out, but don't you think that means I'm weak; don't you think that makes me stupid. I'm not going to be a pushover, like she was.'

'I'm sure that whoever she was, she wasn't a pushover,' he simpers.

'You don't even care that I've seen your face, do you? Who's going to believe me, an out-and-out nutter? – That's what you think, isn't it? I'll find you, you know, whichever rock you live under. I'll track you down and serve to you what you served to her.'

'I'm sorry. I think you must be confused. I should get on. 'Bye, Mary.'

She knows as soon as he says her name that she's meant to be fearful, that this knowledge of her identity is a latent threat, but she's ready for him because she's been expecting him to come back to this house, this tree from which he plucked such gratifying fruit.

She watches his figure diminish down the long pathway, his hips swaying beneath the thin polyester of his trousers, and buttoning her violet raincoat, she follows.

Thirty

Mary squints again at the house that she watched him enter. An ancient flabby woman answered the door and her face was illuminated with a grin of welcome and recognition. He raised his arms to be helped out of his coat in a way that Mary found abhorrent, and he stayed inside only an hour before returning to the street and hopping onto an omnibus, whose emptiness precluded her entry.

There is something here, she feels sure. This woman might be in alliance with him, she might be a co-conspirator, but equally she might also be his next victim and if so, Mary feels she should warn her. Although, if they are in cahoots, then such a warning could have fatal consequences for herself. Yet what genuine business could he possibly have in this tall Victorian mansion standing like a fortress in the heart of seafaring Devonport?

She passes through the wrought-iron gateway and on to the arched front entrance. Taking a deep breath, she taps on the black wooden door and is answered with silence. She waits a moment and then taps louder, only to be met with the same result. Finally, she bites her lip and rains several hard blows down on the door.

'Strewth, fit to wake the dead, that is. Hello, how can I help you?' The same obese elderly woman stands at the door, bearing a toothy grin. She has a dockyard accent that Mary finds distasteful.

'I'm here to look at wedding dresses. *Cheap wedding dresses 4 hire,* it says there.' Mary points to a number of wrinkly newspaper cuttings, advertisements evidently, which have been framed and hung around the entrance. The woman inclines her head.

'That's right, dear. I'm Mrs Lough; come in now. They do say it's never too late to be a bride. Come in, come in. Second time around the merry-go-round, is it?'

'Pardon?'

'Widow, are you?'

'I am not. This will be my first wedding, thank you very much.'

'Well, come through, come through, don't just stand there. I'm sure we can find something flattering for you. This way. I'll just get these out of the oven and we'll go down to the basement.'

She leads Mary past the foot of the stairs and into a hot kitchen where Mary stands, the scent of bread swirling around her, while Mrs Lough scrunches warm bread in her hand. Mary doesn't mean to, but she can't help but ogle the plate of gooey buttered rolls, tasting phantom mealy warmth in her mouth. Then, her pulses racing, she spots a photograph in a splintering pine frame.

'Is this you here?' Mary asks, looking at the retouched image of a bosomy lady in a flared oxblood skirt standing next to a gingery boy.

'It is. I was a knock-out back then, never walked down the street without being whistled at. I miss them whistles the most.'

'He's a nice looking young person with you.'

'What's that? Oh, that's my son. Queer boy,' she says, rubbing a wart on her nose.

'Queer – how so?'

'Funny; quiet. I never thought that boy would amount to anything. He had some strange ways. Found him wearing one of my wedding dresses once and thought he'd turn out to be a poofter. But I was wrong, and he's done well for himself. Fancy artist of sorts; made a lot of money, they say, though I don't see any of it.'

'How lovely. And does he live with you?'

'Heavens, no. He bought his own house years ago. Big old ramshackle place, he says, not to my tastes, but there you go. He knows if he wants to visit me, he's got to come here. I'm too old to be traipsing around the countryside.'

'The countryside? Whereabouts in the countryside?' asks Mary, her heart racing.

'I'm not rightly sure. I had the address written down somewhere but I lost it and I've never been there. Not that I'd let a little thing like that bother me. Roo said I'd take a disliking to it anyway; very cold it is, very cold. Roo's never had heating put in and I can't abide a cold house.'

'Roo?' asks Mary ponderously.

'Roo, my son Roo,' Mrs Lough says, nodding.

'Roo as in...?'

'What do you think as in? Not blooming *kangaroo*.'

'I don't know,' says Mary, her eyes glazing.

'What do you mean, you don't know?' says Mrs Lough frowning.

'They used to tell us at school that *kangaroo* was the Aboriginal word for 'I don't know.' But they were wrong. The word *kangaroo* comes from the Aboriginal word *gangurru* which refers to a species of kangaroo.'

Mary can't trust her own mind; her thoughts are streaking through her consciousness in a blur.

'You've lost me, dear,' says Mrs Lough.

'I'm sorry. And does your son have his own studio?'

'That's right. His utilities come to a hundred thousand pounds a year, just on electric and gas. Criminal, that is. Now when's your big day, petal?'

Mary considers her hurriedly-collated lie-manifest, but finding no answer, she decides to go with the traditional.

'I suppose that would be June. The end of June, to be precise. Of next year.'

'Sorting it out early? That's good. Some of these young girls show up a week before their big day and I've nothing left for them. Especially in June.'

'My gentleman friend likes to be on top of things.'

'I'm sure he does. Anyway – it's *fiancé* you mean, not *gentleman friend*. There's a ring on your finger now. Oh. Where is the ring?'

'We're having it made.'

'Very nice. What are you having made, then?'

'A diamond.'

'Oh, a diamond.'

'A yellow one. We're having it made from my mother's ashes. She died. You can do that now – it was in the paper. You send the ashes away and they send you back a diamond. It costs a lot, but my gentleman friend is rich.'

'Lucky you. Sounds a bit morbid – a bit Victorian to me, mind, but each to their own. Want one?' she offers, tantalisingly holding out the plate of rolls. A small fragment of bread and spittle lands on the kitchen's chequerboard floor.

'No, thank you. I've just had lunch.' Although Mary is repulsed by the sight of her eating, she wishes instantly that she had not denied herself the bread; her stomach aches with hunger and the smell of the bread roots her.

Mrs Lough eventually finishes chewing her roll and leads the way out of the kitchen, down a winding stairway and into a dark basement. Devonport's *Barad-dûr*, Mary thinks, and suppresses a shudder.

Racked up around the room are swathes of bride fabric, browned satin, lace and polyester, billowing skirts, beads, bows and netting. Spawned decades ago, worn by a hundred other brides and barely cleaned since. Designer dresses, these are not.

'What size are you, lover?' Mrs Lough runs her hand through the dresses, abominably, fondling their worn old fabrics.

'I don't need to try anything on today. I'm just looking, thank you kindly,' says Mary, hastily.

'You might as well, seeing as you're here. What size?'

'Really, it's not necessary.'

'For heaven's sake, lighten up. You're getting married.'

'I'm perfectly light, thank you.'

'Well?'

'Six. Size six.'

'You sure? You don't seem that thin. Anyhow, tens is the littlest I do. Try this one.'

'And where is the changing room?' Mary ventures, surveying the cluttered basement.

'What's that? Oh, there's no changing room. Here will do. Don't worry: all girls together.'

She grins and Mary hesitates, but sees no means of escape; she reluctantly peels off her clothes until she stands only in greyed underwear, thanking her lucky stars that the coldness of the morning made her dig out undergarments, but acutely aware that Mrs Lough stares at her swollen hungry belly. Shifting from foot to foot, she watches as Mrs Lough wrestles with the foaming body of fabric.

'We're thinking of having a portrait done. Perhaps your son could take it? We'd pay him handsomely.'

'Here we go, now: one foot here.'

Stepping into the gown, the only bridal gown that she has ever worn, Mary yaws as her foot catches in the lining; but, recovering her balance, she pulls the scratching monster up and over her tender skin.

Trapped inside its living tissue, it grazes her and squashes her larynx with a button. As if this is not enough, Mrs Lough presses a veil to her head with sharp pins, and Mary is then led, like the blind, to a cracked mirror. The fat woman stands behind her and cups her, twisting pink bows on her bosom.

Mary looks at herself and stiffens. The thin straps of her once-black bra contrast with the billowing yellowed dress: black and yellow. A warning: wasps.

Memories sting her consciousness: the hot summer when she climbed her favourite tree, a sycamore studded with six-inch nails for footholds. Reaching up, hand over hand, accidentally grasping the wasp nest, fingers sinking deep into the honeycombs. Her mind flicks painfully over the severed wasp that had been wallowing within her cheese and onion baguette, stinging her three times as her throat sought to swallow it. She hadn't seen the black and yellow. She'd missed the warning.

'Best take that brassière off. See the full effect.' Mrs Lough inserts her age-spotted hand into the back of the dress and releases the clasps, sending Mary's bra slithering to the floor. Mary is furious: she wants to rip this awful dress off, hack at the monster with a saw, watch it bleed in a heap on the floor. Betraying tears graze her face; they sting and she could swear these bastard teardrops are cutting tracks into her flesh, and then the dress speaks to her.

Weird rustling, malevolent voices. Voices of brides that have died – or worse, divorced. They curse the dress; their spectres inhabit it; seams tighten as cold fingers wrap around her throat and she must get this straitjacket off.

'Ain't you just perfect, lovie? Aw, she's crying! It's all too much, isn't it?' Mrs Lough dabs her stinging face with the back of her hand, nudging her eyes with knuckles: Mary's tears stop abruptly. She looks towards the stairs, the exit, and she untangles herself from the dress, pushing it onto lumpy arms, hastily dressing in her own clothes.

'About the portrait?' Mary perseveres.

'My son isn't that sort of artist, dearie. He makes glass. Lead crystal: vases, plates, ornaments, candelabras, that sort of thing. Fancy bric-a-brac.'

Of course, thinks Mary, of course. The glass birds. It makes sense: he is not a collector, he is a creator. This is how he has given her clues, goading her, daring her to find him. How could she have been so stupid? – All of this time she has been searching for a collector, when the man she sought was the maker.

'What a shame! And yet, now I think of it, we were also thinking of commissioning an inscribed plate to commemorate the day.'

Mrs Lough looks at her with an expression that Mary fears is suspicion, and says sharply: 'I suppose he could make it, but you'd have to get somebody else to engrave it.'

'That would be fine. Where does he work?'

'I'll give you his card in a second. Now stop blathering and tell me what you think of the dress.'

'Lovely. How much is it?' Mary asks, her face no doubt losing in the battle to mask repulsion.

'Hundred pounds for the day. That's not including shoes or veil though, my dear. But seeing as the last blushing bride spilt cherry wine on the hem, you shall have your shoes for free. Can't say fairer than that now, can I?'

Mary's eyes drift over the pile of dirty satin shoes stacked up in the corner.

'I can't find any of his cards. Just you go to the Crystillery, they'll sort you out. Now: do we have a deal on the dress?'

The Crystillery! He works at the Crystillery. How did she not think of it before? She has been blind; she has been moronic.

'I'll get back to you tomorrow. I just have a few more appointments,' Mary mumbles, bounding up the shadowy basement steps. She reaches the top and her eyes fix on the front door. In contrast to the black exterior, the inside of the front door has been painted with white gloss and it shimmers like some fantastical dream exit, with a promise to lead her to the real world.

'Wait a minute, there. Scampering away like a coney.' She's close behind; this portly old woman can move, and she's mounted the stairs with a celerity that can only be construed as demonic.

'Yes?' says Mary impatiently. Now that she has got what she needs, she is desperate to leave.

'You forgot my business card, dearie. My telephone number's on it.'

'Thank you.' Mary gingerly pockets the card in the front of her raincoat, careful not to touch it for too long. She doesn't want its vileness contaminating her fingers. God only knows where the card has been. Sitting on the kitchen worktop probably, with Mrs Lough spitting bread slime all over it.

'Now, haven't you forgotten something else?' Mrs Lough peers with watery, penetrating eyes. Mary lifts her eyebrows in response.

'What about the bread, now, lover?'

'No, thank you.' Even as she says it, rumbles echo around her belly. She ignores the urge to eat and turns to the door once more, which stands there white and reassuring.

'What, lover? No, I mean the dough, dolly.' A quizzical look. She takes a pace forward and Mary is almost certain she can smell body odour.

'No, thank you. I really don't want any bread, or bread-related products,' says Mary with more energy than strictly necessary.

Mrs Lough holds out her right hand expectantly. 'Deposit. Ten pounds.'

'Oh. Of course.' Mary fumbles with her purse and Mrs Lough squints at her appraisingly as she hands over a ten-pound note.

'I'll phone you tomorrow,' Mary lies, the fine film of sweat around her throat condensing into rivulets.

Mrs Lough nods.

Mary stumbles away, glad to be free of the loathsome woman, but she's acutely aware that the front door hasn't been shut – she's watched.

'Give my regards to my boy.' Mary does not look around, but feigns deafness, and finally there is a bang. Feeling around her inner pocket, she lets Mrs Lough's business card flutter to the ground.

Thirty-one

There is an assistant, a woman. She has caught his eye. She has been here for a year already, and for a year he has denied himself. He has left her in the fridge to be consumed later. She is old, she is short and she is enfleshed with lard, but her eyes are still bright. She is the product of a postgraduate degree. She has trained for a new career, even though she is far beyond retirement age.

In the summer she does her hot work at night when the workshop is cooler, and she sleeps in the day. Daylight makes blowing torturous for her old bones, she says; the gigantic windows swamp the room with light and make the space unbearable. 'Thirteen hundred degrees, that furnace is,' she informs him, smiling, 'and sunlight is the final straw, my boy.'

His lovely vampire likes the night and so he is here, watching her, peering through the waxy latticework of the rhododendron while she beavers away at the furnace, blowing jewel-like sculptures that glow in every colour and transform as the light shifts. He watches her often from this small amphitheatre which overlooks the Crystillery, ensconced in bushes which have been artfully landscaped into spaces pocking the concrete, and he whispers his desires to her across the void of the night. Although she can't hear him, he recites his homilies in a soft, choked voice:

'I hope your progeny die, too. I want you to see them abused, front and back – as you stand there suspended impotently in the corner – abused long and hard and determinedly, then set upon with psychopathic solemnity, cut and stretched and pierced with beautiful weaponry, shredded by antique torture devices. I want them slit into slices by the bluntest devices, one little finger, one little vertebra cut out at a time. I want you to hear their screams until their tongues are ripped from their throats and eaten raw so they may scream no more. I want you to hear their bones break one at a time, I want you to witness the grotesque swellings, the loss of their faces as they turn to mush under fierce blows. I want you to watch while their eyes are gouged out and dispensed with, as in *The Story of O* – don't plead ignorance, you know that you know *The Story of O* – I want you to see them grope in their darkness trying

195

to find you, but never finding you. I want you to know that once they're done, I'll start on you. I want you to beg me to be quicker with your family so that you may watch no more, then I want you to change your mind and wish – once I've started – that your darlings suffered longer, so that you could have one more pain-free minute before your agony begins. I want you dead. I want you all dead.'

He follows her every move with his eyes, watching her dipping her blowpipe in the molten lava crucible, being careful, for molten glass is no laughing matter and there is a technique to be mastered. It is just like taking honey from a pot, he has told her: be frugal, just take a bit, a little bit at a time, for if you're greedy it'll drip all over you.

She has a globule spitting from the end of her rod and she blows it hard, harder than women are wont – he asked her one time whether her cheeks get sore too? She said they didn't, but she was amused by the question – and she rolls the gather across his prized graphite marver table that is hardy enough to take the heat, bending over, rolling out the gather, blowing and tooling, blowing and tooling.

He watches intently as she works the glass, building up more and more layers, and she is absorbed in her work, totally unaware that she's watched, and this pleases him. She takes a swig from a water bottle and turns back to her piece, stopping off the end with another rod to trap some air, which expands and forms the cavity.

He appraises her skills as she manoeuvres her bubble in the colorant that will eventually decide its hue. He cannot see from here just what colour her piece will be, for now it is molten and orange and it will not transform until it has cooled, yet he's intrigued to know what she's picked. Powdered oxides may turn the piece any colour of the rainbow, except for red: for red they must use gold, as gold yields the bloodiest red that can be imagined, and he hopes ardently that she has opted for a bloodshot auriferous piece.

He is electrified to note that though she has technically worked enough, she is a perfectionist: she keeps rolling, and even when she must be convinced she has rolled sufficiently, she rolls some more.

She retrieves her tools: pincers, battledore, parrot-nosed shears, straight-nosed shears and duck-billed shears. All at the ready for manipulation, and she sets to with determined ferocity. Glass needs a lot of manipulation, he's told her, and he watches her now, adeptly using tweezers to yank out imperfections.

She could do some serious damage with that collection of hardware, and it makes him smile just thinking about it.

She lets the glass cool to annealing temperature – 440 degrees, no more and no less – then she locks it in the Lehr oven, bit by bit reducing the heat and every so often taking it out to scrape away the layers of impurities that ooze through to the top.

He watches her reading a book to pass the time. He cannot see the cover, but it is thick, a tome: perhaps a Dickens or a Tolstoy. She's dedicated, though; she never forgets her piece, never becomes absorbed in her book. She is like clockwork; she is a machine.

He doesn't know whether it's the heat from the furnace or the book that she's reading, but something's making her hot, making her pink and damp. Her grey hair is darkened by streaks of ash and her face is marked by sweat runs and, even dirty – especially dirty, he thinks – she is superb.

He will kill her with a tourniquet. He will strip a slice from her red apron, he will wrap it around her neck and he will use his pontil rod to tighten it, winding the fabric tighter and tighter until her windpipe is crushed and her neck snaps.

He will continue to get away with it because he is a professional, because he has had years to hone his craft and, excepting the Armenian, whom he killed grandiosely for the sake of infamy, he leaves no evidence.

He knows all about DNA. He knows as much as the police, if not more, and he knows exactly what to wear to preclude leaving any genetic markers. And he knows that in order to be successful there cannot be crimes of passion: he must wait until conditions are exactly right.

No-one will know of his assistant's death, because he will leave no body. She will just be one more addition to Plymouth's higher-than-average missing persons statistics.

It is just as he is thinking this thought that he hears the rustling of leaves, and on the leaf-strewn path that leads from the Crystillery, he sees Mary's silver-clad figure run lightly away.

Thirty-two

She has followed him at a distance on the last three consecutive days, and she understands his routine. He works odd hours at the Crystillery, seeming to come and go as he pleases, and often, of late, he has slept there. He must have a bunk room of sorts, as she hasn't once seen him return to a house.

She knows from her vantage point that he will come, as he came last night, to this amphitheatre at the back of the Crystillery where he will sit and talk to the stars or the moon or the Devil or whoever it is he talks to, and this time she will be close enough to hear.

Crouching in the bushes that overlook the miniature amphitheatre, dark leaves engulf her and render her invisible, but the algid night wind finds her. It snakes through the bushes, rustling vindictive leaves which catch and graze her skin.

Hiding. Freezing; no coat. She must stay calm; she must not think about the cold. She must think of something else, anything else, but not the cold. But it's hard when she's garbed in only in the sheerest of cotton nightdresses: the nightdress her mother made three short months ago, which has pastel-coloured flowers – the sort of flowers that exist only in fairytales and fabric.

She imagines such flowers might possibly exist in Swiss meadows, but only in May.

Like edelweiss: tiny but perfectly-proportioned blooms. And coloured, instead of white: pastel pink, yellow, green and palest cataract blue. Her mother embroidered them with silk thread whilst Mary was absent, probably out walking – a mossless rover is what she once aspired to be, a rolling stone of the best kind. It must've been whilst she was out walking, because Mary didn't see the nightdress until she found it on her bed, wrapped in brown paper and string.

Usually if her mother made her something for Christmas or her birthday or some other special occasion, she would petition her help with measuring, cutting, fittings; but for some reason, which baffles her, her mother wanted the nightdress to be a surprise.

It's pretty; Mary acknowledges that. It must've taken many hours of sewing, worked on over many weeks. She's counted the flowers that adorn the hemline, and found there to be fifty-eight exactly. Her mother sewed a flower for every year of her life, and in a way Mary is still reeling from this odd gift which has caught her so off-guard. For love has been woven into these impossible flowers; why else spend so long when plain fabric would have sufficed? Every broad sweep of her mother's arm as she hand-stitched the embroidery must've been tiring: more tiring to an old woman than anyone else.

But then, Mary is aware that she has a proclivity for grasping at straws, for reading affection where there is none. Like the time she fantasized a relationship with the Eggman. Not just a daydream, but a fully-fledged relationship with all the bells and whistles, with all the folly and the disaster, and all the while the Eggman and she were only on first name terms.

An overactive imagination is a blessing (it eases loneliness) and a curse (it exacerbates feelings of inadequacy) and in her simple, fraught existence imagination is a complicating factor that she could probably do without. It is a handicap: like her arthritic knee, her myopia, her frizzy hair, it plays against her.

Life is a game in which she has repeatedly proven herself to be a dunce.

The problem is the rules: a set of complex and interconnected understandings that go without being said. Even the most savvy, the most street-smart of persons must trip up sometimes, and Mary is barely able to cross a road without stumbling in front of oncoming traffic.

A rabbit in the headlights is how she has always been described by unimpressed commentators. Her startled eyes unnerve people; her expression of permanent surprise annoys them. Perhaps, she thinks, her stare seems to be questioning. Asking them, are you serious? Can you *really* be coming to run me over? And so, just like the rabbit, Mary feels in her bones that she'll inevitably be squished. In the fullness of time she'll be obliterated and scraped off the road by a young person with NVQs.

But the nightdress, the wonderful graspable nightdress: doesn't it speak for itself, through its very existence? It's irrefutable; it's tangible; it's hers, and her mother made it.

Her mother got so tired from sewing – especially embroidery – and yet she made it for her.

She wishes she could have talked to her, thanked her properly, but she was so stunned at receiving a gift that she could think of nothing to say. She wanted to go downstairs and kiss that cool old cheek but she couldn't, she was frozen, and she thought her affection would most likely have been spurned.

Her mother didn't love her. She thought she knew this categorically, but she was wrong. When she first received the gift she was discombobulated, to say the least. The only possible conclusion, she thought, was that now, in her twilight years, her mother had been feeling some guilt. Perhaps she knew that her time was near, sensed it'd be the last year she'd ever spend with her, the fifty-eight flowers symbolising the fifty-eight arctic years they'd endured together. But she was wrong; the reason for the gift was simple love.

The nightdress is so beautiful; in future it must be saved for the Sabbath. It's the grandest article she owns. She would, of course, have preferred to have changed into proper clothes before she left, but that was impossible: she had no time.

It's cold, so cold. How much longer will she have to wait here? If she can just get through this night. She supposes she'd look rather ridiculous to a casual onlooker, possibly a bit strange, but luckily there are no onlookers at this time of night – what sane person would choose to wander the amphitheatre in the dark hours before dawn? No, at three in the morning the amphitheatre is deserted; even the trash-talking youths have found their way home. She closes her eyes and feels it: something in the air has changed. Her body tautens. He's come.

She did everything she could: she knotted together her bed sheets, she hooked them around the bedpost, she climbed through the window. Even as she slid downwards, she heard him enter her chamber. Footsteps above reverberated through the house. She neared the patio and the sheets slithered to the ground, taking her with them.

Now, from beyond the stage, the short figure appears. Robed in a flapping black raincoat that is three sizes too big for him, he wears a tight balaclava that reveals only the dark pools of his eyes. He walks into the square and pauses.

Frozen, she waits for his move. His head begins to move, scanning from side to side.

He fixes his gaze upon the west side of the amphitheatre, where she crouches. He raises his fists and with a sudden flick of the wrists, he shoots his digits at her, unfurling them like gypsy scarves, long fingers snaking out into the air.

Stumbling from her old hiding place, tentacular undergrowth clawing her, she flees. Worms in overdrive; she fears she'll soil her nightdress, as she can't cross her legs and run at the same time – it's a physical impossibility.

Up the wide steps, over the sheer drop at the back of the amphitheatre, thudding on the concrete slabs below. Searing pains shoot up her ankles for the second time this night and she uses all her might to run towards the distant church. The greenness underfoot deliquesces and though she runs, she feels as if she's falling. She must get to the church; she must reclaim her religion and stand beneath the red globe of the Tabernacle Lamp, the Sanctuary Lamp, which burns eternally to signify the presence of God.

He counts to seven, slowly. She hears him as she runs; his voice is high-pitched, it reverberates through the soft night, it flies around the amphitheatre and overtakes her. He pursues, short legs striding through the battle-ground, eating up the distance between them.

She gasps, chest heaving, legs not running fast enough. The rear of the church is almost within reach but her ankles are agony, they'll give out and she can feel him behind her. She reaches the church and clings to the wall. She's here.

Warm waves pulse through her and she's stronger: The House of The Lord energises her. She edges around the perimeter of the church, hands inching across the wall, scuffing them, maintaining contact. In the shadow of the mock-Gothic arch, she pushes herself onto the door – but is stopped short. The door is locked.

The door is locked. She stares at the door, but it remains locked.

She breaks contact for the merest fraction of a second to turn to face her enemy.

He appears. Stock-still, or moving very slowly; she can't tell.

'Fuck a duck,' she shouts wrathfully, and she scrabbles with the handle, a rush of fear energising her; and then she knocks at the door, fierce whacking blows crashing on the timber.

'Help me, Father!' There is no answer from the church and she hears the voice behind her.

'Hello, Mary. Why are you following me?' His unholy voice is shrill upon the air.

'You can't hurt me … not in the church.' She won't turn, she won't look at him again, but she can feel his cold breath on her neck, her soft nuchal tissues polluted by foulness.

'But you're not in the church; you're outside.'

'Don't kill me,' Mary says firmly. 'Not here, not like this…' she tails off.

'I'm not interested in the middle-aged, although I might look you up in twenty years,' he says softly. Mary throws her whole body against the door, a bone in her shoulder cracks and she hits the deck.

'You killed Mother,' she says, pathetically.

'So what? If I handed you the knife, and you knew you'd never be caught, you'd kill your enemies and lick their blood up off the floor. You'd take over willingly, and chalk it up to experience. We're all alone, Mary; existentialists know it, we all know it in our hearts. The only people we care about are ourselves. Just say, perchance, there was a killer in your house who wanted you or your spouse. Don't tell me you wouldn't feel a hint of remorse as you sacrificed yourself because you thought you must? Don't tell me as you were dying that you wouldn't be thinking about your spouse's next lover, who he'd fuck with greater enjoyment than he ever fucked you? *I should have nominated that bastard,* you'd realise, too late.

'There's just one life here to be lived, and it's yours. So get on with it and forget about me.'

'I don't have a spouse,' says Mary.

He laughs with genuine amusement. 'No, you don't, do you? You only had your mum, and I dealt with her.' Mary groans, despite herself.

'So, Mary, do you want to see something swell?' he asks in a breathy, suffocating voice that is laden with innuendo.

'No, I do not want to see anything swell.' She turns now and she is aware of the deep furrows, the laughter lines around his eyes and then she sees the orbs themselves and they are black and penetrating and they burn; they are laser eyes.

'Then stop following me. Or I'll make you an exception, and make you a vase.'

Thirty-three

It is a raw, grey day and she is here at the Crystillery, surveilling him from the camouflage of the ornamental garden. She watches him come and go through the workshop and onto the sales floor and into the stockroom and back again and he is as a barely-noteworthy ant in his endeavours: he is short indeed, and perhaps, she thinks, it is this vertical deficiency that has lured so many women into finding him unthreatening. He is in his early fifties and thin, attenuated, as if his growing body was stretched like bread dough over his skeleton – bread dough that has not risen.

His cheeks are hollow and he has a wide forehead and a pronounced brow-bone, all of which gives him the air of a foreigner. His eyebrows are wild but the rest of him is spruce; he is neat in a pressed shirt with a small blue and green check; neat, with a green and white Chinese serpent tie; neat, in his dark trousers and red apron. His darkly-dyed hair is swept back and held in place with gel. An unctuous lickspittle around the ladies, he simpers and smiles when expected, and laughs when jokes are cracked: polite, unassuming, charming.

She sees his fiery face reflecting the light of the furnace and watches him using his tools with martial gusto. She watches through the glass windows as he has watched so many others, and she waits. She waits all day in the rain until afternoon segues into evening, until the shop-women have gone home, until the customers bearing heavy bags have sauntered through sliding doors. She waits until it is just him, and then leaning heavily on her sodden khaki umbrella, she walks through the gloaming to the building's façade and the doors glide silently apart.

The workshop overflows with an eclectic selection of glassware: rows and rows of multi-coloured vases are lined up around the periphery of the room. They shine. Some are sandblasted and translucent, some are clear and limpid, yet all are vibrant and are cast in shades of mulberry and amethyst and rust and turquoise and emerald and hundreds of other colours that she doesn't have names for.

She cannot believe that this base despicable man can create such beauty, for these vases have been tended with great care and skill, and then she comes to the armoury of tools: rods, pincers, shears: sturdy metalware, and it occurs to her that glassmaking is an act of self-assertion. He makes, he uses his tools to cut and shape and force his works into submission; he fashions as he sees fit.

There are colorants in pots, each carefully labelled with colour swatches indicating the shade they'll turn the glass.

She feels woozy and she hesitates, reaching her hand to the wall to regain her balance, uncertain of how best to proceed, when she realises she has been holding her breath. She summons her strength and, clutching her raincoat to her throat, she continues. She rounds a corner and sees the back of his body.

Arranged around him are shelves and shelves of glass animals: blue dolphins and sharks, grey and pink elephants and birds of every species.

She would thunder down upon him like a cavalry charge, but she cannot. Instead, she gathers all of her strength and inches towards him, following her outstretched index finger.

Terrific heat hits her as she passes the furnace; it is hotter than a sauna, but there is not even a drop of perspiration on his exposed neck: he is used to these hellish temperatures, to this inferno.

She dabs her forehead and feels sweat. She stares at his back.

He stands at a grinding machine, filing away the base of a lead-crystal greenfinch. The noise of the machine is deafening, a screech of glass on diamond, and there is a sharp metallic smell in the air. She taps him on the shoulder.

'Hello, Roo. Remember me, sir?' she asks, holding her dripping umbrella tightly. Her voice jolts him and he swings around violently.

'Do I know you?' he asks, peering out from overgrown eyebrows, which also appear to have been tinted.

'Well, I wouldn't say you *know* me as such,' she replies sarcastically, 'but you have often visited my house and you accosted me at church last night, and I'm almost certain you knew my mother.'

His face is saturnine as he glances at her umbrella. He flicks a switch and the disc ceases its lightning revolutions.

'I'm sorry, madam; I think you're mistaking me for someone else,' he murmurs softly, leaning against his grinding machine as if it were a lamppost.

'I'm quite sure I'm not. In fact, now that I look at you close up I remember you from somewhere else. It was you, was it not, with whom I spoke at Carkeel? Your hair was different: it was light then. You've dyed it since, and feigned the crass air of a Swilly Billy, but it was you. Was my mother still alive then? Was she stowed in the attic, bewildered and terrified as I talked with you of horses?'

Her eyes are stinging, her nose is full of prickly heat and her cheeks are reddening painfully.

'I don't know what I can do for you. We're closed.' His purring voice is as oily as his hair and it reviles her.

'You can tell me where she's buried. Mrs Sibly: foreign, old, in case you don't remember. I'm sure she's merely one of a long list.'

'Don't misconstrue my honesty as incivility, but you are mistaken.' He is softly mocking and his eyes are liquid lustre.

'Give me her body. I want the bones of her.'

'You're insane.'

Mary pulls the knife from her pocket: the knife she has kept with her every day since her mother's disappearance; the knife she has been saving until she was sure. She's spent many hours sharpening it, and it'll suffice.

'Tell me where she is. Did you feed her to the ducks in the boating lake? Is she buried? Is she in the tunnels?'

His face registers alarm at the sight of the knife, and he wrings his hands, making a cathedral of his fingers.

'Put the knife down,' he says, *sotto voce*.

'Is she in the tunnels? Answer me.'

'What tunnels? I don't know any tunnels.'

'You know what tunnels. The tunnels that lead to Drake's Island, from the Citadel. Is that how you got her away, without anyone seeing? Or did you put her on a boat and feed her like a pollack to the porbeagle sharks?'

'You're mistaken. This is madness.'

His colour darkens and he applies himself to a bottle of spring water. She watches him gulping the liquid, his Adam's apple rising and falling with each sip.

'I know it was you.'

'Your problem is that you have a cornucopian imagination.'

'I don't know what you're talking about,' Mary answers, a lump of humiliation forming in her throat.

205

'Cornucopia: the horn of plenty. The horn of the goat that suckled Zeus, which broke off and filled with fruit. It filled with whatever its owner desired. Your imagination is cornucopian; you pull from it whatever you think you need. *Cornus* means *horn*, you see?'

'Unicorn: one horn,' she murmurs, softly.

'Yes, like unicorn.'

She considers the possibility of innocence and shakes her head, sending splinters of pain down her neck.

'It had to be you. You left a jay feather in her chair and a trail of glass birds and you're a glassmaker.'

'I've sold thousands of birds in my time,' he says, sensing her confusion, his face a mask of perfect sangfroid. 'I think you should go. I can't help you.'

Mary will not be defeated so easily. She'll not leave just because she's told: she'll not allow him that power.

'Oh yes, you can help me. I'm not leaving until you've told me where she is. I don't care if that's before or after I've snipped off your testicles.'

'If you touch me, you'll go to prison for a long, long time and I don't think you could cope in prison,' he says in a new nasal voice. He sidles up to her slowly until he is an arm's length from her and his eyes, it seems, are pitch black.

'I don't care. As long as you're stopped, it's worth it.'

He turns his back to her and views her over a lowered shoulder, his eyes sharp now, and glittering.

'Stab me in the back, will you?'

She tightens her grip and ponders a killing thrust, but he turns like lightning and before she knows it, her hand is empty and the knife is gleaming in his.

Mary backs away, her thighs meeting the wooden workbench behind her.

'Sit down,' he orders. His voice has acquired a new authoritative tone, which seems to suit it most of all.

She pulls out a chair that scrapes on the concrete floor and she sits hastily, made clumsy by adrenaline. 'It's like I always say,' he remarks: 'you cannot educate pork.'

'I am not pork,' she says definitely.

'Those who are born stupid will stay stupid, like dogs. You can tell if a puppy's got potential just by looking at it. Give it a rag to play with: the ones that get it in their teeth and don't let go are the ones you don't want. You'll never be able to train a dog like that. What you want are the docile ones: the ones that aren't much interested in the rag and look at you as if you're a cretin for jiggling it around under their nose. You want a critter with a spirit that can be broken. Or, better still, that doesn't have a spirit to begin with.'

He smiles his crooked smile at her, but his eyes are excoriating.

'I suppose you judged my mother by the same criteria, did you? Lacking in spirit?'

He titters. 'I don't judge women, Mary. Women judge me. Your mother was my favourite, you know: I never had an Armenian before. She was a seahorse in a pond full of trout.'

Mary is sickened; she shakes her head in deep opprobrium.

'How did you get her to go with you?'

'She thought we were going to see my mother,' he says.

'Why would my mother want to visit yours?'

'Because my mother was Armenian.'

'Your mother's not Armenian.'

'You know that, and I know that. Your mother didn't. Her eyes lit up like a pinball machine when she thought she'd have an hour with a countrywoman. I spent months telling her all about my Armenian ancestors who came from Van and fled during the genocide. She was adorably dupable,' he says.

'You don't even look Armenian.'

'I did to your mum, but then her cataracts were quite severe, weren't they? She sucked it up. I think she was glad to feel a bit of kinship, however insincere.'

'I'm her kin.'

'You're English. I was Armenian.'

So this is how he got to her. He beguiled her with sweet lies. He feigned cultural solidarity, he faked ethnicity, and he tricked her into believing his assumed allegiance to the Armenian people.

It's an insight that she doesn't much like, now that she's been given it.

'No,' she says, petulantly. 'No, no, no.'

'Yes. She was drawn to me, like a collie summoned by an ultrasonic whistle. Inaudible to your ears, but she heard it. We cursed the Turks for hours on end and she was never happier.'

'You anathematised the Turkish people? That's all?'

He runs his finger down his nose and leaves it resting in his wrinkled cupid's bow.

'Oh no, that wasn't all. She used to like me telling her historical things about Plymouth. She loved it when I told her how Drake's Island was used as a prison for twenty-five years after the English civil war.'

'You're not even from Plymouth.'

'I might look foreign, but I'm not. Born and bred here, I was. I've loved my city ever since I heard that The Royal Citadel, constructed to guard against a French Invasion, had most of its cannons pointed over the city – a threat to those that supported Parliament and not the king.'

'So what?' Mary says, confused and unhappy.

'This city is full of rebels. That's why I fit in here, although really I'm just a grass snake in a nest of vipers. There's worse out there than me, I'm sad to say.

'She cooked me a dinner once, you know: a recipe she brought from Armenia. A gouged-out marrow, stuffed with tomatoes and rice and strange spices. *Mashee*, she called it. I didn't like it – it had an unnatural flavour – but I ate it.'

His taunting hurts. He knows where the wounds are; he knows where to prod for maximum pain.

'I'll kill you. I don't care: I'll kill you,' Mary says.

'If you kill me, you'll be caught. You're not clever enough to evade the police; you're out of your depth. You're descended from peasants. I'm aristocracy.' He pauses to think. 'No, I'm better: I'm meritocracy. I've got where I am by my own efforts – by using my intellect.'

Mary shakes her head defiantly. 'You are conflating merit with murder. You are nothing except a blight. An incubus, a nightmare, a shadow. You are a sexual predator.'

'In your opinion, that is – and your opinion, lest we forget, is the opinion of a dull-as-ditchwater shop-madam, a certified loon, and the most hideous spinster of the parish.'

'Do not judge me by my occupation,' Mary answers with perfect calm, holding her head proudly. 'I might have been a shop-woman but I'm no dullard.'

He laughs again, loudly this time, a rolling clangorous laugh, dire and sinister.

'Stupidity is in your genes. I've researched your ancestral tree, looked you up on the 1901 census. Lo and behold, your father's relatives were present! Bricklayers, joiners, labourers, sweet-makers.'

'You know nothing about my family,' Mary says unhappily.

'I know your father died because he valued cigarettes more than he valued you or your mother.'

'That's not true. He had an addiction.' She rakes her hands through her hair and her locks answer, standing up in all directions, wild and dishevelled.

'He was weak. Your mum told me. She confided in me, because who else did she have? She told me all about her weak husband.'

'He was not weak, he was strong.'

'Do you know, in her last days your mum stank to high heaven? She had a gamey reek about her. If body odour could be bottled and vended to cheesemongers, I'd be rich.'

He rubs his mentum and shoots her an odious look.

'My mother was clean as a whistle. Why she ever talked to you, why she ever took your custom, I'll never know. Every moment with you must have been a *saison en enfer*. By which I mean a season in hell.'

Mary's spitefulness, her gall, her vitriol, her caustic cracks: she welcomes them all, she ushers them in and seats them on her right side. They will help her through this.

'I don't know why you want to make me angry. If I kill you, you'll never find her.'

'I already know where she is.'

'And where is that?'

'In here.' She points to her chest and he laughs disparagingly.

'The only thing you have there is frigidity. *Mary, Mary, eyes are scary, how does your hymen grow?* That's what the kids call when you walk by.'

Mary sweats and her breathing grows stertorous under the weight of his vim.

'I couldn't care less what the children call me. They're just bored. Let them enjoy their catcalls; it's in their nature to be hostile. Girls fighting over purloined clothing; boys sulking, looking at me askance, swivellings of the eye the only signs that they're aware of my existence. So what if once in a while they call out unpleasantness? I don't care.'

'Do you care what your mother said about you? She called you a harpy, a harridan. You drove her into my arms. She said you repulsed her,' he remarks, clearing his throat and dabbing his nose with a tissue.

'She would never say that. She didn't even know the word repulse.'

'Well, she did by the time I'd finished with her. She was such a sweet little émigré. She trusted me more than she ever trusted you, and I killed her. Now, does that say more about me, or more about you?'

He brays with laughter and Mary watches as mucus from his pocked nose is forcibly ejected.

'She must have been desperate.'

'That's right, she was desperate. She even told me Armenian fairy stories. There was one called *A Big Pot of Gold*. Do you want to hear it?'

'I don't believe she told you any such thing. My mother didn't even know any fairy stories, or she would have told them to me when I was little.'

'Lucky I recorded her then. I play it for motivation. Listen.'

Thirty-four

He retrieves a Dictaphone from an inner pocket of his jacket, presses *play* and there she is: there are the tones of her mother, the beloved timbre of her foreign voice warm and fluid, rising and falling in unique contralto.

Mary weeps in response to the first sentence; she can take only so much, and she cannot take her mother's voice speaking so trustingly from the grave:

'Once there live poor peasant who own small field and pair oxen. One winter, the oxen, which belong to poor peasant, they die. When spring come and time plough mud, he say to neighbour: "Neighbour, you rent land. I got no oxen do work and shame let land go waste."

'Neighbour come plough land, and work hard all day and when he near finish and go home for *panir*, he hear plough hit something hard, metal.

'When he go look, he feel in dirt and use hand to push away mud and he find big pot of gold.

'So much gold it can give hundred village food for ten year.

'Neighbour so happy he leave oxen in field and run to village to peasant house: "Hey, God bless you, I find big pot of gold in your field, come and take home!" "No, brother, it not mine," answer peasant. "I rent land, you pay for it, so whatever come out of it, it yours. Gold has come out, still better, it yours."

'Peasant and neighbour argue for long time, both think it not belong to him, but to other man. Arguing go bad and turn to big shouting and so they go to king. When the king hear about pot of gold, he happy, all smiling and say: "I solve problem. It belong not you, or him. This gold in my kingdom, so it mine."

'Men not happy but there nothing they can do: can't argue with king, so they agree. King and his men go to fetch gold. They come to little field and he order his men to pull heavy pot of gold from earth and then he tell them to take cover off pot. King look into it and what he see?

'Pot is full of snake!

'Angry he come back to peasant and neighbour and order his

211

men to punish ignorant peasants who dare lie to king. "Long live the king," cry poor men, "but why you kill us?"

'"There snakes in your pot gold!" "No, no," they say, confuse.

'"You not look good enough, there no snakes there, it gold, pot is full gold coin, enough to feed hundred village for ten year."

'King give one more chance and he send new men to find who is right.

'Men come back and tell confused king that in pot, there is gold, as peasant say.

'"What?" say king. "Maybe I not look well, or maybe it another pot I look in." And so king go to field again. He looks into pot and just like before it full of snake. "It magic!" say king, even more confuse. "What it mean?"

'King tells wise men to come. "Tell me, wise men, what miracle this? This farmers find big pot of gold in they field. I go there, but pot full snakes, but when they go, there gold. What means?"

'"Highness, if you not get angry, we tell you," say wise men. "Pot of gold is for farmers, gift for honesty, gift for long labour. When they go to pot, they go to reward they deserve and find gold, but when you go, you go to take other men fortune, so for you, it snake."

'King is quiet. He not find any answer for many hour. "Okay," he say. "You wise men tell which farmer take pot of gold."

'"To landowner," say neighbour who rent land. "To neighbour," say landowner.

'They argue.

'"Well, well, stop argue," say wise men and they calm things down.

'"What children have you, son or daughter?"

'It turn out that peasant have son and neighbour have daughter. Wise men say peasant son and neighbour daughter must marry. Then peasants give them pot gold as present.

'Honest peasants say yes and all smiling. Arguing all gone and wedding festival begin. Wedding feast last seven day and seven night and all village people invited.

'In this we learn that it better to give neighbour, than keep. It not good to argue with king. And is best give everything to children.'

'Is that the end, Meghranoush?'

Mary hears his purring voice radiate from the Dictaphone.

'Yes, end. You like?' her mother asks.

'The king was not nice,' is his considered response.

'All king is not nice,' answers her mother.

'Do you think I'll find a pot of gold, Meghranoush?'

There is a silence as she ponders the chances of him stumbling across a windfall.

'Maybe yes, maybe no,' she answers thoughtfully. 'You work hard?'

Mary listens in traumatised horror as her mother converses so reposefully with this madman.

'I do,' he says. 'I do work hard.'

Her mother is silent and there is a small cough.

'Work hard and tell truth and gold he comes to you.'

'It already has,' he replies.

The tape ends with a click.

'Why did you pick her?' asks Mary, finally asking the one question that she is most desperate for him to answer, 'when you could have picked anyone?'

'Her eyes – her ancient, glittering eyes – were gay. Yeats.' He purses his lips and looks up to the heavens.

'It must have been more than her eyes.'

'She ensorcelled me. She was different, she was special,' he says. 'You could say her heritage piqued my interest.'

These words are galling, but he is right: her mother was special. It was only her continuing presence that allowed Mary to forget this.

'Why did you leave me the raven?' she asks, suddenly remembering the birds.

'I was bored. I thought I could tip you over the edge by hanging around your house,' he replies, jubilantly.

He swallows an abundance of spittle and as Mary watches his throat, she has a desire to rip it out with her teeth.

'These trinkets you make – your glass – in time they'll turn back into liquid and everything you've ever made will be destroyed. And you can't undo destruction with creation, you know. A fancy vase does not cancel out a murder.'

'Murder is an act of creation in itself. I take something that is whole and create something that is fractured. I take a life and create a death.'

213

There is no rationalising with this man: he is deeply damaged, a lost soul. He is dark matter.

'Why did you kill her at the war memorial?'

'You are so full of questions,' he says. 'You are positively overflowing.'

'It costs you nothing to answer.'

He considers this and nods. 'True. I killed her at the war memorial because I am interested in war.'

'An interest in war is not a motive for murder.'

'Motive?' He sneers, patting down parts of his body, exploring imaginary pockets. 'No, I can't find any motives for murder, but there was a motive for picking the war memorial.'

'What?' she asks with what she hopes is dignity.

'It pleased me that I could conquer what war couldn't.'

How could a person be twisted into this abomination before her?

Reading her mind, he replies, 'I am Janus: two faces. One is law-abiding, the other is not.'

He snaps his jaws together, opening and closing his mouth as if in the business of catching flies.

'You have no conscience. You're morally benighted. You are dark to the core.'

'I don't have a conscience? At least I saw your mum was gold. To you she was snakes.'

'I loved my mother,' she says sharply, her eyes staring into his.

'Only after she was gone. I coveted her. I loved her for the whole time that I knew her, and I loved her most when I cut her throat,' he says, flooded with pride.

He feels the ultimate *schadenfreude* in her mother's destruction, and this enrages her.

'You are a killer. Dress it up however you like, but you're nothing but an animal – a beast.'

'Sticks and stones,' he jeers, 'sticks and stones.' And, waving the knife in front of his eyes, he asks: 'Art thou but a dagger of the mind, a false creation, proceeding from the heat-oppressed brain?'

He is angry now; a cold calculated anger, and she can see he has crossed the line from mockery to wrath. A red aura swirls from his body; it comes towards her.

'Why did you dismember her? Why wasn't death enough?'

214

'I like them FUBAR,' he says softly but with perfect clarity.

'Fubar is not a word.'

'An acronym that stands for *Fucked Up Beyond All Recognition.*'

Unbidden tears prickle in her eyes.

'You're depraved, you are: sick.'

'And what medicine can you offer?'

Within Mary something snaps. Rage takes over and she charges at him.

She hears his leonine roar and watches incredulously as he lashes out with the knife and hits her hard in the mouth; she sees a flash of yellow and some teeth hit the floor, shearing away a portion of her lower lip, leaving it hanging by a thread.

His hand is blood-strewn with her blood and the liquid running from her mouth is pink and foaming. He is stronger than she imagined, and she is terrified to see that she has engaged in a fight that is unwinnable.

In the confused scrimmage he drops the knife and grabs her throat, pushing her down to the ground and she's light, so *nothingy*, he could snap her neck. He's not holding her tight enough, though; he needs to be stronger, to hurt her more. He holds her down with his right hand, and hits her with his left. He's blind – red mist in his eyes. He wants this woman – this witch – to die.

It is a strange and sad feeling to know that whilst he bears down upon her, he is the first man to have ever touched her. Truly, this monster, this woman-eater, he is the first. And as he pins her arms with his knees and moves his hands to her neck it is a surety that these are the first male hands to have touched the bare, smooth skin of her throat, so long hidden by restrictive collars.

And the truth, the stomach-lurching truth is that this killer, this man-most-foul, doesn't even want her. Not really. He is taking her, touching her, only under duress; only because he has had his hand forced by circumstance. The eyes that look down into hers are not malevolent: they are seriously cool; they mean business. She is but a task to him.

Before her eyes blur, she looks higher, above his uncanny eyes, to the smear of ginger at his hairline and she marvels at it. This chameleon, this gentleman of many guises, this slave to peroxide and ammonia and artifice, is a carrot-top. A human being with all

215

the frailty and weaknesses therein, and with her last resources of strength her limp legs become animated and her left knee contacts brutally with the warmth of his groin and he recoils, and his eyes are saucers, alive with outrage.

But she's not done yet: her knee does not stop when it meets resistance. It continues, it follows through, as boxers are meant to with punches, until he is prized away, until he falls and lies twitching fitfully at her side, coiling his body around his injury – a foetus jabbed by an abortifacient needle.

Mary grabs the nearest thing to her – a pale blue vase streaked with white, bulbous with a narrow opening – and it is so heavy in her hand that she almost drops it – but she grasps it tightly, drawing up her fists and feeling power surge up from her belly, through her breasts, and into her arm.

She strikes his head, the blow landing so hard that it almost shatters the bones of her hands, which redden and swell.

His body, taut with adrenaline, becomes limber and softens, his eyes glazing and rolling upwards.

In a tempest of wrath, she smashes it down upon his cranium again, and still the vase does not break. She hits him until she's sure he won't get up.

The work is almost bloodless except for a small spatter that finds its way into her eye socket and which she wipes away with her ring finger as she exits the premises.

She takes the blue vase with her, for a souvenir.

In the times to come, Mary will cherish this vase. She will talk to it; she will fill it with daffodils and crocuses, and boughs of horse chestnut in the autumn. She will revere it, because it stopped him in his tracks.

She forgets about her mutilated lips until she arrives home, whereupon she sets to stitching them in place with pink thread and a needle that she has sterilised on the hob.

And they are stitches of such smallness and neatness that even her mother would be proud.

She hears on the news the next day that a pillar of society has been attacked, discovered unconscious and found to be upon the brink of death. Solicitous reporters inform the public that he has been committed to intensive care and that, although hopes were high and prayers were sent to heaven, he has not regained consciousness, and even if he does, there is little chance that he will be able to rekindle his phenomenal career.

They have investigated such things as reflex action and cerebral activity, and the results are not encouraging: it seems likely that his paralysis will be permanent.

Mary listens calmly, but with regret that she did not quite finish the job.

She does not worry that she'll be caught, even though she undoubtedly left her own blood at the scene. The police will never track her down – first, because her DNA is not on file; second, because she took the printed weapon with her; and finally and most important, because that is not the way of karma.

She feels not one pang of guilt.

Only lightness; only loss. Because now that he is gone she can grieve; she can cry good clean tears.

She hopes, without much conviction, that if the police dig up his past, they'll find tokens of his victims. And perhaps, one day, he'll sit handcuffed in a courtroom and receive his condign punishment. But for now, his crippling is enough.

In his paralysis, he will be painfully aware of a fact that he cannot share.

He committed her to the flames of his furnace. He used the calcium of her fired skeleton to turn a vase blue, and this devastating vase that stole his life was created with the ash of Meghranoush: the most strong in a string of them; his favourite, his masterpiece.

Fiction from Two Ravens Press

Love Letters from my Death-bed
Cynthia Rogerson

There's something very strange going on in Fairfax, California. Joe Johnson is on the hunt for dying people while his wife stares into space and flies land on her nose; the Snelling kids fester in a hippie backwater and pretend that they haven't just killed their grandfather; and Morag, multi-bigamist from the Scottish Highlands, makes some rash decisions when diagnosed with terminal cancer by Manuel – who may or may not be a doctor. Meanwhile, the ghost of Consuela threads her way through all the stories, oblivious to the ever-watching Connie – who sees everything from the attic of the Gentle Valleys Hospice.

Cynthia Rogerson's second novel is a funny and life-affirming tale about the courage to love in the face of death.

'Witty, wise and on occasions laugh-aloud funny. A tonic for all those concerned with living more fully while we can.' **Andrew Greig**

'Her writing has a lovely spirit to it, an appealing mixture of the spiky and the warm.' **Michel Faber**

£8.99. ISBN 978-1-906120-00-9. Published April 2007.

Nightingale
Peter Dorward

On the second of August 1980, at 1pm, a bomb placed under a chair in the second class waiting room of the international railway station in Bologna exploded, resulting in the deaths of eighty-five people. Despite indictments and arrests, no convictions were ever secured.

Exactly a year before the bombing, a young British couple disembarked at the station and walked into town. He – pale-blue eyes, white collarless shirt, baggy green army surplus trousers – and twenty yards behind him, the woman whom, in a couple of years he will marry, then eventually abandon. He is Don, she is Julia. Within twenty-four hours she'll leave for home, and he will wander into a bar called the *Nightingale* – and a labyrinthine world of extreme politics and terrorism.

More than twenty years later their daughter Rosie, as naïve as her father was before her, will return to the city, and both Don – and his past – will follow...

'Nightingale *is a gripping and intelligent novel; it takes an unsentimental and vivid look at the lives of a small group of Italian terrorists and the naive Scottish musician who finds himself in their midst in Bologna in 1980. Full of authentic detail and texture,* Nightingale *is written with clarity and precision. Peter Dorward tells this tragic story with huge confidence and verve.'* **Kate Pullinger**

£9.99. ISBN 978-1-906120-09-2. Published September 2007.

Parties
Tom Lappin

Gordon yearns for a little power; Richard wishes reality could match the romantic ideal of a perfect pop song; Grainne wants life to be a little more like Tolstoy. Beatrice looks on and tries to chronicle the disappointment of a generation measuring the years to the end of the century in parties.

Parties, the début novel by journalist Tom Lappin, is a scathing, insightful and profoundly human commentary on party politics and the corrupting effects of power. But above all it is a satire: a black comedy about young people getting older, and learning to be careful what they wish for, lest they end up finding it.

'*Compelling and absorbing: the story of five friends growing up in the '80s and '90s, through the voyage from idealism to disillusion that was left-wing party politics through the turn of the century.*' **Paul Torday** (author of *Salmon Fishing in the Yemen*)

£9.99. ISBN 978-1-906120-11-5. Published October 2007.

The Most Glorified Strip of Bunting
John McGill

The United States North Polar expedition of 1871-73 was a disaster-strewn adventure that counts amongst the most bizarre and exciting in the annals of Arctic exploration. Commanded by Charles Francis Hall, a romantic idealist with an obsessive interest in the frozen north, the converted river tug Polaris carries a multinational crew of scientists and sailors, assisted by two Inuit families, along the so-called American Way to the North Pole - the icy channels between Greenland and Ellesmere Island. For Hall, the planting of the Stars and Stripes on the top of the world is a sacred and patriotic duty, but his enthusiasm is shared by few of his companions, and the expedition, under the strain of conditions in the high Arctic, quickly disintegrates into warring factions. With their ship embedded in the ice, the explorers plunge into a maelstrom of anarchy and paranoia fuelled by the clash of two civilisations – Inuit and European – and the mutual misunderstanding and hostility that arise from it.

John McGill's novel chronicles the events leading up to the strange and suspicious death of the commander, and in a parallel narrative, tells the astonishing tale of the nineteen crew members separated in a storm and cast adrift on an ice floe. Their story is one of the truly great Arctic adventures, a six-month drama of narrow escapes coloured by the ever-present threats of rape, murder and cannibalism, and acted out on a shrinking platform of ice exposed to all the horrors of the most inhospitable climate on earth.

'A compulsive adventure story encompassing the struggle to reach the North Pole, an unsolved murder and a long-drawn-out fight for survival among shifting ice floes, The Most Glorified Strip of Bunting *turns every imperial value on its head.'* **Margaret Elphinstone**

£9.99. ISBN 978-1-906120-12-2. Published November 2007.

Short Fiction from Two Ravens Press

Highland Views
David Ross

Military jets exercise over Loch Eye as a seer struggles to remember his vision; the honeymoon is over for workers down at the Nigg yard, and an English incomer leads the fight for independence both for Scotland and for herself... This debut collection of stories provides an original perspective on the Highlands, subtly addressing the unique combination of old and new influences that operate today.

'I'm a big fan. A fine organic collection that advances a viewpoint, culture and history quite other than the urban central belt that still lopsidedly dominates recent Scottish literature.' **Andrew Greig**

'A view of the Highlands with a strong element of political and social comment. Ross explores these concerns in convincingly human terms through the lives of his characters.' **Brian McCabe**

£7.99. ISBN 978-1-906120-05-4. Published April 2007.

RIPTIDE
New Writing from the Highlands and Islands
Edited by Sharon Blackie & David Knowles

This diverse collection of new fiction and poetry from the Highlands & Islands showcases the work of established writers and new names to watch.

Contributors:

Pam Beasant, Sharon Blackie, Robert Davidson, Angus Dunn, Eva Faber, Alison Flett, Yvonne Gray, John Glenday, Clio Gray, Andrew Greig, Nicky Guthrie, Mandy Haggith, Morag Henderson, Elyse Jamieson, Laureen Johnson, David Knowles, Morag MacInnes, Anne Macleod, Kevin MacNeil, Daibhidh Martin, John McGill, Donald Murray, Alison Napier, Pauline Prior-Pitt, Joanna Ramsey, Cynthia Rogerson, David Ross, Mark Ryan Smith, and Peter Urpeth.

'...*a force of creation, the kind of irresistible tide into which we should dip.*' **The Scotsman**

£8.99. ISBN 978-1-906120-02-3. Published April 2007.

Types of Everlasting Rest
by Scotsman-Orange Prize winner Clio Gray

From Italy and Russia in the time of Napoleon to the fate of Boy Scouts in Czechoslovakia during the Second World War, Clio Gray's short stories are filled with intrigue, conspiracy and murder. Laden with sumptuous detail, each story leads the reader directly into the compelling and sometimes bizarre inner worlds of her fascinating characters.

'*Clio Gray is a master of atmosphere and sensuousness. She combines historical realism with the bizarre, whimsy with the macabre. Reading her is like being at a sumptuous feast in a palace, just before it is stormed.*' **Alan Bissett**

£8.99. ISBN 978-1-906120-04-7. Published July 2007.

Poetry from Two Ravens Press

Castings: by Mandy Haggith.
£8.99. ISBN 978-1-906120-01-6. Published April 2007.

Leaving the Nest: by Dorothy Baird.
£8.99. ISBN 978-1-906120-06-1. Published July 2007.

The Zig Zag Woman: by Maggie Sawkins.
£8.99. ISBN 978-1-906120-08-5. Published September 2007.

In a Room Darkened: by Kevin Williamson.
£8.99. ISBN 978-1-906120-07-8. Published October 2007.

For more information on these and other titles, and for
extracts and author interviews, see our website.

Titles are available direct from the publisher at
www.tworavenspress.com
or from any good bookshop.